PRAISE FOR M. L. BUCHMAN

3x "Top 10 Romance of the Year"

— BOOKLIST

13 times "Top Pick of the Month"

— NIGHT OWL REVIEWS

I became completely immersed in this story and it had me at page one. Entertaining and full of emotion.

— FRESH FICTION, *WHERE DREAMS ARE BORN*

A delightful family drama with a feel good storyline. Readers will relish this entertaining contemporary.

— MIDWEST BOOK REVIEW, *WHERE DREAMS UNFOLD*

A favorite author of mine. I'll read anything that carries his name, no questions asked. Meet your new favorite author!

— THE SASSY BOOKSTER, FLASH OF FIRE

M.L. Buchman is guaranteed to get me lost in a good story.

— THE READING CAFE, WAY OF THE WARRIOR: NSDQ

I love Buchman's writing. His vivid descriptions bring everything to life in an unforgettable way.

— PURE JONEL, HOT POINT

Buchman has catapulted his way to the top tier of my favorite authors.

— FRESH FICTION

The only thing you'll ask yourself is, "When does the next one come out?"

— *WAIT UNTIL MIDNIGHT*, RT REVIEWS, 4 STARS

Superb! Miranda is utterly compelling!

— *BOOKLIST*, STARRED REVIEW

Miranda Chase continues to astound and charm.

— BARB M.

Escape Rating: A. Five Stars! OMG just start with *Drone* and be prepared for a fantastic binge-read!

— READING REALITY

WHERE DREAMS UNFOLD

A PIKE PLACE MARKET SEATTLE ROMANCE

M. L. BUCHMAN

Buchman Bookworks

Other works by M. L. Buchman: *(* - also in audio)*

Other works by M. L. Buchman:

Contemporary Romance (cont)

Love Abroad
Heart of the Cotswolds: England
Path of Love: Cinque Terre, Italy

Where Dreams
Where Dreams are Born
Where Dreams Reside
Where Dreams Are of Christmas*
Where Dreams Unfold
Where Dreams Are Written
Where Dreams Continue

Science Fiction / Fantasy

Deities Anonymous
Cookbook from Hell: Reheated
Saviors 101

Single Titles
The Nara Reaction
Monk's Maze
the Me and Elsie Chronicles

Non-Fiction

Strategies for Success
Managing Your Inner Artist/Writer
Estate Planning for Authors*
Character Voice
Narrate and Record Your Own
Audiobook*

Short Story Series by M. L. Buchman:

Romantic Suspense

Antarctic Ice Fliers

Delta Force
Th Delta Force Shooters
The Delta Force Warriors

Firehawks
The Firehawks Lookouts
The Firehawks Hotshots
The Firebirds

The Night Stalkers
The Night Stalkers 5D Stories
The Night Stalkers 5E Stories
The Night Stalkers CSAR
The Night Stalkers Wedding Stories

US Coast Guard

White House Protection Force

Contemporary Romance

Eagle Cove

Henderson's Ranch*

Where Dreams

Action-Adventure Thrillers

Dead Chef

Miranda Chase Origin Stories

Science Fiction / Fantasy

Deities Anonymous

Other
The Future Night Stalkers
Single Titles

ABOUT THIS TITLE

Fashion and opera collide in a story of romance in the heart of Seattle.

Bill Cullen *is the Stage Manager for Seattle's Emerald City Opera, and a single father with two precocious children dedicated to making him nuts. The last thing he needs? A free-spirited costume designer for his new opera production.*

Perrin Williams *left behind her past to become Seattle's premier boutique fashion designer. But Bill and his children see right through her defenses and into her heart. A heart she's always been very skilled at hiding.*

Confronting their pasts, strains the fabric of their futures Where Dreams Unfold.

·

CHAPTER 1

*P*errin Williams hung up the dress bags and collapsed onto the tattered gray sofa in her design studio. Exhaustion rippled through her in familiar waves. She felt both the dull ache and the immense satisfaction that typically coursed through her after an exceptionally long bout of clothing design, her favorite form of play.

The gentle light of the warm late-April-in-Seattle morning filled her boutique and design studio with a soft glow that made her want to just sprawl here and giggle madly. Somehow, against all odds, her life had brought her to work and create in this wonderful, safe space.

This time the exhaustion had been earned at the wedding of one of her two best friends. "Jo" Thompson had married Angelo Parrano at an event of grand proportions in the heart of the Pike Place Market.

Many of the Seattle elite had attended. More than a few had commissioned dresses from Perrin's Glorious Garb. Which elicited another giggle that might have been a chortle of self-satisfaction.

No one around yet to tell her if her tired brain had tipped

over the edge to gloating, so she let herself revel in the wonder of it all.

To see her designs flashing among the wedding crowd had filled her heart in a way that had left her speechless more than once last night. Because it was a Market wedding, after all, Jo was the new director of the Pike Place Market, the finest street musicians had added their music—including some great dancing music from the rolling-piano guy.

The food was perhaps the finest Maximilien's had ever made. Perrin had put a giant sign on the kitchen door, "Angelo not allowed past this point." The groom, one of Seattle's most highly acclaimed chefs, had it coming. Everyone, including Perrin, had made sure he was reminded of that sign often throughout the night.

The bride and groom had looked so beautiful dancing beneath the moonlight. They swayed together out on the patio overlooking Elliott Bay, a backdrop of scooting ferries and the brilliant glow of the ice-capped Olympic Mountains beyond. The couple had looked so in love. So happy.

Perrin shot to her feet and paced around the studio. She'd gone past tired and tipped right over into hyperactively awake. At some point soon she'd crash for a day or two, but not yet.

She unzipped the first bag. Jo's dress of shimmering pale blue cascaded forth. She'd have it cleaned and properly boxed before Jo and Angelo returned from a week in Hawaii. Neither of them had ever been there, and a week was all either of them could afford to be away at the moment. April was perfect weather in both Seattle and the resort on Kauai's eastern shore, especially known for relentlessly pampering its guests.

Perrin pulled Jo's dress in front of her and posed before the tall antique tri-fold mirror of beveled glass and dark oak. She turned on the lights; the early morning sun didn't reach into this corner of her studio. The pale blue had complimented Jo's Alaskan-dark complexion and flowing black hair. There had been no need for the dress to accent the curves, Jo's body had provided those perfectly.

Perrin tilted her head critically, and then had to roll it around a bit to loosen the crick from a serious lack of sleep. The dress wouldn't do at all on her own pale skin and slender frame. She hung it on the "to be cleaned" rack.

From the second bag she pulled out the bridesmaid dresses that she and Cassidy Knowles had worn. They had been as softly gold as the bride's dress had been softly blue. The gold had picked up highlights in the best man's suit that Perrin had put on Cassidy's husband Russell.

She'd also accented the mother-of-the-bride's dress with just a bit of the soft gold as well, which had made the photographs really pop. Russell had shared a few tips with her that only a professional fashion photographer would know. Seeing Eloise giving away her previously estranged daughter had brought tears to everyone's eyes.

Perrin sighed and hung the other dresses beside the wedding gown. Cassidy and Russell. Jo and Angelo. Even Angelo's mother had recently met and married the true love of her life.

That left only Perrin herself without a man anywhere on the horizon. Part of her didn't want one.

"Avert!"

It was like some order from a space-captain's chair, "Evasive maneuver delta." "Avert!" It always made her smile, and because it was such a silly and simple thought it usually did track her away from thinking of her life prior to meeting Cassidy and Jo in college.

She didn't want a man because of the nightmare example of her family, but she also desperately did want one. One like Cassidy or Jo had found. The rough edges of Russell, the sensitivity of Angelo. And as long as she was making a list...

A knock on her door had her checking herself in the mirror: a simple light wool skirt appropriate for fall and a bright spring shirt topped with a summery sheer batik scarf. She was missing a season. Which one? Oh, winter. She really was tired, something to do with not having slept except for occasional catnaps in the last four or five days.

Something had brought her to stand in front of the mirror— but what?

"WILSON. Please tell me this is one of your crazy jokes." Except the Director of the Emerald City Opera was not given to jokes, at least not practical ones.

Bill Cullen glared at the display window of the fashion designer's storefront that Wilson had led him to while Wilson thumped on the locked door once more.

The outfits in the window were cute, urban. He guessed it would draw a woman passing by into the shop, just as well as a dozen other places that he seemed to pass every day. They cropped up, more dreams than solid basis in either business acumen or common sense. Then they went away and someone else moved in the next day with their hopes and dreams clutched tight.

He turned away and studied the neighborhood.

Wilson Jervis had dragged him into the heart of the Belltown area to meet a designer. The old brick building did nothing to inspire his confidence. After Pioneer Square, this was one of the oldest portions of downtown Seattle, just north of the business core. Most of the area had been rebuilt, turned into condos and ad-agency-slick small business fronts. This block had been completely bypassed by the neighborhood's recent rejuvenation and gentrification.

Its age showed in many ways, darkened brickwork, cracks in the sidewalk. An abandoned tattoo parlor across the street with a "Half-off for Two" sign that might have once lured customers, but was now superseded by the "Out of Business" sign across the glass. Next to it, a small bike shop looked to be doing okay. Belltown wasn't dangerous the way Pioneer Square had been before its restoration, this part of it was just old.

"My wife found her. Trust me," was all the reassurance the rotund icon of the Seattle theater scene offered. He'd been leading the Opera with a confident and mostly unquestioned hand for decades. He'd taken a small company on the verge of insolvency and turned it into one of the five largest opera houses in the U.S., and one of the most respected in the world.

All that still didn't make Bill trust Wilson about this. They were mounting a new opera and it was up to Bill as stage manager to see that it happened perfectly, or at least on schedule and near budget. It was his job to make sure that every piece from set design and costumes to lighting and singers came together by opening night, only six weeks away. What they were doing in Belltown, too early on a Monday morning, was beyond him. Well, not totally beyond him.

Carlotta Gianelli had thrown one of her world-famous tantrums and stalked out yesterday to fly back to Milan and now they needed a costume designer who could perform a six-month miracle in only six weeks. Gianelli had burned up over four months and achieved nothing except some sketches that no one liked or could interpret.

He glared back at the shop as a light flickered on deep in the shop.

The glass door bore bold-colored lettering so close to graffiti that he could barely read it. Except he could. The "P" and "G" were actually oversized, ornate letters in the Victorian style. Perrin's Glorious Garb, the second two words attached to the same "G" were actually artful slashes that he recognized as a variety of fashion styles ranging over the last fifty years, somehow done so that they made a unified whole. What he'd almost dismissed as tacky was actually a deeply nuanced under-standing of design.

He peered into the window. The shop was dark, but for the light shining in back. He spotted a waif coming through the store toward them, silhouetted by the light behind and pulling on a hat despite the warm day.

"We're not open yet," she called through the glass but was already unlocking the door.

She was dressed like some teenager that had been thrown bodily into a closet and crawled forth wearing whatever she fell against. She wore a form-fitting silk turtleneck of new-grass green, an unlikely mauve skirt that evoked autumn swirled in pleats about her calves, and a filmy batik scarf the red-orange of a summer sunset that looked as if it had attempted to throttle her. All mismatched and crazy, the unlikely ensemble somehow looked good on her in a way he didn't care enough about to attempt to fathom. She'd topped it off with a knitwear winter hat of orange and russet with earflaps and a ridiculous pom-pom pulled down over pale-blonde hair that brushed her narrow shoulders.

Wilson introduced them and talked his way into the shop as easily as he'd talked Bill away from the San Francisco Opera four years before.

Adira's death had made Bill a single dad at thirty-three years old. His need to escape "their" city and the needs of their two children had been the biggest factor by far. But Wilson hadn't played that card. Instead, he'd offered a new and interesting job in a different city, leaving it to be Bill's own realization that such a change was exactly what he needed to do for both himself and his kids. Tricky SOB. To this day Bill still didn't know quite how that had happened.

Bill followed Wilson into the shop, letting the director deal with the sloppily dressed clerk. The shop had been set up like a 1950s diner, all chromed metal and red leatherette. Mannequins sat in booths in a quirky mash-up of eras. A '20s flapper cozied up with a '50s greaser and a '40s housewife.

Yet that wasn't what they were.

The housewife's wide, white collar wasn't on the housewife dress, it was on the flapper's, and it distinctly accented the cleavage. The greaser actually sported the classic lines of a '20s linen suit, but sewn in denim and flannel.

He could hear the girl bubbling away at Wilson about something. Sounded like a chickadee mixed up with one of those small singing birds. Disconnected flighty bits that, even if gathered together, wouldn't really communicate much.

The next booth included Victorian brocade set in a modern blazer, and a gown design that would be formal enough for an opera opening night yet remained racy enough for the hottest club. Even studying the piece didn't reveal how the two distinct messages had been combined in a single garment.

He glanced over at the shop girl, wondering when the owner was coming in.

This girl was all arms and legs and nerves. Her slender build was only emphasized by her height. Fingers flashed out to emphasize points, her gestures were twice life size. She made a grand sweeping gesture which suggested she might be a dancer as well.

She had rolled out a short rack which bore a set of dresses, wedding and two bridesmaids, and was showing them to Wilson as he slouched next to a particularly voluptuous mannequin in a Wall Street business suit. Cutting a suit to a full-figured woman was hard, and she'd made the outfit pop; that it was in hot '50s poodle-pink wool only made it more so.

Then he focused on the wedding and bridesmaid dresses. Exceptionally fine work, yet wholly inappropriate for the stage, as the ensemble was a masterpiece of subtlety. He'd bet that the clerk would look particularly good in the gold one.

Wilson had really lost it this time.

All of these clothes were studies of craftsmanship and nuance. But they weren't costumes, especially not ones that would play to the vast three-thousand seat expanse of the ECO Opera House at Seattle Center. To play at the Emerald City Opera they need scale and impact.

"Where's the designer?"

"Why?" The woman pulled down her winter cap as if to shield herself.

"We're here to see her for reasons that wholly escape me." Up close the girl wasn't so much of a girl. She was a woman, long and sleek. Her hair a long, thick, pale blonde that looked too substantial for so elegant a neck. She looked him nearly in the eye despite, he checked, bare feet.

The hat of garish orange wool had been pulled down almost far enough to hide her eyes, but they shone brilliant blue past pale lashes.

"Why?" Her voice was soft.

"Why what?"

"Why do the reasons escape you?" There was a real "duh" tone to her voice as if he were the one being exceedingly dense and not the other way around.

"Wilson wants to hire her and I want to tell the woman to her face that there's no way in hell I'll work with her."

She regarded him with those bright blues for so long that he had to fight to not look away. There was a mind behind those eyes. And a force of personality all out of balance with the crazed attire and flighty first, second, and third impression.

"Boy, it's going to really suck being you."

"Why?"

"Because Director Wilson Jervis of the Emerald City Opera has just offered me the contract to design the costumes for *Ascension,* your next opera. And because it sounds like fun, I," she turned briefly to Wilson, "thank you Mr. Jervis, yes" then she turned back to him, "have as of this moment decided to accept. Perrin Williams at your service."

She held out a hand and shook his numb fingers strongly when he held them out in shock like a trained puppy.

She was right, it was going to really suck being him.

"WILSON, you can't do this! What are her credentials? What productions has she designed for?"

Wilson lounged back in one of the booths next to the hot poodle-pink business suit. He propped his feet on the opposite seat next to a mannequin sheathed in a dress of tiny mirrors, like a human disco ball—except it wasn't some gimmick dress, it made the figure look hot as hell. As Wilson landed his feet there, it shimmered. Rather than the expected heaviness, it was a light fabric that moved easily, catching and changing light. Every breath the wearer took would be dramatic and impossible to look away from.

"Ask her yourself, Bill. She's standing right in front of you. This rude chap is Bill Cullen our Stage Manager. Getting the show up is his responsibility. Picking the right people is mine."

Bill turned to look down at her. Except, it still wasn't down. It was across. And she was no longer on the verge of disappearing into her hat. Now she was very present, watching him. He couldn't quite tell, but she almost looked amused.

"Sorry if I was rude, but—"

"No, Mr. Cullen. I've never designed an opera. I've never even been to one."

All he could do was gasp. He held out his hands to Wilson and the damn man just did one of those seraphic smiles of his. The same smile he'd confronted Bill with four years before when he stole him from San Francisco for the Emerald City Opera.

"Further, Mr. Cullen. I have designed for no movies, plays, dramas in the park, or poetry readings. Though I have attended all of those."

Bill reined himself in. He could hear the disdain in her voice, carefully tempered to slap him back with his own attitude. She'd have made a fine dramatic actress, no use to him on an opera stage, but still a precisely balanced performance.

"Then..." he took a deep breath and felt not the least bit better, no matter how much his daughter insisted it would help him. She'd also told him to try using "please" once in a while. "Then, please, tell me why you think you can do this."

"Would you prefer a list of prior creative works, a sworn deposition, or a demonstration?" She was definitely mocking him.

"A demonstration? What are you talking about?"

"This way." She turned and walked away as if he was just expected to follow along.

He looked at Wilson who simply worked his way back to his feet and moseyed along behind her. Bill cursed under his breath and brought up the rear. He didn't have time for any of this today; not that he'd been given any choice.

She led them through the dimly lit shop and through what had once been the doors to the kitchen.

The shadows were deep here. The only light source was the morning sun, reflected off the tattoo parlor across the street and shining in through the front window and the cook's window.

The mannequins in front of the stove looked so real that he thought they were alive for a moment. Dramatic designer coats indicated this was where the outerwear must be sold. One was an apparently typical black leather coat except for massive red buttons as big around as his palm. There was something odd about the cut, but he couldn't tell in the dim light. The other wore the cape that clearly went with the mirrored gown. It would swirl and flutter and draw every eye until the moment it was removed to reveal the mirrored spectacle form-fit to a woman's body.

There was a theme here. Bill didn't have it until he was following the other two into the walk-in freezer lined with shoes and accessories, and then through another swinging door into the design space beyond.

The common theme was that this woman designed for people who wanted to be noticed. Every single piece of clothing was an absolute attention grabber. On the right woman— women, for each design was impressively distinct—they'd be irresistible.

Again, Bill imagined the golden bridesmaid dress on the woman who was now waiting by her cutting table. That *would be* a vision to behold.

"Tell me about your opera."

Bill looked around the room. He'd been in near enough a hundred of costume design studios over the years. From this woman he'd expected chaos and disarray. Instead, it was one of the neatest and most organized spaces he'd ever seen.

The cutting table was large and immaculate, topped with a green self-healing cutting mat marked in standard one-inch squares with thin yellow lines. Two top-of-the-line sewing machines, a long-arm embroidery machine, and a five-thread serger were lined up along the back window. He almost missed an old Singer Featherweight sitting to one side on a small oak desk with the black, curlicued, wrought-iron base. Not only did it appear well cared for, it was the only one that hadn't been tidied up, as if it were the latest used.

He turned and was confronted by a wall of fabric neatly stored in cubicle shelves that ranged floor to ceiling down the long wall. Whatever else this woman might be, she was serious about her workspace.

Bill kicked free a stool from under the edge of the cutting

table and sat down next to Wilson, across the table from the designer.

"Well, it is an entirely new opera, not just a new mount."

He saw her confused expression. Great. Time to get remedial. He made a show of checking his watch, but Wilson merely cocked his head in her direction and he was left with no choice but to continue.

"Operas are typically done one of two ways. A packaged opera is one that has been previously designed. We pull everything from storage: sets, costumes, props, and so on. Or we rent someone else's. Sometimes we'll mix it up; rent a set from Houston, but use San Francisco's costumes. All we have to do then is adjust, fit, and perhaps replicate a couple pieces that are too worn or too drastically the wrong size. Then there's a new mount. All new sets and costumes. That's expensive and takes a lot of planning."

"But you said this one was more than that." She had remained standing and he had to look up at her. He wasn't complaining. Despite her incoherent taste in clothing, she was fine-featured and genuinely nice to look at. When was the last time he'd really looked at a woman? There had to be someone in the four years since Adira's death, but he couldn't think of one at the moment. Maybe single dads of two pre-teens didn't have enough extra brain cells unoccupied to handle such a task.

"Yes. A new opera is a new mount with many additional nightmares because no one has ever staged this opera before. We will be the first to present the work which has been in development for over two years. We will be making a statement that will enter the repertoire of dozens of opera companies—or that disappears quietly taking several million dollars of investment with it. Now you see why you aren't acceptable. You make nice clothes, but that is a whole different matter from costuming a new and successful opera."

PERRIN WASN'T REALLY LISTENING. Wasn't even worrying about the gauntlet she had cast at his feet of a "demonstration" whatever she'd meant by that. She was too tired to make much sense of what Bill Cullen was actually saying.

All she knew was that the page on the sketchpad she'd dropped before her on the cutting table was still blank. A square white hole in a sea of green cutting mat. She started looking around the table for a Yellow Submarine and then stopped herself. Not tired enough to hallucinate…yet.

She didn't care that he kept saying she wasn't qualified, that kind of statement only ever made her that much more determined. Too many years of proving her parents wrong about her, that lesson was deeply ingrained. Up until now repeating himself appeared to make him happy so she'd let him do it. But she needed more.

"You still have told me nothing about your opera. An opera must have a setting, a place, a feel, a story, or it would just be noise. Clothes are the same. Without the story, they are just coverings."

"Yes, Bill. Do get on with it."

Perrin liked Wilson Jervis. He was a generation, or even two older than she was, but he had an easy-going manner that was totally belied by his well-known success. She'd never been inside the Opera House, except once to hear an Indigo Girls concert during the Bumbershoot music festival. But Perrin had been commissioned to make enough opening-night-of-the-opera gowns to know of him and what he'd achieved.

And wasn't part of Jo's new job being on the opera board? Or maybe it was Cassidy. One of her two best friends… Or maybe both? Again, brain too tired to remember or care.

Bill Cullen she hadn't quite figured out yet. He studied her through narrowed eyes, wary and suspicious. He was like

Jeffrey, a bulldog she once knew—all rough and grumpy. She wondered if he also had a mushy heart beneath that bristly exterior, or if he was irascible to the core.

He was certainly far prettier than Jeffrey. Bill Cullen stood six feet tall. He wasn't all shoulders like her friend Russell, not that there was any fat on him. He was simply built of a squarer stock. His deep brown hair and disdainful expression, combined with his strong features, lent itself to two different avenues of expression.

She flipped open her pencil set and selected a simple gray to start with.

He began describing a dark adventure. Part Jules Verne and part Hobbit, evil staff of power. He talked about it being quite different in character from Wagner's "Ring Cycle" which meant nothing to her. Somewhere in his explanation he mentioned a tragic love story. It was his voice that caught her attention. It was a good voice, expressive, clearly practiced at storytelling. She let herself simply enjoy the tones and emotions he wove.

Perrin sketched two side-by-side figures. One stern and foreboding, one the romantic hero. She began adding color and lines to both, letting his deep voice and evocative words wrap about her as she sketched. To the left, grays, browns, boots, and towering shoulders...high collar. To the right, purples and blues of royalty and inner majesty, thin lines of white to promise hope. The valiant savior riding to the rescue. But the trim was in darkest red to suggest that heart's blood would be shed despite the nobility. The white hope quite in vain.

Her hand ached by the time she pulled back enough to again be aware of her surroundings. Dozens of colored pencils were scattered about the table. The room was silent. The cramp in her hand told her she'd drawn for twenty, perhaps thirty minutes without interruption.

As she flexed her fingers, she inspected the drawing before her. The same man, twice presented. The Dark Overlord, and the forsaken nobleman doomed before his time to a tragic end. They would work well at a distance. The overemphasized shapes of one and the powerful colors of the other.

She would never make street clothes like these, far too depressing. She wanted clothes that made people smile, or want to get married in. But designing to embody an individual's power itself was intriguing.

She practically yelped when she became aware of the two large men flanking her. She'd forgotten they were here.

Bill Cullen was leaning in, studying her drawing intently.

Wilson Jervis smiled at her broadly after little more than a glance.

"Ooo, she's seen right through you, Bill Cullen. You absolutely nailed him, Ms. Williams. We'll have a contract for your review by tomorrow."

Perrin turned back to see Mr. Cullen's reaction. He was no longer studying the sketch. He was studying her, from mere inches away. She could practically see the thoughts churning in his head. His dark brown eyes, the way two vertical lines appeared on his brow when he was concentrating, the unexpected laugh lines around his eyes and mouth, as if he did that a lot... She knew she would be able to draw his face from memory.

"But can you execute your vision?" His voice was still rough.

She waved a hand to indicate the room they were standing in.

"Actually, Bill," Jervis stopped the man. "Her contract is to design. Any costumes she actually constructs earns a bonus but is not required by the contract."

Cullen's expression slowly shifted to one of chagrin though he didn't look away.

"Tomorrow. Nine a.m. At the—"

"Tomorrow at nine a.m.," Perrin interrupted him. "I will still be asleep. I've been awake for four days for one of my best

15

friend's weddings. I might be up by noon. Maybe." She knew that she couldn't let him have control. He struck her as the sort of man that once he had control, he'd never let it go.

"Would tomorrow at two in the afternoon be satisfactory?" His growl didn't sound all that different from Jeffrey the bulldog's. She couldn't decide whether to be deeply peeved at his tone, or amused at how cute he was at being all male and growly.

"That… " she almost said it was fine, but changed her course just to push him and see what he would do. "Would be far more likely than nine a.m. Do people get up at nine a.m.?"

"I have kids. My day starts at six." He nodded curtly and the two men showed themselves out.

Perrin felt a surge of disappointment that she didn't understand. She hung onto the edge of the cutting table, weaving with exhaustion while she tried to figure out the source of it.

Kids. Bill Cullen had children and was married. She hadn't noticed a ring, but she was so tired she could easily have missed it. Some men didn't wear them, but she didn't like men who did that.

Perrin dreamed of a man who was so glad to be with her that he'd want to wear a ring so that he could brag about her. He would need to feel the connection between them even when they were apart.

And she wanted the same for herself.

She'd seen her two best friends find it. But she also knew that such dreams would never be reality for Perrin Williams. With her past, why was she the one who ended up being the romantic among her group of friends?

That still didn't explain the disappointment. Perrin had long ago learned to chase down her emotions until she understood them. When she was younger, her acute reactions and reckless actions had been sources of grave personal danger. The ride down that path had only been averted by meeting Cassidy

Knowles and Jo Thompson on the first day of college, and a million painfully careful steps since.

That was it. She'd taken a step without being aware of it; a step she took far too often with men, her great weakness. Because while she knew it would never come, she still wanted the dream of true love. That feeling of let-down could be traced back to the fact that Perrin had liked Bill Cullen despite his irascible self.

But he was married. He'd also scoffed at the only thing she did well, had ever done well, which didn't earn him a lot of points. She gazed back down at her drawings. The dark and the tragic stood side by side. Wilson Jervis had been right. She had captured Bill Cullen.

Without being aware of it, she'd drawn both costumed men with his features and build. And the two images... The Dark Overlord who had so carefully inspected each of her designs, appreciated them, yet deemed her unworthy. Him she'd been far too aware of from the moment he entered her shop. And the Tragic Prince who only showed through when Bill Cullen wasn't so busy being himself.

She took up the lead pencil and clarified a few of the details on his face. The way his hair shaded his eyes: not with its length, but with its rich darkness. The least bit of curl that she hoped his wife appreciated toying with.

Then she began sketching a third image. The face was less clear...a woman's face? A woman's body. Yes. Tall. In her mind's eye, the clothing became clearer.

CHAPTER 2

*T*wo-thirty. Damn the woman! Five more minutes and Bill was going to Jervis and make sure he didn't send the contract to this damned woman. He'd tear it up himself if he had to.

It wasn't like the day had been off to a good start to begin with. The kids had been in rare form, Tamara showed all the signs of having read a book until the middle of the night. She was lethargic, grumpy, and had snapped at Jaspar. He in turn had added salt to his sister's cereal when she wasn't looking. Bill actually had to snap at them before they pummeled each other, or even worse, messed up their school clothes ten minutes before he had to drop them off.

Then he'd spent the morning finding out that the costumes weren't his only problem. The set designer had been timely, thorough, and innovative in his scenic design. He'd also shown absolutely no concept of what it would cost to build, to move about the stage, or store between productions. Then his lead scenic painter had broken her wrist... Bill ground his teeth and tried to beat down his e-mail that had decided today was the day everything should be labeled urgent.

At two-thirty-three, past the limit of his patience, Bill went to hunt down Wilson to fire this Williams woman before she signed any damned contract. His office was empty.

The old office building had been built into a hillside, with rooftop parking and a flight of stairs descending to the top story where the main offices were. They were a labyrinth of white-painted concrete rooms chopped up with open-plan cubicles. It had once been a moving company's storage facility. The towering storage racks had been removed and the tall ceiling lowered with dropped T-bar and acoustic tiles. The result had been a nice enough office environment with inexplicably long flights of stairs between the tall stories. Rising from the industrial-gray carpet, the walls were magnificent with large production photos of every opera performed over the last forty years by Emerald City Opera.

Timothy, the Production Manager, had seen Wilson about an hour earlier. No one since, not Marci, Consuela, or Chloe. Where had the damn man wandered off to? Bill swung by the front desk where Nia reigned as the eyes and ears of the organization.

As he was asking, he felt someone come in through the front doors. He turned around part way to see if it was Wilson or his missing designer, then forgot how to breathe when he saw the apparition entering the small lobby from the stairs.

The woman who had walked in wasn't the costume designer, but she was an incredible sight to behold.

He heard Nia gasp behind him, but he couldn't turn to gauge her reaction. He couldn't even gauge his own. He'd been slapped by a gestalt vision that his brain was now having to unravel.

Amazingly, it was Perrin Williams—yet it couldn't be.

In place of the crazy-clothed blonde waif, he now faced a towering woman of power and majesty. Her hair was the darkest, purest black, except for a stripe of her original coloring. A pale-blonde stripe started at her right temple in a three-inch wide band and disappeared behind her head in a sloping spiral. It reappeared on the other side, just meeting the tips of her hair at her left shoulder.

From there, in fabric, the white stripe was picked up and continued its downward swirl across her gown, widening as it went. The dark purples and blues of her second drawing from yesterday had been incorporated. The thin white stripe of hope on her "tragic noble" was now a blazing banner. The white transitioned, by an exceptional job of hand-dying, into a gold of true glory. If he remembered correctly, every place that had been blood red in her drawing of the Prince had been turned golden in this dress.

She was hope embodied. But its message didn't stop there.

The left shoulder extended to a tall collar encasing her neck from clavicle to tight under her chin. But the right shoulder was bare, a line of flesh was exposed down her ribs and that opening extended around the side reappearing at the far hip.

A thigh-high side slit revealed even more skin in long legs of startling perfection. Every muscle enhanced and accented by the knee-tall, high-heel boots of the dark destroyer sketch. In the boots she was several inches taller than he was.

It was a dramatic statement that would play as well from the back of the house as it did from ten feet away. She was joy and hope and immense power all wound together.

And beauty. Gods, she was incredible. Her slender frame had been shifted from waif to sleek by the design. Every womanly shape and curve was accented until her gender struck such a hard slap in the face that it left him reeling.

"Well, I guess that worked." She sounded incredibly pleased with herself.

Bill blinked hard. "Huh? What worked?"

She twirled on one foot proving that the look was as powerful from behind as it was from the front, and at the same time totally destroying the persona. The swirl of her hair and girlish laugh matched the crazed designer of yesterday.

"The look on your face. It so totally worked." She did a little stomping victory dance in her high-heel boots.

He heard a laugh beside him and turned to see Nia nodding in agreement.

"What worked?" He knew he was repeating himself like a child, and not a very smart one. He couldn't help himself.

He turned once more to admire the woman before him.

She was breathtaking.

BILL CULLEN really was so cute. Perrin knew she had the ability to shock. But to make a married man turn into a gibbering idiot, that was a new one. Well, not really. But she did thoroughly enjoy doing it.

Had the last thirty hours of frenetic work been worth it? She was now so tired that her body had gone past aching and numb right into zombie. Zombie girl. Her body so disconnected it could wander off on its own and she'd never notice. She giggled at the image.

"What?" Bill was still being monosyllabic, she'd really gotten him good. "What's so funny?"

"Wow! Back up to polysyllabic, Bill Cullen. Well done, you! Gonna go for three syllables together anytime soon?"

That brought the Dark Overlord scowl back.

She decided that made him fair game. "Me. As a zombie, you know, green-and-ghoul makeup, singing opera in a killer dress. It has real possibilities."

She started dancing, Madonna-style bends and hair swoops, and began singing a KT Tunstall song that she didn't really know the words to, so she made them up as she went which was okay because sometimes she wondered if KT did just that. On the third dip and whirl she was so lightheaded that she almost collapsed. She stopped and had to brace herself to remain upright while her head spun.

Her palm landed in the middle of Bill's chest. He didn't waver, the man was solid as if built from the rock of the Earth's very core. She could feel the hard muscle through his thin shirt. She'd always been a fan of hard muscle.

"Are you okay?" His deep voice rumbled in his chest and tickled its way up her arm.

"Solicitous? Are there no ends to the wonders of Bill Cullen?"

The receptionist actually snorted with laughter.

Perrin shot her a smile, but she couldn't stand up on her own just yet. Her head still whirled viciously.

"I'll try once more. Are you okay? Do you need to sit down for a moment? Can I get you some coffee?"

"Coffee? Shit no. If I'm like this normally, can you imagine me on caffeine? So not a pretty sight. I need sleep and food, in that order." Feeling a little steadier, she managed to stand on her own, brushing his shirt smooth as she did so. Nice chest. She wanted to pet it, but it belonged to another woman so she stopped herself.

"How about we go to my office? We can talk over the schedule and then tour the scene shop so you can see the sets, to let you see the tone of the production."

"Uh, as long as we can sit down real soon. It's been so long since I slept that I'm starting to hallucinate tiny conga lines of opera-singing mice swirling about my ankles." She might have slept an hour or two last night, she usually managed at least that —even when a design bit her hard. If she had, she didn't remember it. This design had been ripped out from somewhere deep.

Bill offered his arm. She steadied herself with a hand on his elbow, the only thing that made her steady enough to walk. As he led her back through the offices, a ripple of whispers ran ahead of them and gawkers were soon lining the aisle. Bill was mumbling something about ticket sales department, production design, education…indicating one cluster of cubicles that looked exactly like the last.

A guy walking along carrying a computer monitor actually ran into a wall while looking at her.

By that time she was able to make some sense of the whispers. "The Empress!" said with a touch of awe that she found quite cheery. That was all that sustained her until she reached Bill's office.

It was a smallish space that had a window looking down over an old section of the warehouse district that now housed a Taco Del Mar fast food restaurant and an Asian furniture importer, despite the ancient paint on brick that declared it as "Johnson Expeditors 1914."

The office walls had drawings done by children. There were several framed photos of Bill with two kids, but she couldn't seem to make her eyes focus on them well enough to even pick out gender or age. Then she spotted the couch along the side wall. The last thing she remembered was planting her face into one of the cushions.

"HELLO, Ms. Thompson, my name is Bill Cullen. I'm with Emerald City Opera and we met last week at a board meeting. Do you by any chance know a woman named Perrin Williams?"

He felt stupid for calling one of Seattle's movers and shakers with such a dumb question, but it was all he could think to do. He'd had to shake Perrin fairly hard to rouse her at all. When he'd asked who he should call, she mumbled, "Cassidy or Jo." At least that's what he thought she'd said before collapsing back onto his office sofa.

There were two women he'd met recently at a Friends of the Opera board meeting, where he'd gone to give a presentation about the new production. One of them had been Cassidy Knowles, a leading wine entrepreneur. And Jo Thompson who had replaced the powerhouse Renée Linden and appeared to be no less formidable. He couldn't imagine the association a small-time fashion designer would have with these two, but the names were unique enough that he decided to give it a try.

"Actually it's Jo Parrano now, but yes, I know her. Is she okay?"

"I'm not sure. She collapsed on my office sofa and fell asleep."

He heard a long-suffering sigh over the phone. "She does that. My recommendation is to make sure she's comfortable, then throw a blanket over her."

"But she's in my office," Bill once again felt as if he were being dumb. And like he was whining, which was even more embarrassing. He took a breath and tried to calm down. "I don't quite know what to do with her."

"Welcome to the club, Mr. Cullen. Well, I'm in Hawaii on my honeymoon and I think Cassidy is in France for a vintner's conference. We closed the restaurant and gave the staff a week off, no idea where they will have scattered to. If she still hasn't slept since before the wedding, she'll be down until sometime tomorrow morning. My best advice is to just let her sleep." The woman spoke as if this were somehow normal behavior.

"But in my office?" It hardly seemed appropriate, or convenient.

"Oh, you can work. Nothing much on the planet will wake her. And she'll wake very hungry, so having some food around would be a kindness. She eats anything. Sorry I can't be more helpful."

"Uh, I guess she's okay as long as I don't need to rush her to the hospital or back to the mothership or something."

Jo Thompson had the decency to laugh. "That latter option wouldn't surprise any of us even a little bit. Is she okay there? I could try to rally some troops... "

Her voice was very tentative.

"No. I'll take care of it from here. Congratulations and thanks." He hung up the phone wondering what in hell he'd just signed up for. Well, for damn sure, he couldn't just leave her there like that. His hormones would kill him looking at her in that amazing dress for hour after hour.

He picked up the phone and buzzed downstairs for some help. Then he sat back to wait and allowed himself just a moment to admire the revelation of such exceptional beauty in the woman who wore that amazing dress.

Jaspar and Tamara arrived about the same time that Jerimy, the head of the Costume Shop, arrived from the floor below. The kids ran in and gave him huge, after-school hugs. Whatever else he was messing up, he was doing this right...mostly. Tamara was drifting away and he had no idea what to do about it. She still hugged him when she wasn't really thinking about it. Other times it was suffered, and recently she'd avoided his hug a few times. As a single dad, she often left him with his moorings cut loose and no channel markers on where to go from there.

Jaspar was just gone ten, a cocky, know-it-all, splendid fifth grader. Dark-haired like his dad, but with his mother's wide eyes.

Tamara was a sophisticated thirteen-year-old acting like she was in high school rather than tolerating the last months of middle school, and who thankfully hadn't yet decided her dad was a crime against nature. She looked so like a young version of her dead mother—a thick mane of dark red hair, and Italian-dusky skin—that she broke his heart every day, though he would never let it show.

They waved hello to Jerimy and turned for their usual after-school-debrief hangout of the couch, then stumbled to a halt.

"Who's she?" Jaspar tipped his head sideways to study Perrin sort of right side up. "Is she real or a mannequin?"

"She's breathing, dummy." Tamara tipped her head so like her brother that Bill had to cover his mouth to not laugh at them.

He shared a smile with Jerimy over the kid's heads.

"Wild dress," Tamara's voice was filled with a bit of wonder.

"Yeah," how in the hell was he supposed to explain this one? He almost went with spaceship alien as being the most plausible. No, he'd better go for the simple truth, that was bizarre enough on the credibility scale. Jerimy was leaning comfortably against the door frame enjoying the whole scene.

Tamara brushed Perrin's crazy hair back from her face. "I like her hair."

"Don't get any ideas, kiddo. No crazy dye jobs."

Tamara squinched her eyes shut and stuck her tongue out at him. He did the same right back. A good moment. When had he started hoarding those?

"She's our new costume designer, but I think she was awake for five days straight or something."

"She okay?" Jaspar was whispering. They all were.

"I called a friend of hers who assures me that she just needs to sleep. Jerimy, I'm going to take the kids out for some ice cream," there was a small round of quiet cheers. "Before they start their homework," a chorus of less soft boos.

He stood up and grabbed Jaspar around the waist and held him upside down until he was giggling. Been a long while since he'd been able to do that with Tamara. Probably since Adira's death when Tamara had decided she had to become the lady of the household. Hell of a burden for a then nine-year old girl. He and Tamara had both grown up a lot that year. Jaspar had been six, too young to do more than be in shock.

"Ms. Williams," he figured remaining formal in front of his kids was a good thing. "She was modeling a costume design for me when she fell asleep. Jerimy, I was hoping that you could gather some more comfortable clothes, arrange for a discreet change, and then toss a blanket on her. I'm assured that she will be almost impossible to wake for some time yet."

Jerimy nodded. "I'll go gather some supplies, and help." He tickled Jaspar's belly button where being held upside down had made his shirt pull out of his pants. Jaspar squirmed and giggled harder as Jerimy left.

"She's beautiful," Tamara was still studying the sleeping Perrin Williams.

"She's even prettier when she's awake."

His daughter eyed him with a far too thoughtful look.

He shook his head, a clear "no way!" Tamara had alternated over the years between trying to matchmake him, and assuming that he no longer loved Tamara's mother if he even glanced at a woman walking down the street.

Well, she didn't need to worry. This woman was nuts. Not no way. Not no how.

He herded the kids out of there before there were more questions.

But Bill could still feel the outline of where Perrin's palm had rested over his heart. The touch of the Empress, a great curse or a great blessing in the new opera's story. Always unknown, but always powerful.

CHAPTER 3

*P*errin woke slowly. She always enjoyed the crawl back from her "hibernations" as Cassidy had dubbed them. She didn't do it often, but when a design really grabbed her, like Jo's wedding dress, or that outfit for the opera, she just had to chase it until it was done and purged from her system.

She became aware of voices as she languished beneath the warm blankets.

A deep voice rumbling that she recognized easily. Mr. Bill Cullen. He had such a great voice, a far-off thunderstorm brushing soft sounds across an otherwise peaceful summer evening.

A higher voice, still male, but with a definite swish to it. "This is amazing work, Bill. I've been doing costumes since I was a teen, and I can barely tell how she did it. And the hand dyeing here from the white to gold, it's just magnificent. That's a technique that I'd like to learn."

She opened her eyes and looked through the brush of hair that had slid over her face. Black. When had her hair gone black? Last she remembered it was blonde.

Oh, the costume. What had people called it? "The Empress."
She liked the sound of that.

Peeking through her hair, she could see two men closely
inspecting the costume where it hung by itself on a rack. One
was showing the inside of the seams to the other. The second
one was Bill Cullen, in his classic, arms-crossed Overlord pose
that made her smile.

Further inspection revealed that she was on an office
couch and it felt as if she'd been here quite some time. But
she'd arrived wearing the dress. She was fairly sure of that. So,
she lifted the blanket. A black Emerald City Opera t-shirt,
with a lemon-yellow stylized ECO logo over one breast. She
brushed her legs together under the blanket. Sweats and bare
feet.

Then the last of her came awake and she smelled sugar. That
got her upright. Bill and the other man whirled to look at her,
but all she cared about was the large cheese Danish that had
been placed on the low table in front of the couch she'd apparently slept on.

"Good morning."

"Uh, hi!" she mumbled around a mouthful. "Morning, huh?
How long... Never mind. Overnight. You have milk or tea or
something?"

Bill moved to a small fridge and pulled out a carton of
chocolate milk. "After school treat for Jaspar. Tamara is now
above that, so I also have ginger ale."

"How old are they? Milk's fine." She took it from him, and
knocked back half a carton to clear the Danish so that she could
speak properly.

"Ten and the oldest thirteen there ever was."

She hoped not, for the kid's sake.

By thirteen the world had held no more illusions for Perrin
at all.

"And you give her ginger ale? You'd get way more dad-points

if you stocked in some caffeine-free diet Coke or Pepsi. Trust me on that."

He opened his mouth, clearly to say something about knowing his own kids well enough. So, she cut him off by holding out a hand to the other man.

"Hi, I'm Perrin."

"Jerimy. I'm the manager of the costume department for ECO, I hope you don't mind that I changed you yesterday. You were really out of it, honey." Jerimy was a trim man with a shock of bottle-red hair moussed up into a chaotic hairstyle that suited his blue eyes and narrow features. He wore a very tailored white shirt and black pants with lines that narrowed the hips, and good shoes. He looked sharp, standing hipshot like a runway model.

Bill was wearing jeans and an open white shirt from some off-the-rack store, Sears probably. Bought at the same time he was buying a reciprocating drill or a forty-two-tooth screwdriver or some such.

"Was he here?" She nodded toward Bill and took another bite of the Danish. Weird combo with a swirl of chocolate milk, but okay.

His jaw dropped to protest his innocence. He must really be gone on his wife to have passed up on the opportunity to see her mostly naked. The bra had been built into the dress after all. Not that Perrin really needed one very often; the one and only advantage to never really growing breasts. Well, that and she could get away with wearing almost any high-fashion design.

"Just me and Patsy, she's straight and I'm so not, so your secrets are perfectly safe with both of us," Jerimy offered her a broad wink. She liked him, and not just because he appreciated her dress.

She eyed it critically as she continued to chew.

"The Empress?"

"Yes. You really captured her," Bill turned once more to the dress.

"Wow! You actually paid me a compliment there, Mr. Cullen. You may want to go easy on that. Making my head spin. You, uh, told me about the Empress?"

Bill looked up at the ceiling in exasperation. Well, what did he expect? She'd been asleep on her feet during their visit to her shop—even before she'd started this dress.

"It just sort of came together from the other two designs I drew." Perrin remembered Bill rambling on at some length about the opera's story, but she couldn't remember a word. This design had simply been a natural extension of the story about the first two male characters. Maybe the tone of Bill's deep voice as he'd described the character was in there somewhere, but she couldn't pick it out.

The dress' lines were good, the balance of sex and power.

"Is the Empress good or evil?"

"No one is sure. Even at the opera's end, she is still enigmatic. The powerful unknown."

Perrin cocked her head trying to see the color and tone without wholly discounting shape and line.

"I think it needs a blood-red lining then, to balance the hope of the gold."

Jerimy caught his breath and she knew it was right.

But it had come out well for not knowing anything about the story. She remembered Bill's eyes going dark with heat as he'd first looked at her in the Opera's lobby.

Yes, the dress had come out very well.

JERIMY HAD SPREAD out Carlotta Gianelli's watercolors along the Costume Shop table. They really had quite an amazing setup here. He'd given her the full tour.

"A really major production can have three hundred costumes, which is easily over a thousand pieces not counting shoes and accessories. And sometimes we have two casts for the leads, that means building some costumes twice, in two different sizes."

There was a sewing area that had a dozen machines. Perrin's studio had one four-by-eight foot cutting table. The opera had two matted tables, eight feet wide by twenty-four long. A dozen people could work at each table, though only a half dozen people were in the entire room at the moment.

They had a vented paint booth where red shoes were repainted as blue, fabrics were sprayed with texturing, and papier-mâché headdresses were magically transformed into golden crowns, bishop miters, and magician hats. There were boxes and boxes of shoes simply labeled: Men's 9, Women's 8, Child's 6. Each was a treasure chest filled with shoes, boots, sandals, platforms, and more of almost every imaginable type.

What had surprised Perrin about the costumes themselves was the way they were constructed. Only rarely were they of the fine-finished construction she was used to.

"We only do that for the most special pieces," Jerimy had informed her. "And we never manage anything as spectacular as the one you built." The more typical costumes were well-built, but with massive six-inch seam allowances. They must be uncomfortable for the singers but allowed for the costume to be adjusted to different-sized singers without rebuilding them each time. Take out a couple seams, fit, and restitch.

"The typical costume will last through twenty or more productions, each of perhaps a dozen performances. They're used for a dozen years or more at ten or twenty different opera houses. So, we try to make the costumes as adjustable as possible."

Perrin looked down at Carlotta's drawings. They were little more than blurs of colors. They were cohesive in their color palette. The lines were dramatic. But they didn't relate. It was like a runway collection that really didn't work. Each piece would be fine, but it wasn't a whole story.

Perrin hadn't really understood that until she started doing weddings. For years she'd made couples' clothing, that told a story of two people. But a wedding told the story of the main couple, with their friends supplementing that, and family the next layer beyond that. All of them designed and built to focus back on the couple.

Bill Cullen wandered in, probably to check up on them. She ignored him, as well as she could. He was way too attractive to be allowed out in public. Not rugged like Russell or ever so handsome like his best friend Angelo. Bill Cullen's face was striking because it was rich with character and his emotions brushed so close beneath the surface.

She did her best to ignore his presence and spoke to the head of the costume department.

"There's only one story here, Jerimy."

"What do you mean?" He and Bill came up to stand to either side of her. She'd definitely have to make sure that didn't keep happening with Bill, it only made her body all too aware of things it couldn't have.

She rearranged Carlotta's drawings, at least getting the story's hierarchy correct. Empress and Overlord side by side, Prince and his court below, separated for the good, the evil, and the overly neutral drabness of the townspeople.

"Damn!" Jerimy cursed. "I didn't even see that. So that's how they're supposed to go together?"

"I didn't see it either," Bill commented. "But you said it only told one story, what's the other one?"

"Other two. Maybe three, but I have to think about that. This," she waved a hand at them, "is the story of the opera. Or at least one part of it." Then she pointed at the dress now hanging behind them.

"That is the story of the individual, of what she is inside. Each must add together to explain where they came from before the opera and where they're going after."

Bill did his arms-crossed thing. Maybe that was how he always stood when he was thinking.

Jerimy returned, as he had a dozen times, to inspect the costume closely as if the answer was somehow in the material itself rather than the design. Perrin recognized that blind spot, she had suffered from it for years, too fascinated by the construction to step back and see how it went together with the surrounding context.

"The other story is the audience?" Bill barely whispered.

Perrin twisted to look at him, she'd never expected Bill Cullen to understand. So few people saw that. From somewhere deep inside, a laugh of sheer delight bubbled forth.

Perrin's joyous laugh rocked Bill back on his heels. The smile that lit her face made him feel ten feet tall, as did the approving hand resting lightly on his arm. It was ridiculous to feel so gratified about being right, but Perrin made it easy.

"Yes! Exactly! High fashion design is about who we are, but even more about how we wish to be perceived. So few people see that. Jo in her power suits, Cassidy in her ever so tasteful black, Jerimy sharp and snappy, and you... " her giggle was absolutely ridiculous.

"What? Finish it."

She pushed him around like one of Jerimy's dress forms on wheels until she stood behind him. Then she pulled at his shirt collar. "JC Penny. Well, I was close."

He turned back to try and explain about finding a minute to grab a shirt while riding herd on a ten-year-old who kept trying to sell his need for hundred-dollar sneakers, and a sullen thirteen-year-old who kept trying on clothes, and hating all of them right along with her body that was maturing far too fast for his fatherly vision of her.

Before he could speak, he heard the kids pounding down the stairs. He always let Nia know where he'd be about the time the school bus dropped the kids off. For the four years since Wilson had convinced him to move to Seattle, they'd practically grown up at the Opera's offices; everyone knew to keep an eye out for them. Most days, he could just work another hour or two while they did their homework, then they'd all go home together. He often did paperwork in the evening or after they went to bed; impossibly it all worked. As a family, they'd found their groove.

The kids plummeted into the Costume Shop. Jaspar came right up for a hug, but Tamara pulled up short when she spotted Perrin. Her assessing gaze snapped his attention to just how close the designer was standing to him. He took a step away from Perrin and toward Tammy, but she detoured wide and moved to the design table.

"Are these yours?" Tammy looked down at Carlotta's drawings.

Perrin turned her attention as fully on his daughter as it had been on him the moment before.

"First tell me if you like them, truthfully, then I'll tell you."

TAMMY DIDN'T LOOK up from the drawings spread across the table. She didn't like them, and they probably were this lady's work or her dad wouldn't be acting so weird around her.

Last night before they left, he'd been all fussy, making sure he left a big note with his cell number in case she woke. Even tucking in her blanket as if it was normal for people to sleep on his office couch. Even at home he'd been saying, "Ms. Williams this" and "Ms. Williams that."

So, Tammy delivered her verdict, which actually wasn't that biased.

"Major yawn."

"Jerimy!" Perrin cried out, startling all of them, causing Tammy to take a quick step back in case she'd upset her. The woman was waving her arm like a pirate captain from the quarterdeck. "The young lady has spoken! This calls for the rubbish bin!"

Jerimy swung one out from under the bench.

"Do it, girl!" Ms. Williams cried loudly enough for her voice to echo about the large space and draw everyone's attention from the other parts of the Costume Shop.

Tammy picked up the plainest drawing. She glanced up at the woman, but still couldn't detect one way or the other what she thought. When Tammy looked at her dad, he shrugged.

Tammy dropped the drawing carefully into the trash can and looked again for everyone's reaction. She'd been around the opera enough to know the value of an artist's work as well as their temperament about it. The time when Jasp was four and had drawn green flowers around someone's set drawing had almost gotten him murdered.

Dad opened his mouth. She could see he was about to tell her it was okay, when the lady poked Tammy's shoulder hard enough to make her turn away from him. The woman put her fists on her hips, glared down at Tammy, and blew out a huff of air that would have stirred her bangs if she'd had any. Instead she had that black hair with the blonde stripe that was even prettier now that she was awake.

Here it comes. Figures. Another crazy adult saying it was okay one minute and gearing up to chew you out the nex—

"Where did you learn how to do that?" The lady didn't wait for an answer. Instead she pointed at Jasp without even turning. "You! Boy! What's your name?"

"Jaspar," he didn't quite stammer in his surprise at suddenly being the center of attention.

"Jaspar, show this girl how you throw out an ugly drawing."

With only a brief backward glance at Dad for reassurance, he took up a drawing, crumpled it a little. Then he glanced at Tammy. She grinned back at him; he was gonna show Ms. Williams but good.

Jasp made a whole spectacle of crushing it into the smallest, wrinkliest ball he could, then ran back a couple paces and shot it into the trash like a basketball.

Tammy could see her dad. Jasp might not get it, but she knew. Each of those paintings represented untold hours of painstaking coaxing and wheedling to get "Carlotta Nightmare," as Jasp had dubbed her, to produce them. They were also the only designs they had, and there were less than six weeks to production.

Last night Dad had been groaning, in between worrying about Ms. Williams, about how the publicity shots were supposed to be this week and there were no costumes yet and—

"Better," the lady told Jasp.

He checked in with Tammy, but she could only twitch a shoulder in a shrug. She didn't know how to read Ms. Williams yet.

"Better, but still lame. Now, watch carefully."

Tammy had to figure out what was going on. Even without the fancy dress, she was very tall and very pretty.

Tammy liked the black hair that matched the opera t-shirt. And she wouldn't mind trying to have a blonde swirl in her hair. It pointed like an arrow to the bright yellow ECO logo over her breast. The t-shirt clung to her body. Tammy glanced at Dad through the fall of her own long hair so that he wouldn't notice her attention. He was staring hard at the woman, which Tammy didn't like much.

The lady handed her and Jasp another drawing and took one

herself. So slowly that it was almost painful, she tore it in half: the paper making a long, drawn-out cry of protest. The half-dozen costumers doing touch-up work on the clothes for the present opera rushed over to see what was happening. They stopped and stared, with their jaws down.

She glanced to Dad for permission, but Ms. Williams called them back to attention like they were both still in third grade.

"You have to just do it!"

Jasp raised one eyebrow in question then waited to see what she'd do. Tammy set her jaw and tore it with the same agonizing slowness, Jasp joining her part way through.

Then Ms. Williams overlapped her two pieces and tore them the other way, a little faster.

Tammy and Jasp did the same. Then faster and faster they all tore their paintings and tore them and tore them until they were little more than large confetti.

With a fistful of torn paper, she sent Jasp the tiniest head nod toward Dad. He was sharp and chucked his into the air right over Dad's head. Dad ducked and cringed beneath the shower of bits of paper. At the last second, Tammy changed her target and launched her own fistful of paper over the woman's head who burst out with a wild laugh and threw hers right back, saving a few to sprinkle over Jasp.

BILL WATCHED in amazement as three of Carlotta Nightmare's drawings fluttered about them in tiny pieces. He tried to think of something to say, but couldn't as Jaspar scraped up a fistful that had fallen on the table and launched them right at Bill's face where they burst apart into a colorful flurry just inches away.

Perrin dove for another watercolor and began tearing madly. The kids joined in. In the midst of the mayhem that ensued, Perrin very solemnly handed one painting to him.

It was harder than he expected, making that first tear. It was the Overlord, at least he thought it was, it was hard to tell on Carlotta's work and she'd certainly been above explaining her "Art"—always with a capital A—to anyone who couldn't simply "intuit" it themselves. The second tear was easier, then the third.

In moments, he too was showering bits of paper over his kids' heads.

After the last drawing was destroyed, and Jerimy had the honor of stuffing the last fistful down the back of Jaspar's shirt, they all set in to clean up. Bill saw Perrin take Tammy a little to one side. He moved as unobtrusively as he could to collect some confetti that was closer to them, so that he could overhear.

"That," Perrin pointed at the floor. "So not me." Then she turned Tammy to face the Empress' dress.

"That," Perrin nodded as if reassuring herself. Though he could hear the doubt in her voice as if she didn't believe in her own power.

"That is me."

It was absolutely her. So powerful that she actually unnerved him a bit. And now she'd made friends with his children.

That he was far less sure about.

CHAPTER 4

*P*errin would have liked to have someone to call. But with Jo's wedding over and the week-long closure of the restaurant, everyone was gone. Even Maria had taken the opportunity to go on a belated honeymoon with her Hogan. They were taking some extra time and had rented a sailboat for two weeks to cruise along the Amalfi coast of Italy.

She wasn't even sure why she wanted someone around at this moment. She was fine on her own for days at a time. Especially when a challenging design tackled her. It wasn't that she wanted to talk to one of her friends about anything in particular. Perrin just wanted to be around them for a time.

They were her sanity benchmark. She sometimes needed reminding, even now at thirty, that she was okay—a good person and not some product of her childhood. That people liked her who weren't merely looking for ways to use her.

So, she sat by herself at Cutters Crabhouse, just her untouched iced tea, some focaccia, and her sketchbook. It was mid-afternoon. Through the towering windows the Seattle waterfront lay spread out below her. Pike Place Market, a close bustle of tourists and hundreds of cool little shops perched on the cliff edge. Out of sight on Post Alley, Angelo's Tuscan Hearth Ristorante with its "Closed for Honeymoon" sign on the door. Below, the long piers of the waterfront reached out into Elliott Bay. The sun glittered off the water and the snowy Olympic Mountains loomed high in the west on the far side of Puget Sound.

This was as close as she could be to her absent friends. This is where they usually gathered, in Cutter's upscale bar. All dressed to the limit, shimmering together around a too small, wood-and-steel table, perched on high-leather stools, and teasing waiters far and wide.

This time, instead of too much alcohol and too many appetizers and laughing until her sides ached, she sat by herself and ordered a cup of chowder and half of a hot pastrami on rye.

It was still a bit early for the after-work crowd, so the bar was uncharacteristically quiet. It would be hopping in a couple hours, but for the moment there was mostly just her, a few stray tourists, and the wait staff.

At the Opera, after they'd all finished the cleanup and the kids were tucked into handy cubicles outside his office, chipping away at their homework, Bill had told her the opera's plot again. He also gave her a script.

"No," he corrected her. "It's a libretto not a script, everything is sung." Even in *The Sound of Music* Julie Andrews didn't sing everything. Singing meant the clothing needed to provide room to breathe even more than room to move.

He'd shown her photos of the lead singers. The Empress was okay, the lead tenor singing the Tragic Prince was a big guy. The Dark Overlord, a rare true bass singer, even bigger. Now she understood some of Jerimy's comments on construction. These were people who made their livings with their chest and gut muscles. Making the proportions balance out would take some doing.

"There was a great tenor," Jerimy had informed her. "Whose

chest grew so massive and his legs so out of shape that it actually ended his career when he could no longer stand through a whole performance." She'd stepped through a door into a whole other world.

She'd read the libretto, doodled a little, but she still didn't have any ideas flowing. Perrin wasn't worried, yet. She was supposed to go see the final performance of the current production of *Turandot* this weekend. Bill had assured her it would have a happy ending. Cassidy would be back by then. She'd agreed by e-mail to go with Perrin and Russell had begged to not be forced to go, so that should be fun. A mini girls' night out.

Tomorrow, she'd see the sets and the first rehearsal of *Ascension*, opening in just over five weeks. That's what she was counting on. The libretto gave her plot, but it still told her so little of the world and the people involved.

She doodled quick images of the three designs she'd already done as thumbnails across the top of the page as a reference.

The chowder and sandwich arrived. She ignored the waiter's mild flirt and paid attention to the smells of the sandwich, rich pastrami and tangy sauerkraut. The first taste didn't disappoint in the slightest. She tried to savor it as Cassidy would savor a wine—the interaction of the caraway-seed rye bread and stone-ground mustard—but instead found herself just chewing it. Food kept her body running. So many of her friends were foodies that some appreciation had rubbed off on her, but eating alone didn't make it fun enough to be worth the effort.

There was a benefit to ignoring the waiter and paying some attention to food that she usually saw as merely sustenance. If she did those things with the front of her mind, she didn't pay too much attention to her sketching, shutting out that inner editor. She'd continued to idly doodle more ideas to go with the first three as she ate.

Powerful colors, but simpler.

Less complex than Prince and Empress.

More hopeful, brighter lights. But understated.

Costumes to match the character rather than enhance them. To let the person show through without declaring the role outright, avoiding the dynamism of a chosen mantle that so overshadowed what nature had provided. That choice to cloak oneself was so adult. Use the greens and golds of nature. The simplicity of youth.

Youth.

The children. There they were, smiling at her from her sketchpad, clothed like the parental Overlord and Empress. But they didn't have their older brother Prince's tragedy imprinted yet on either them or their costumes.

She paged open the libretto and inspected the cast of characters. There was a younger daughter, a child soprano. But no little boy. Well, they could just go ahead and add a non-singing boy-child role who could follow after his older sister.

That actually gave her drawings for one whole side of the cast, the Empress' lineage. But what of the other side of the house, the marriage-sworn Princess and the Tragic Prince's True Love? Before tomorrow's rehearsal, she could start building the prototypes for the children's costumes.

Jerimy had assured her that they could build whatever she drew, or create patterns from anything she'd sewn. Though he had seemed less sure about the Empress' outfit. But she always finished her design concept while *doing* the construction herself. That was her creative process. She'd have to build all of the major pieces at least once herself.

Models. Jaspar and Tammy. Maybe Bill would let her borrow his kids as models. That would really help. She hadn't done children's clothing since her own first efforts, and those had been to hide, blend in, be invisible. Back when—

"Perrin!"

Perrin startled from her dark thoughts and almost dumped her cup of untouched chowder over her now-cold sandwich.

"Josh! Come here, cutey. Give your Perrin a hug!" Josh Harper was so handsome. Totally safe, but fun and funny. Tall, with wavy, light brown hair and an easy smile.

He gave her a big hug that she let herself be lost in for just a moment that washed away the last of her uncomfortable memories.

"How are you, my love?" he teased her.

"Still pining away. Waiting for you to throw over that woman you're married to."

"Yes, I know. If only I didn't love her so much. Alas, we're never meant to be." He gestured for permission then took the seat across from her.

"I could take out a contract on her. I do know some really scary guys. Ones who would, like, do anything for me. Maybe, I dunno, Russell."

"Oh, now I'm really scared." Josh wasn't in town very often, but he, Russell, and Angelo had become good friends at first meeting. It didn't hurt that Josh was a senior food-and-wine critic for *Gourmet Week* magazine and had consistently raved about Angelo's restaurant both in print and on-line.

"But what are you doing sitting alone, my love? Why is there no suitor begging at your feet? And where the heck is everybody? 'Restaurant Closed for Honeymoon.' It was my fifth anniversary, so I couldn't make it to Jo and Angelo's wedding. I went by to pay my respects and it's closed. You have to tell me everything!"

Perrin, glad for a friend, closed her pad and pulled her lunch in front of her while Josh ordered. Then she settled in and filled him in on all the details of Jo's wedding, especially teasing him about the great food he'd missed.

BILL COULDN'T BELIEVE he was doing this. He had a thousand things to get done and here he was playing Seattle tour guide to a tenor and his supermodel girlfriend. They'd flown in together for tomorrow's first rehearsal of *Ascension*.

This was Wilson's kind of job, but he was rubbing shoulders with some of the high-rolling donors at the Seattle Men's Club.

Jerimy had dropped the kids off with Bill's sister for a couple hours, God bless Lucy, and he'd been dragged out on the town. He and Lucy had issues that made it hard to be in the same room together, but none of them were about his kids.

In her soft French accent, the towering blonde model, several inches taller than Perrin, had suggested this Cutters Crabhouse place and he'd been thankful. He knew the whereabouts of every IHOP, Mitzel's, and pizza house in all of Seattle. In-crowd bars and upscale waterfront restaurants, not so much.

This place was near the Pike Place Market and oozed urban professional without actually flaunting it in your face like so many modern bars. It was all chrome and high tables with tall leather stools. Waiters in black pants and white shirts scooted about looking immensely sharp, unhurried, and efficient all at once. A wall of windows looked out toward the Seattle waterfront and the Market.

Actually, if he ever again in his life found time to have a date, this would be a nice place to bring her.

"Perrin!" The model cried out while they stood in the entry debating between the bar and the restaurant.

There couldn't be two women in Seattle named Perrin.

Sure enough, he spotted the woman at the far side of the bar making grand and ridiculous gestures as if reenacting the Greek battle at Troy for an audience of hundreds instead of the one man who sat with her.

Bill couldn't believe Perrin was here. But her hair, hanked back into a ponytail, revealed the swirling blonde stripe that proved her identity even at this distance. She still wore the black opera t-shirt, now partly covered by a knit vest of a rather electric blue.

She was sitting by the window, practically huddled together with some far-too-handsome man. Bill and Carlo di Stefano dutifully followed in the model's wake, who was so cliché that her waist-length blonde hair actually floated along behind her. In moments, the two women were embracing like long lost sisters.

"Melanie," Perrin responded in full, bubbling flight. Again, the madcap waif revealed herself in full airhead-blonde mode.

Assuming she really was blonde with dark-dyed hair, rather than dark-haired with a blonde stripe or....

"You've never met Josh, I don't think. I'd introduce you, but he's married and he's mine if his wife ever leaves him because it is sure he'll never leave her. He doesn't even waver when I throw myself at him."

The model towered over the seated man, fists on hips. She glared down at Josh. "You would deny my friend Perrin? What sort of a cad are you, *monsieur?*"

"A happily married one, I'm afraid." He smiled easily up at the long blonde.

"Pity, or I might try to steal you from her. You are so very pretty," the model sighed, then leaned down and kissed him cheerfully on both cheeks.

"He is awfully pretty, isn't he?" Perrin agreed.

Bill wondered if all women were mad in this day and age. He was so out of touch with "the scene" now. Not that he'd ever really been in touch. He'd met Adira during senior year of college and that had been it for him. She'd been his quiet center, the diametric opposite of Ms. Perrin Williams in every way.

Introductions were made and they moved to a larger table. He ended up sitting farthest from Perrin, clearly she was a favorite. What he found interesting was he felt a bit put out by how the seating wound up. He hadn't been jealous of Josh

Harper when he'd first spotted them so obviously enjoying each other's company.

Had he?

Gods above, maybe he was the one who was going mad.

No, he was simply bothered by the fact that she was sitting there chatting with someone over lunch when she should be back in her shop working on the new designs. Though she had her libretto and sketchpad with her, closed, he noted with some chagrin. He did his best to not grind his teeth while finding something to chat about with Carlo while his model girlfriend ignored both of them.

The problem was that while Carlo could sing beautifully in several languages, he spoke only German and Italian fluently. Bill's German was almost as bad as Carlo's English and his other languages were nonexistent beyond what was needed to manage opera schedules and stage directions.

Here he was in an urban watering hole, which was slowly filling with the young and beautiful of Seattle. And all he really wanted was to go fetch the kids and bribe their happiness with take-out pizza.

One of these days he was going to have to kill Wilson Jervis. At least sitting kitty-corner from Perrin, he was able to watch her, for he couldn't seem to look away.

PERRIN COULD FEEL Bill Cullen's attention without turning to look. Why did his attention so affect her that she *couldn't* turn in his direction?

She'd also overheard his stumbling attempts to talk with Carlo. She wanted to tease him about it. See if she could goad him into a blustering defense about how he hadn't followed her here because he'd fallen in love with her while she slept on his office couch.

She also wanted to find out more about him and his family. He was so sweet with the kids. Perrin couldn't imagine what that was like. Cassidy's dad had been a good guy even if he didn't speak much, letting Perrin come and stay during college vacations so that she never had to go home. Jo's dad had been a sullen fisherman who lived on his boat or in a bar. Not a drunk, just an every-night regular until the day he'd died. Her own dad… She wouldn't think of him.

Jaspar clearly worshipped his dad, and Tammy, once she'd loosened up about being too careful, had leaned against him happily while she'd reached up to stuff confetti down the back of his shirt.

"So, Perrin. I will be needing a terribly sexy dress." Melanie was laying it on a little thick, sliding her hands down her sleek form, perhaps for the benefit of the others.

A quick wink showed that Perrin was absolutely right.

"I will be coming to the opening night of Carlo's opera. I must be the most beautiful woman on opening night so that Carlo will not be able sing without thinking of me. I must have another of your dresses."

"Did you know I'm designing the costumes for the opera?"

"No? *C'est vrai? Très bon!*"

"Yes! And the best part?"

"*Oui?*"

"It's making Bill absolutely nuts!"

Melanie and Perrin both turned to look at him. He turned from one face to the other, then he blushed.

"Ooo," Melanie rested a hand over Perrin's and whispered after Josh had started a conversation with him. "This one, he likes you."

Perrin looked back at Bill's profile a little more closely. "No… I don't think so. Besides, he's married. You should see his kids. They're wonderful. So alive. So un… " She'd almost said undamaged.

Melanie squeezed her hand. They had recognized that in each other at their very first meeting, a common bond even Jo and Cassidy didn't understand more than intellectually.

"So uninhibited," she corrected. Then she glanced once more down the table at Bill. If she was being objective, she'd say that Melanie was right. That he did like her.

But that made no sense.

BILL TRIED to sort out his own feelings, but wasn't having much luck. He'd expected to spend the afternoon trapped in a yawning chasm of boredom as wide as the world, instead he was intrigued despite his better judgment.

Perrin, so overdramatic when talking to Josh or teasing Carlo in broken Italian, was a different woman when talking to the supermodel. With Melanie, Perrin was calm, close, intimate. Her smile warm rather than madcap. Her gestures fluid and graceful rather than flamboyant and occasionally hazardous to those seated nearby.

When at last the party broke up in late afternoon, he figured his duties for the Opera and Wilson were well paid. Melanie had certainly enjoyed herself, which appeared to be enough to keep Carlo happy. They were within walking distance of their hotel and headed off with many hugs between the two women.

Melanie and Perrin were a little daunting to watch actually. Melanie was several inches taller, but they almost could have been sisters. Rather than having that emaciated look that so many models did, they were both simply slender, healthy-looking women of truly exceptional beauty. They were certainly easy enough together to be related.

Josh was headed to Kirkland to review some waterfront restaurant that had just been opened by a two-star Michelin chef. He'd given back his stars, closed his major New York restaurant, and moved west to open a small bistro in the upscale suburb.

Bill watched as Perrin stepped out into the afternoon light and raised her arms as if she were a goddess greeting the setting sun and the glistening waterfront. She strolled toward the waterfront to walk through the city park that lay between Cutters and the Pike Place Market.

It was a beautiful spring evening, the breeze cool, but the air warm. Other people gathered in the park, sitting on benches to stare out at the ferries and container ships working their way through Seattle's harbor. Nothing brought out the people of this city quite like a sunny day.

Bill didn't stop moving long enough to enjoy the view very often anymore. But the view here was stunning, in more ways than one. When Perrin saw that he'd accompanied her, she turned to him.

"I'd like to borrow your kids."

"What? No!" The last thing Bill wanted was his kids under this woman's influence. Or getting more attached to her. They'd already started asking him questions this afternoon once she'd left.

Jaspar liked her, dubbing her as "cool." His current "retro-word." Bill had just introduced the kids to Travolta in *Grease*. There was more going on than "cool" though. The little twerp was always hunting for a new mother to marry his dad.

For a while his choice had been Nia at the front desk, then his fifth-grade teacher, and now Perrin was on the verge of replacing Olivia Newton-John. Jaspar didn't quite understand that Olivia Newton-John, while still a fine-looking woman, was in her sixties and his dad wasn't. Jaspar's only measure? Being older than his big sister, which meant you were old... just like his dad. Great!

Tammy had been just the opposite, though making the same assumptions. His pointing out that he'd met her on Monday and this was only Wednesday did nothing to appease his daughter's suspicions. A teenager who was in and out of crushes almost weekly wouldn't understand that actual, adult relationships didn't happen overnight.

"Why can't I borrow them?" Perrin asked as she arrived at the thick brass railing that overlooked the waterfront. "I promise I'll give them back."

"What do you want them for?" He moved up beside her, giving that anonymous nod that Seattleites always traded with strangers to the guy just a few feet farther along.

Perrin flipped open the sketchbook and pointed to a drawing. Three thumbnails across the top and then the two larger drawings of children. His children!

"Having them as models would really help." Perrin had drawn Jaspar and Tammy in costumes.

She'd captured Jaspar with his wide-eyed wonder at the world. His costume vibrated with that energy as if always reaching for the next thing. He looked caught on the verge of his favorite question: "Why?" He'd gone through the "Why" phase when he was four, just like every other child on the planet, but now he'd circled back around to it, and this time really wanted to know rather than just being assured that there was indeed order to the universe.

Tammy was different. Perrin had caught her on the edge of becoming a woman, but less ready than she thought she was. In ways Bill couldn't sort out, Perrin had captured both her surety and the slight fracturing that occurred from being overeager to grow up.

He glanced around to see if anyone else was watching this shocking exposure of his children's true characters, but everyone was interested in their own world, not his. The cool breeze sent a chill up his spine.

Who was this woman?

Had she been researching his kids somehow?

No, she was just…what?

A psychic?

A…

"There's no boy character in the opera," Bill retreated to the known. He had to, to cover just how perfectly this enigmatic woman had captured his children, as if she'd known them their whole lives.

She waved the libretto at him, "Hello. Not stupid. So add one who doesn't sing. Jaspar would love the role."

"Little twerp would," Bill had to admit with a smile that he hadn't intended. "But his sister would be some kind of pissed if he got to wear a cool costume on stage and she didn't."

"Is the girl's part cast yet?"

Bill tried to think through the cast list.

The major singers had all been cast a year ahead for scheduling reasons, and the standing Emerald City Opera Chorus would fill all of the villager and guard roles as well as most of the courtiers. Those with half-solo contracts could fill the Chief of Guard and Missionary roles.

But a couple of the middle characters weren't yet cast. That included the child. Children?

"Tammy doesn't sing, except with her guitar."

"So teach her! She only has seven lines and three of them are only one word long."

Bill looked up from the drawing to study Perrin. The sun was almost directly behind her, making her face hard to see. As if she were deeply inscrutable, mysterious, so powerful that she wore the sun as a halo.

She couldn't have had time to read the libretto more than once since she'd left the Costume Shop this afternoon, there simply wasn't time. And the child's lines were spread out. Odd thing to tally on a single reading, unless she'd somehow tallied everything. To avoid feeling totally humbled by the shining Empress, he'd let that one go unremarked.

The light breeze that always ghosted along the Seattle water-front on even the calmest days made her hair, now out of its ponytail, dance on her shoulders. The brightest blue eyes he'd ever seen argued that the blonde stripe, or something near to it was her proper hair color, though the dyed-black look was a nice contrast to her pale skin. It also accented her strong cheekbones.

She'd added a fleece jacket. It was strange in a way that took him a moment to identify.

"Black t-shirt, blue knit vest, REI jacket. You look almost... " He bit his tongue to avoid saying it.

"Almost human." A wicked glint came into her eyes.

"Uh, I was going to say normal."

"Normal compared to what?"

Bill grinned at her, "I think this would be a fine time for me to be in a different conversation."

She grinned and leaned against the rail but stayed facing him.

He couldn't help noticing that the guy a little further down the rail was admiring the view, and not the one of the water-front. He turned away when Bill glared at him.

"Okay, Mr. Cullen. What conversation would you like to be in? Shall I go get one of those first-date conversation deck of cards for you? I'm sure I saw some in one of the game stalls in the Market." She waved a fine-fingered hand over her shoulder indicating Pike Place Market behind her.

"You're amazing!" He didn't know where that came from, but she was. Intelligent, funny, wild... amazing.

After a long pause, she slowly stood up straight, took her sketch pad back from him, and, closing it, slid it beside the libretto. Pulling her jacket closed against a sudden gust, he could feel a type of shield forming around her, like on the Star-ship *Enterprise*.

"I think I should be going."

It was only then, like he'd been caught in a time warp while watching her change, that he realized that he didn't want her to go. Not at all.

"Why?"

She began moving off.

"No, wait."

She stopped.

"Why?"

For a long moment she stood still, rigid, then turned to face him. There was no sign of the wild blonde, or the powerful Empress. Instead, in their place, stood the waif with the saddest eyes he'd ever seen.

"The likes of you aren't for the likes of me, Mr. Cullen. You should go home to your wife and children, I'm sure they're missing you."

"Wait!" he called before she could turn away once more. "Just wait."

So she did. Standing there all alone, the lost girl fighting off a shiver on a warm sunny day, her jacket still clutched closed across her chest. The wind still toyed with the tips of her hair.

"I'm not married." Where the hell had that come from? He wanted to work with Perrin, not bed her.

She eyed him skeptically.

"She died four years ago. A drunk hit her with a car. Broad daylight in a crosswalk." God Almighty! Why was he ripping his guts out in front of this woman? It almost killed his heart all over again to say the words out loud.

The change was instantaneous. Sympathy poured out of her as her hand shifted from holding her jacket closed to holding her palm over her heart.

"I'm so sorry. And I was teasing you about— You must hate me."

"No." Bill closed his eyes, not knowing what he was feeling. "No, I don't hate you. It's just hard sometimes."

Perrin took a step closer and rested a hand on his arm. "You're such a good father."

"What? What makes you say that?" He screwed up more days than he didn't. His daughter was drifting away and he didn't know why or how to bring her back. He didn't spend enough time with Jaspar. They were both growing up so damn fast that he—

"Because it's hard for you. If it wasn't, it would mean you didn't care. Trust me, I know." For a moment longer, the sad-eyed girl patted his arm. Then she began brushing at his shoulders, as if dusting him off.

"What? What are you doing?"

She dusted harder, squinting her eyes as if it were arduous work. She moved around him until she was practically pounding him on the back.

He tried to turn to face her, but she shoved against his shoulder to keep him in place and continued her way around him. Passers-by were eyeing them strangely. When she arrived once more in front of him, she brushed her hand lightly a few times over his heart.

"There."

"There what?"

"There," Perrin now stood quite close before him, those sad eyes brightening. "You can now leave all that 'bad father' crap behind, I brushed it off you."

Bill could feel his jaw slacken, but clamped it shut before he looked even dumber than he felt. But he couldn't help looking down to see what now lay at his feet. Nothing but the gray concrete of the walkway.

"You think it's as simple as that?" What kind of a ditzy—

"Of course!" Perrin chirped merrily. "Wait. It didn't work? What's wrong with you?" She moved even closer and lifted up on his eyebrows and inspected one eye and then the other, her fingers cool on his brow. "That's strange."

"What?" He was having trouble breathing she was so near. Her eyes were an incredibly pure blue. And the way she smelled. He'd expected perfume or at least an exotic-scented soap. Instead she just smelled immensely, deliciously female.

"I have a terrible diagnosis for you, Mr. Cullen. Are you ready for it?"

This should be good. He nodded with only a little hesitation.

"You're human. I can't just brush that off you. Not even the Empress can do that." Then she grew solemn. "If it were so easy, Bill, we'd all be so much happier, wouldn't we? I'll see you at rehearsal tomorrow. And I'm expecting you and your children in my shop tomorrow evening for dinner. I'll get the pizza."

His light touch on her arm stopped her from turning. Toe to toe he let himself enjoy the sensation of being so close to her.

"I think, Ms. Perrin Williams, that you may well be the most startling person I've ever met."

"I'll take that as a compliment."

"You should, I think... Yes. You should." He really was a lost cause. He couldn't even pay a beautiful and kind woman a decent compliment without screwing it up.

She rested a hand on his cheek. Then she leaned forward and rested her cheek against his.

An electric shock rippled through him, like a static discharge on a doorknob, but without the pain. A sense of simple wonder coursed down through him. The small pleasure of being touched by an attractive woman for the first time since Adira. That's all it was.

Perrin pulled back, but didn't remove her hand from his other cheek. She studied him carefully from just inches away. Then she leaned in and kissed him.

Bill forgot to breathe, or think, or anything. He simply marveled at the sweet tenderness of her lips on his. He leaned into it: the warmth, the sensation, the trust. He didn't know which overwhelmed him the most, but there was no question that "overwhelm" was the operative word here.

Whether the kiss lasted a second or a handful of minutes, he'd never know. He just knew that when Perrin once again moved back, she'd left a taste of her behind. A taste that he couldn't compare to anyone. Not to Adira, not to his first-ever kiss. This was wholly Perrin Williams. Whoever in the world that might be.

"Well," she whispered from a bare inch away, "that was certainly interesting."

"You sound like the Empress, but you look like the wacky designer."

"I'll try switching that." She composed a serious expression that he wasn't buying for an instant. "We gonna have ta try that kiss again some day soon. Because if that was real... Holy Shit, Batman!"

She'd done it. Perrin Williams now *sounded* like the wacky designer. But she looked like the empress. As to the kiss?

"Oh yeah!" Bill finally managed to speak. Try kissing her again? "Real soon."

CHAPTER 5

*P*errin sat in the rehearsal space on the upper level of the Seattle Opera House about a mile from the Emerald City Opera's offices. It was a beautiful space, nearly the same size as the main stage without all the extra space off to the back of the stage and the sides that Bill told her were called wings. The rehearsal space was actually on the top floor of the building, off the side of the upstairs lobby behind an unmarked door. Decorated in a soft beige, it had been turned golden by the tall windows at one end letting in the Seattle sunshine. A shining black grand piano replaced the orchestra.

"This is just our first sing-through," Bill had informed her. "We need to start getting the cast comfortable with the new music. If this were a repertoire opera, they would arrive three weeks before the opening rather than six and we'd move right into staging because they'd already know their roles."

Perrin sat between Wilson Jervis and Melanie in a row of folding chairs along one wall. The principal singers sat in a circle in the middle of the stage, along with the orchestra conductor, the director, Bill, and the Chorus Master who would sing all of the minor roles for now.

Bill had greeted her briefly, barely offering a smile, back in his bustling Overlord role. Perrin could be okay with that. One kiss didn't change the world. She wouldn't even try to count how many men she'd been in and out of love with over the years. Not as many as Jo and Cassidy thought by a long shot— Perrin enjoyed giving them a good story and something to worry about—but still, more than she'd care to admit.

Some part of her was irritated at Bill's apparent lack of ongoing interest. That kiss had certainly rocked her charts. The Tragic Prince, all his hopes and desires and needs had been wrapped up in that kiss. That she was the woman who had drawn that out of Bill Cullen ranked as a startling concept.

That she had lost herself in that kiss, losing track of where she was and who she was, and simply been present in that moment was an even greater surprise. The one thing Perrin never was? Out of control. Deep inside, she had a very rigid grip on who she was and what she would do.

But for a kiss like Bill's, perhaps losing a bit of her control wasn't a terrible thing.

The more she watched Bill as he organized the rehearsal, the less put out she felt about his simple greeting.

Everyone came to him with questions. He had two assistants who constantly brought him questions, some about *Ascension*, some about the *Turandot* closing this weekend. Singers took cajoling.

The writer—the librettist she'd been corrected—and the composer were both there because it was a new opera. The former, a thin young man who practically shimmered with nerves and the latter a staunch woman who apparently thought lyrics were a waste of time and should be changed to fit her music or better yet, removed entirely so that they didn't interfere with her creation. Clearly they were not on speaking terms and Bill had to handle any communication between them.

All of this took Bill's attention. As she watched him, she

began to see quite how good he was at what he did. The conductor had heavily marked his score with questions, but Bill had found a way for the composer to work with him rather than slugging him as she seemed more prone to do. The singers actually cared what order they sat in around the circled chairs. One man was so big that a sturdier chair had to be found.

When Renata Donatello made her entrance, the room had gone quiet as all attention shifted to her. Renata had taken one look at the Empress' dress and insisted on wearing it to the rehearsal. Perrin and Jerimy had made some quick alterations this morning, thankfully ones that didn't require rebuilding the whole costume, then added the red lining. The compliments that swirled about the room upon Renata's grand entrance left Perrin feeling a little giddy.

"That is the dress I want," Melanie leaned in to whisper. "I want to be powerful like that. That's how every woman wants to feel. You have such incredible skills, my friend."

Now Perrin was having trouble breathing. To have one of New York's most successful models say such things… Perrin could only marvel at what it took to actually feel a stamp of approval, as if what she'd done for over a decade didn't count until this moment.

Two years ago, she'd still been struggling on her own. Now she had practically abandoned the front of the shop, adding a manager and an assistant, and was spending most of her time designing and building. Not that she was complaining, that's what she loved best, it was just surprising.

And to have a woman who was constantly clothed in the finest designer labels insist on having one of her dresses… It made Perrin feel oddly capable and twice as uncertain at the same time, as if she were faking being a designer as hard as she was faking being even close to normal.

Melanie had a point though.

While the Empress' dress wouldn't be quite right for her,

something closely related would work. Melanie was too sensual a woman for the austere look of the Empress. The punch of power would look good on her, but she needed something other. Perrin flipped to a fresh page on her pad and began sketching a few ideas while Bill organized the singers.

Perrin became focused on the design, building layer upon layer of detail for the dress she'd design for Melanie until she realized that a rush of sound was carrying her forward. She looked up startled to see the singers already well into the first act.

Opera had never been part of her repertoire. She preferred a good band for dancing and didn't really care what era. Blue Scholars, The Band Perry, and The Black Keys shared her playlists with Maroon 5, Madonna, and Styx. Nothing had prepared her for the powerful wall of sound that the opera singers produced with just their voices.

It was in Italian, which didn't help her much, but it didn't matter. Renata was not ordering around Carlo; instead the Empress was crashing a mandate down upon the Prince's head.

When the barrel-chested deep bass of Geoffrey Palliser joined the fray, the room practically shook with the Overlord's derision.

The Prince's soaring tenor fought for freedom, but found little space between the wall of the Empress' power and the bulldozer of the Overlord's driving rhythms.

It was so completely different from anything she'd heard before it was hard to make sense of it. Even the symphonies that Jo and Cassidy had occasionally dragged her to were no comparison. These weren't instruments, these were people. They weren't hurling music at each other, but rather it was a battle of pure emotion expressed through singing.

The sound swept her along.

The mezzo-soprano Princess, her lower-voiced, contralto Maid-servant Confessor, and the high-coloratura True Love vied for the Prince's attention. The audience's hopes and fears would swing back and forth between them. Whichever one triumphed, it would reshape the future of the kingdom, perhaps alter the fabric of the very world.

The final five-voiced chord of Act I crashed Perrin back into her seat and the dim world of reality.

It took her a moment to reorient herself in the rehearsal studio space.

Several of the singers were talking about the roles, but Carlo and Geoffrey, apparently old friends, were catching up on the latest Italy versus England soccer rivalries.

"What do you think?" Bill was squatting before her chair and looking at her with the kind smile she'd been missing earlier.

"I think I'm in love!" Perrin could still feel the sound of the music vibrating through her.

"Not with Carlo, I hope. I might get jealous."

Perrin placed a finger on the center of his forehead and pushed until he fell back on his butt.

"Wow! This is so cool!" Tammy had taken up her brother's adjective.

Jaspar, on the other hand, had only one comment to make about Perrin's shop, "Ugh! Girl clothes." And then he'd immediately put on his best bored look, one that Bill knew all too well.

Though his son did stop to admire his reflection from the dress made of little mirrors. Bill convinced himself that the mannequin's chest was simply the largest expanse for Jaspar to observe himself in and that Bill shouldn't read anything deeper into it. When Jaspar started making faces at himself, Bill felt better. A little.

Tammy took her time. She'd spent enough afternoons down in the Costume Shop with Jerimy that she actually inspected how some of the clothes were made. She "just happened" to pass close to him at one point during her inspection to ask him a question.

"Are these really good, Dad?"

"Yeah," he acknowledged just as Perrin came over from chatting volubly with a customer now departing in a brand-new blue silk jacket that was clearly a custom fit. "*Really* good."

Tammy nodded and wandered off while Bill inspected the vision headed his way.

Perrin wore a blazer of green and yellow that made her look like nothing so much as a leprechaun. She even sported a bright green hat, shaped like that of a racy secret agent, slanting forward and left, partly covering one eye. When she approached, he saw that she still wore the opera t-shirt beneath the blazer. It made for a deep pseudo-cleavage of black that reached to her sternum, without being the least bit indecent. No one should look good in such an outfit, but she certainly did.

She greeted the kids and then leaned close enough that only he would hear. "I thought about not wearing the t-shirt just to make you crazy." And then in the same breath but a louder voice, "Come on, kids. Let me show you something cool I just made for someone getting married in a couple weeks."

The kids followed her happily enough.

Bill tried, but couldn't. She'd riveted him right to the floor with the image of her in nothing but that deeply plunging blazer.

"Pizza as promised!" Tammy followed Ms. Williams as she led them like a girl scout troop into the back room carrying the just-delivered boxes.

Jasp had offered Ms. Williams an "okay I guess" on the new wedding clothes she'd showed them. Then he'd rolled his eyes at

Tammy in long-suffering pain. Dad had taught them good manners, but he and Tammy both knew Jasp's pretending to have any interest at all was complete baloney.

"She's pretty," Jasp offered up just in case Ms. Williams had caught his eye roll.

Tammy couldn't look away from the female mannequin, all dressed up for her wedding. It was like the dress in the photo on Dad's bedside table. Well, not really, but it was enough to remind her of what it had felt like to have a mother and how much she missed her every day.

Her dad was acting all weird when he finally joined them in the back room. And Ms. Williams was looking awfully pleased with herself. Then she set the pizza boxes on the big table. They hadn't even spoken together, never mind anything else. Tammy had made sure to stay close to Ms. Williams, just to be sure. But she must have missed something that was going on.

"I ordered two pizzas. Half a pepperoni for Jaspar, because all boys like pepperoni. Half a combo with extra meat for your dad because he probably eats too much of what you kids want and not enough of what he wants." The boys dug right in.

She turned to Tamara, "I got us half veggie and half Hawaiian. How'd I do, Tamara?"

"Everyone calls me Tammy."

Ms. Williams took a slice of the veggie and looked at her over it. "I don't know. I think I'll stick with your full name, it sort of fits you better. You're no longer a little girl."

"Only Mom ever called me Tamara, Ms. Williams."

Ms. Williams didn't look embarrassed, or apologize like other adults Tammy pushed back against.

"Your call. But it sounds like your mom was a smart lady. I'm Perrin by the way. I have no idea who that Ms. Williams person is." She actually shuddered which made it kind of funny.

"Tamara is okay, I guess." Then she looked away. She needed to think about Perrin being all human and normal. She didn't talk down to her at all, which was weird for an adult. It could be a setup, but it didn't feel like one.

Jasp and Dad had each taken huge bites. They were grinning at each other like idiots as they both hooted out cooling breaths over too-hot pizza.

"Well, you certainly nailed those two lame-os."

Tammy took a small bite of her pizza—Hawaiian was her absolute favorite—then figured out how to tell if the woman was being fake-nice to a child. She kept her voice low, so that the lame-os wouldn't hear.

"Have you kissed him yet?"

Perrin looked at her carefully, but didn't stop chewing on her pizza. If she was really shocked, she didn't show it.

She sat on one of the stools and waited for Tammy to climb up on one as well. They were closer to the same height that way.

"Once. And I wonder just how pissed your dad will be that I told you that."

Tammy had only had conversations like this once or twice with her girlfriends, and half the time she lied and she bet her friends did too.

She'd also bet that Perrin had just told her the truth.

"You kissed any boys yet?"

Tammy shot a quick look over at her dad, but he wasn't paying attention. She could feel the heat rushing to her cheeks and did her best to hide it with another bite of pizza, but her stomach was suddenly all twisty.

"A few," she tried to shrug it off, and wondered why she'd just told this woman who'd kissed her dad the truth. "Still don't know what the big deal is."

"When it's the right boy, trust me it will be."

Tammy looked up into those blue eyes. Perrin was talking about kissing as if it was the most normal thing on the planet. As if it wasn't a matter of social standing, or social media hell if you kissed the wrong boy. She tried to find a response, but she couldn't. Perrin was just watching her.

"And until it is a big deal… " Perrin leaned in and whispered. "So not worth the rest of it."

Tammy hadn't thought of it that way. She thought about the boys who wanted to grab, some of them were already asking if she was still a virgin, she knew three girls in her class who for sure weren't. But they were kinda slutty.

But what if she simply said she was waiting until it was a big deal? It just might work. It would sure avoid a lot of hassles.

Maybe Perrin knew what she was talking about.

BILL WATCHED PERRIN WORK. He worried about exposing the kids to her, but he shouldn't be. He'd also "exposed" them to every woman at the opera, both the full-timers and the artists who came in on a freelance contract for just one opera then moved on. Several had made him offers and he'd been tempted more than once, at least for a couple nights of no-strings sex. But he'd never figured out how to actually date with the kids around. They knew his schedule as intimately as he did. Aunt Lucy's on show nights and the occasional crisis at the opera, but nothing else. Evenings were their family-together time.

So, why was he worried about Perrin?

He'd watched her with his kids and she was great. Better than Nia or Jerimy or a half-dozen of the others at the opera? Maybe, maybe not. But they appeared comfortable around her.

Jaspar thought it was all just a lark. He'd giggled when Perrin had measured him, though she'd let Bill do the in-seam measurement while the two girls tactfully were busy down at the other end of the room. He'd eaten so much pizza that Bill was afraid he'd be sick, but instead he finally settled at one end of the worktable with a book of Kipling's *Captains Courageous* that he had to read for school.

Tammy was a different matter. There was something between her and Perrin, something that he hadn't seen happen. It was like two matadors dancing about a ring with no bull present. Testing each other cautiously yet on the same side. Tammy had followed Perrin around and watched everything she was doing, asking a lot of technical questions along the way. Bill had no idea she'd picked up so much from Jerimy and the others in costuming.

Perrin slowed down enough to show her what she was doing, but wouldn't let her sew. "No, not the machines. These aren't like home sewing machines. Maybe I can teach you some other time if it's okay with your dad."

When Tammy had complained, Perrin hadn't turned for Bill's support. She stepped right up to the plate, much like a good parent would.

"You can try the Singer Featherweight some other day."

Tammy's, "Oh man! That's so lame!" groan only elicited a smile from Perrin.

"That's my first sewing machine. It's the first gift that was ever given to me—by my best friend's dad before he died. I taught myself to sew on it. Good clothing isn't about cool machines. It starts here," she tapped Tammy's chest over her heart. "Later it goes here," she tapped Tammy's head. "Figuring out how to build it, that's the easy part."

Easy part. Bill remembered Jerimy's comment about the construction of the Empress' costume, that even seeing the finished gown he wasn't sure how it had been done.

Perrin had pre-built both of the children's costumes she'd shown him yesterday. Just yesterday? Didn't the woman ever sleep?

Now she trimmed, pinned, and seamed with an easy assuredness in her own skills. No sign of the sad waif. And with shedding the leprechaun blazer, she'd also shed most of the eccentric crazy-girl.

In the wake of dropping those personas, they'd left behind a very pleasant woman with a crazy hair dye-job.

A very competent one.

It took less than an hour for both costumes to come together. He was shooed to the far end of the studio and forced to sit with his back to them for the final fitting. He'd seen the clothes all evening on the worktable, he didn't know what the big deal was. But by then she had both kids on her side, and Tammy gave him one of her, "Don't be a dork!" looks. He finally complied.

For lack of anything better to do, he began reading the Kipling. He'd forgotten the story. Two young boys, one arrogant and lost at sea, another raised on a Gloucester fishing vessel working the Grand Banks. And how the boys grew into men. He really wasn't ready for Jaspar to be doing that, not anytime soon. No more than he was ready for Tammy to grow into a woman which was happening much faster. She—

"Okay," he jumped when Perrin spoke close beside him.

He started to turn, but she stopped him with a quick hand on his cheek, exactly where she'd placed it yesterday as they kissed. They shared a look that proved he wasn't the only one who'd been thinking far too much about that moment.

"Close your eyes." He did, though reluctantly. It was the first excuse he'd found to be this close to her all day. She took his hands and guided him to his feet and back down the workroom. He squeezed her hands in his, an unobtrusive enough gesture. She stumbled. Using their shared grip, he had to steady her as she continued to lead him. He liked having at least some of the effect on her that she had on him.

"Okay, are you ready?"

He nodded.

She let go then gave him permission to open his eyes.

There Jaspar stood, not merely as he'd been drawn. He'd become the youthful promise unfulfilled by the Tragic Prince. He was still so pure, hope for the future brimming over with energy and life. The contrast on stage would be shocking when the boy entered in Act II Scene II. The Prince would be abruptly diminished in the audience's eyes, because here, embodied in Bill's ten-year-old child, was everything the Prince had been given as a birthright but been unable to attain.

And then a young woman stepped from behind the screen. Her dark mane of red hair swept up off her shoulders. Her dark eyes watching him with a frankness and a knowledge that no child could possess. There was a tragedy about her, as if she understood her elder brother's failure where the younger did not.

The clothes revealed nothing beyond her sweet shoulders, nothing except the promise of everything she was to become. It would be she who survived the ultimate tragedy. She who carried on to become the next Empress. This was not some young girl, this was a young woman, a woman just born from the child she'd been and discovering her own power.

"Tamara?" he managed only a whisper. He hadn't called her by her given name since the day the woman who had given it to her died. But this was no young Tammy.

Her smile bloomed.

His children hooted, "Oh, we got you, Dad. We got you so bad." And the two operatic figures dissolved back into his children as they threw themselves into his arms.

All Bill could manage was to hold them both tight and kiss them atop their heads.

When at last he looked up to thank her, he saw that Perrin had left the room.

CHAPTER 6

"*W*hy did you leave? Where did you go?" Bill had finally chased Perrin back to her lair in the store. It had taken three days, but he'd done it.

She'd done more than leave for the few minutes after she'd transformed his children into operatic wonders, perhaps to do some busywork in the front of her shop. In the days since then she'd become invisible. Arriving at rehearsals mere minutes before they started, departing immediately after they ended.

She'd delivered the children's costumes to Jerimy. The photographer had been thrilled and photographed them with Renata the Empress for the publicity campaign. Perrin hadn't shown up for the photo shoot.

And the opera had gone crazy. Okay, no crazier than usual, but he'd been unable to get a single minute to track Perrin down in three days.

Carlo's girlfriend Melanie had gone to Paris for a fashion shoot. Carlo, while not dumb enough to begrudge her career, was now impossibly prickly about everything that wasn't absolutely perfect.

Lord spare Bill from opera-sized egos. Geoffrey Palliser

threw a fit about not yet having a costume so he couldn't be on the advertisement. Pointing out that his contract had forbidden the use of his image on precisely such promotions did little to mollify him.

Voice lessons with Tammy had taken another chunk out of his afternoons, though under the Chorus Master's guidance she was coming along wonderfully, showing some real aptitude for the small role. Jaspar wasn't interested in the singing, but did listen carefully when the director provided stage directions.

Twice Bill had come by Perrin's shop only to find it closed and dark. She clearly wasn't a morning person.

It was now early evening on Friday. The last of the light was bleeding out of the Seattle sky. The scent of early flowers in small planters outside her shop hovered on the still air.

Jaspar was at a friend's and Tammy was at the library for some schoolwork. With his single stolen hour, he'd walked into Perrin's Glorious Garb and barely nodded at the clerk before breezing into the kitchen space and through the accessories display in the old freezer and into the design studio.

Perrin had flinched when he walked in. So, he'd sat down quietly across the cutting table and waited for her to settle before repeating his question.

"Why did you leave?"

She began fiddling with the drawings spread across the table. The only light in the room was the worklight directed at the table's surface. She was little more than shape and form, though her hands were caught by the light. Just a glance revealed the drawings of the rest of the cast, but he forced his attention off them knowing if they went down that path, they might lose track of the present one. He'd promised to pick up Tammy in an hour. It was all the time he had to fix whatever this was.

His eyes were adjusting enough to see that Perrin wore a form-fitting silken turtleneck as black as her hair, and wool slacks almost as blonde as the stripe that still remained in her hair. Simple, chic, and a real pleasure to look at.

"Why are you avoiding me?"

"It looked like a great family moment. I didn't want to... " She wouldn't face him.

"Didn't want to what?" Bill wanted to lump this in with his usual job of coaxing along crazy artists, but it didn't feel that way. The dozen drawings spread across the cutting table proved that whatever she needed to create her art, it wasn't coaxing. She'd done them impossibly fast. And if they were even half as good as the first ones, they'd be the finest costumes Emerald City had put on stage in years.

She stood and began gathering them up. "Let's just say that it wasn't my place to intrude and leave it at that."

He stood up and circled the table. When he reached for her hands, she pulled them back.

"Please don't," the sad-eyed girl was back, clutching her drawings as if they were all that anchored her.

He let his hands fall to his sides. "Did I do something wrong? One of the kids?"

"God no!" That snapped her attention to his face. "They're wonderful! And you're so good with them. I didn't belong. It was your moment. So I left."

"A moment you created."

"I. Didn't. Belong. That should be enough for you," she insisted, then moved over to the next table and slipped the drawings into a portfolio. She held the closed case out as a barrier between them. "Since you're here, you can take these to Jerimy."

"Don't you need them to build from?"

"No, they're in my head once I draw them. But it doesn't matter, I was only hired as a designer. There are just a couple designs missing. I'll send those over as soon as I figure them out."

"But you built the first three, I thought you'd want to do the other major costumes. And you know that your contract has a clause paying you more if you do so. I also thought you'd want to maintain the quality of—"

"Here!" She slammed the portfolio flat against his chest so that he had to grab. "You have them. Now just go!"

She turned her back on him and retreated into the darkness, making it only two or three steps before she ground to a halt.

Idiot! Bill shouted at himself. There was something far bigger going on here than any lousy set of drawings. He'd been so slow to see it, that he'd probably just made bad matters worse. He set the portfolio on the table and moved up behind her.

He placed his hands on her upper arms.

She shrugged him off angrily.

He did it again and held on this time. When she didn't protest anymore, he turned her slowly clockwise so that the blonde stripe climbed upward across her hair as she came to face him.

"Why can't you accept that you didn't want me there?" she asked as soon as he had her fully turned.

"But I did."

"You idiot!" She shoved him hard in the center of his chest, forcing him to stumble back a step. He regained his balance just before he ran into a clothing rack. He'd expected to find her weeping, instead he was facing the Empress brought to life.

Perrin stormed several paces away from him until she was blocked by her sewing machines. Then she stalked back toward him, stopping close in front of him in the narrow aisle between the cutting table and a wall of fabric folded onto shelves.

"Those kids!" she jabbed a finger in the direction of the changing corner where the kids had been. "They're precious. You can't have them imprinting on me. You can't let them. Please, Bill, for their own safety, you can't let them. That's why I walked away. So that you don't connect them to me."

"Are you so awful?" He said it as a joke. It was totally ludicrous for her to think so.

NORMALLY PERRIN DIDN'T GIVE a damn what a guy thought, let him get screwed up by being around her. But she'd never been with a single dad. There'd never been so much at stake.

She clamped down on her lips so hard they hurt and then nodded once. Fiercely. Yes, she was that awful.

Bill laughed.

The goddamn man laughed at her.

She pounded the side of her fist against his chest, which did nothing but bounce off.

"You are far and away the least hazardous woman I've ever run into. Whack-a-doodle! Oh yeah! Hazardous, not a chance."

"I'm fucking toxic!" she shouted in his face.

Any man with the least common sense would turn tail and run, glad to be shut of her. She'd been through this enough times to know for a fact that even this little bit of the truth worked to drive men away. She also knew that she truly was toxic. Her past was a poison that ran through her whole life and eventually killed every relationship she'd ever attempted. She was just being preemptive this time, for the kids' sake. She couldn't risk contaminating them with her past.

"Get the hell out and leave me alone!" she yelled again, the pain raking at her throat as she tried once more to drive him off.

"Perrin!" He got right in her face.

"What!?"she shouted back, pissed that it hadn't worked.

He moved forward, forcing her backward into the deeper darkness. *Shit!* She'd pushed too hard. If she screamed would anyone hear her? Raquel had stuck her head in just five minutes ago, but Perrin had nodded it was okay to lock up and leave.

She'd been so stupid. Now she was all alone and Bill was far stronger that she was.

She stumbled back and fell into a chair. She prepared to fight. Her scissors were almost in reach if she just—

Bill pulled over another chair, set it in front of her, then sat down in it.

He didn't attack.

Just sat there.

Perrin fought for a breath. Her heart beat faster than any rabbit's possibly could. *Was she safe?* All of the old emotions were pounding her adrenaline right past redline, and she'd never been able to do anything about it. Ever.

He reached out and took one of her hands gone suddenly nerveless.

"Crap! You're freezing. And your hands are shaking. What the hell? Are you okay?"

She shook her head, it was all she could manage.

"Wait."

Perrin could see a dawning comprehension in his eyes and knew she'd underestimated him and interpreted it all wrong.

"Wait. You thought I'd... I'd never attack a woman!" His shock appeared genuine.

"Heard that often enough." Then she flung up her free arm, wrapping it over her mouth and clamping her hand on her opposite shoulder. She had to stop whatever she was going to say next.

Now Bill looked truly shocked.

She'd given him the unanswerable. No protestation of innocence could work against such a statement. She freed her other hand from his and pulled her knees up until she could wrap both arms around them and her heels were on the edge of the chair.

"I'm sorry," she mumbled through her knees. "I'm so sorry. You didn't deserve that. I told you I was toxic."

He huffed out a breath. He didn't leave. He didn't shout back. He didn't cock back an arm to hit her. He just huffed out another breath.

"Well," his voice a soft rumble. "I'll buy hurt. I'll buy that there's someone on this earth who would be better off dead for whatever they did to you," he actually sounded pissed on her behalf. Then, impossibly he smiled at her.

She had no idea what to do with a smile. Her childhood taught her to never trust it. Her adulthood merely taught her that the man smiling wanted something, usually sex, and was being nice enough to ask first, even if non-verbally. But Bill's smile made no sense. Especially not with what she'd just accused him of. But he still smiled at her nonetheless.

He crossed his arms over his chest and slouched back in the chair as if just getting comfortable. The worklight behind him making him little more than a silhouette. Not quite giving him a halo.

"But if you want the title of toxic, you're going to have to convince me, because I'm not buying it."

"I'm not telling you my life's story."

"You have something better to do this evening?" He was being Mr. Oh So Amiable.

"No. But I'm still not telling." Though if he kept it up, Perrin might find she wanted to smile again, not something she'd done in the last three days.

"In that case," Bill stared up at the pipes on the ceiling as if contemplating the breadth and width of the broadcloth of the universe. "I'll just have to convince you that you aren't."

"Can't fight reality." She wished to God he could, but not even the Tragic Prince could do that.

"Hey, I work in opera. You can't get much further from reality than that. So, here goes. You ready?"

She nodded. Did this man know what he was doing to her? No one had ever been on her side except Jo and Cassidy. Her two college friends loved her and did their best to protect her from herself, and she'd always bless the heavens for the two of them. But no one ever really tried to understand her. To have a man try to protect her from the impossible... That was new and felt amazing inside.

"My first exhibit should be my kids. But I don't want them in the middle of this any more than you do. So I'll simply just happen to mention that what you've done for them in just the first two days since the three of you met has already changed them, and in a good way. Did you know that Wilson Jervis offered them formal contracts which included Union Scale contributions to their college funds? Do you have any idea how proud that made them to be earning money for the family? How proud that made me? And Tammy is really enjoying her voice lessons."

"You said it was unfair to use them, and it is." Though she loved hearing how they were doing. They'd barely met, yet she'd missed them horribly these last days. It was the closest she'd been to tears in a long time, just hearing about them.

"So, for the official first example, I'll offer Jo Thompson."

That startled her enough to sit up and look at him. "You know Jo?"

"Not really. But I called her on her honeymoon while you were passed out on my couch. That one of the most accomplished and powerful women of Seattle loves you so much speaks volumes. By the end of the call, she was ready to get on a plane with or without her new husband. I take it she knows you well?"

Perrin nodded, "No one better, except Cassidy."

"Who is my second official exhibit. You mentioned she will be coming to the opera with you tomorrow. Yet here you are being miserable and still she's not here with you. As I happen to know she's in France, she also must be very attached to you to attend an opera on the same day she flies halfway around the world."

Perrin had forgotten about the jetlag when she'd invited Cassidy.

Bill waited for her to accede his point.

"She's the best." This man deserved some truth. "Cassidy saved my life." She managed to say it without getting too choked up.

He took that as a win without asking for details; another point in his favor even if he didn't know it.

"And third, at lunch, I couldn't get near you because Melanie and Josh were just so glad to be in your company."

She hadn't really thought of it that way, they were simply good friends. "How does all this make your point?"

Bill laughed again, but it didn't make her angry this time.

He reached out and slowly unclamped her hands from around her knees until he was holding both hands, and her feet slipped back to the floor.

"You tell me. Does that sound like someone who's toxic? Someone who sweeps every person they meet off their feet and they never recover?"

"Maybe not. But… "

"No! Cut that out. It's my round. I won it fair and square and you're not going to spoil it. Hell, I deserve a prize. If I'm stuck being human, you are hereafter going to have to live under the cloud of being 'not toxic.' Can you live with that?"

Perrin managed to smile at him. "Guess I'm stuck with it, aren't I?"

Bill just grinned and stroked his nice warm thumbs on the back of her freezing fingers.

She stood slowly, not releasing his hands. Ever so gently, she lowered herself down until she was sitting in his lap.

"You're right," she acknowledged as she settled into place. "You have to get a prize."

"I wasn't trying to get you to—"

And she kissed him. Softly, just barely rubbing her lips over his.

"And that," she deepened the kiss for a delicious moment before pulling back to finish her sentence, "is exactly why you deserve a prize."

Then she stopped any reply with her lips and tongue.

His hands slid out of hers as she reached up to dig her fingers into the waves of his hair. It was even softer than it looked.

He slid his hands around her, snugging her body more tightly against his. His hands hesitated at her waist.

Perhaps she did know Mr. Too-Decent Bill Cullen better than she thought. Reaching down, she coaxed one of his hands upward. They were good hands, big, strong, and they hadn't hit her, not even when she'd pushed him to the edge. When she shifted it onto her breast and clamped her hand over his to keep it there, he was still so gentle. How could she have ever doubted that in this man?

He buried his face in her neck and just stopped there, one hand on her breast, the other equally still on her waist.

She wrapped her arms around him. And he seemed content to stop there, to just remain there.

"You miss her that much?" she made a guess.

He nodded without raising his head.

"Have you even touched a woman since then?"

He hesitated, then shook his head.

She held him against her and stared at the lit worktable. How had she ever thought anything but the best of him? He was too damn decent for his own good.

"Okay," she didn't know quite what to say, but she knew it was up to her to say it. "Mr. Bill Cullen, you listening?"

He nodded against her neck. He brushed his thumb across

her nipple almost absent-mindedly, sending really, really good shivers running down her body.

"Between this non-toxic but whack-a-doodle gal… "

"You heard that," he mumbled into her neck.

"I heard that. Between her and this fallible human guy, we're striking a deal."

"What?" he nuzzled her collarbone and almost stole her breath away.

"There is never a question of right or wrong. Okay?"

He froze, locked in place against her, his hands almost brutally tight on her for just an instant in his shock. Then he eased off, slowly sitting up until they were face to face just inches apart.

"That's what Adira always said. She was the wisest woman I've ever known."

Perrin knew she wasn't wise, but she was smart enough to know when she'd just received the highest compliment of her entire life.

She didn't try to kiss him again. She simply pulled his head back to her shoulder and cradled him there, until a while later when he finally said he had to go and fetch his daughter.

Just inside the darkened doorway from her shop, he did take a few minutes to show her just how much he appreciated her.

After locking the door behind him and watching him drive off, she thought about how much she appreciated him. The aftermath of his final kiss and caress still heated her body deliciously.

CHAPTER 7

"assie!" Perrin sprinted through the lobby crowd awaiting the start of the final performance of *Turandot*. Cassidy had worn her black turtleneck and the sunset sweater that Perrin had picked out for her so long ago to totally slay a blind date. Her clothes had done their magic and they were now married. Cassidy had finished the outfit with a flirty black skirt and the knee-high boots that made her look so fabulous.

Cassidy turned just as Perrin crashed into her. She kissed Cassidy hard on the lips.

"I hope Russell won't be jealous, but I'm just so glad to see you."

Cassidy reeled a bit, but went with the flow as she always did, "Glad to see you too. Wish Jo was here so that we could really make it a night out."

"I know!" Perrin stamped her foot and noticed just how much of the local crowd was grimacing at their PDA, like public display of affection between two women was a crime even in Seattle. So, she raised her voice enough to be clearly heard, "Just like that bitch to run away from us and get married."

The crowd rippled away from them in a slow wave of

evening gowns and suits. The mezzanine and two balconies offered prime views of the main floor. Sure enough, when Perrin looked up they were being the center of attention.

She spun in a whirl. She'd been inspired by the leprechaun outfit and made a Marilyn Monroe *The Seven Year Itch* pleated skirt of the flowiest bright yellow-and-green rayon to go with the green-and-yellow blazer, though she'd left the shirt off this time revealing skin down to her solar plexus. She finished the whirl and stumbled into Cassidy.

"Let 'em dream," she whispered. "Bet half the guys here will be fantasizing about us tonight, not knowing we're both totally straight. Think they'd be disappointed if they knew?"

Cassidy offered one of her staid smiles.

"Sorry, you're all jet-lagged. I haven't a brain in my body. You sure you're okay with sitting through an opera?"

"I'm here."

Perrin gave her another hug, this time as if she were fragile, "You can always sleep on my shoulder, you just can't weep there."

Cassidy blinked at her as if finally coming awake while they climbed the sweeping grand staircase up to the mezzanine entry level.

"Uh, Perrin. What did I miss? You seem even more Perrin than usual."

"I met a guy."

"I'm shocked," her tone was drier than one of her wines that she critiqued for a living.

"I met a nice guy." Not the right reaction yet. "A nice guy with kids."

"That's sweet... Wait! You did what?" Cassidy finally caught up with the conversation.

"I know! Shocked the shit out of me too. Oh, I have to stop saying that in case I run into his kids."

"Here? There are never kids at the opera."

"Oh, I don't know. Maybe we'll get lucky."

Cassidy grabbed her arm and turned her toward the glass and steel rail of the mezzanine level. They leaned on the rail. Down below was the main lobby they'd just climbed up from, still milling with people. A wall of glass five or six stories high showed the outdoor steel scrims. Huge sheets of a fine mesh filled the gap between the opera hall and the next building over, starting twenty feet in the air and climbing to the very top of the structure. They were lit with a bright flow of dancing colors across the mesh. Like a slow kaleidoscope of spring colors.

"How do they do that?"

Cassidy glanced at it, then back at Perrin. "Magic. Who cares? Now spill. I've only been gone for five days. What in the world is up with you?"

Perrin clamped both hands on the top of the rail and sort of pumped herself back and forth. It was all she could do to control the energy bottled up inside her.

"He's really nice. And so damn decent. You know Hogan?"

Cassidy looked at her in utter exasperation. "Maria's Hogan? The man who married the woman who practically raised my husband? The one we all have dinner with every Tuesday evening? That Hogan?"

"Yeah, that one," she loved that she was making Cassidy totally nuts. That would pay her back for being out of the country when Perrin needed her so badly. "Well, I think he may even be more decent than Hogan."

"Uh," Cassidy stopped as she thought about it. "I'm not sure that's possible."

Perrin slanted her best friend a look.

"Okay, prove it."

For the first time Perrin focused on the three-story tall mobile that hung just out of reach. It was made of extension ladders and measuring tapes. It was filled with hammers, pliers, saws, bits and pieces of all the tools she'd been shown in the scenery shop. And a bunch of stuff that looked electrical.

"That's a pretty crazy mobile, don't you think?"

"Perrin!" Cassidy's voice was practically a she-lion snarl. Maybe it was time to answer. But she couldn't quite resist and answered the question with another question.

"You know how you told me after your first time with Russell that really great sex is even way better with the right man?"

"Yea-ah…" she drew it out cautiously.

"Despite every opportunity and encouragement, last night I may have had the best sex of my life and…"

"And what, Perrin?"

"We never even took our clothes off."

Cassidy blinked at her.

Perrin could hear Cassidy analyzing this news. She had the same look that she did when she was tasting one of her wines, that discerning palate and mind that had made her one of the nation's most successful food-and-wine critics before she quit to form the Washington Wine Cooperative.

Her best friend stared at her for the longest moment and then did exactly what Perrin had been hoping for, praying for, because otherwise she was totally losing her mind and she didn't know if she was ready to be doing that.

Cassidy pulled Perrin into her arms and held her tightly. In her ear she whispered, "Oh, I hope so for your sake, Perrin. I really, really do."

"Hey," Perrin pulled back and wiped at her friend's cheek. "You know the rules, no crying or getting drunk unless we're all together."

Cassidy brushed at her eyes and offered a watery smile. "You were right."

"I was? Is that a first?"

"Jo is in such deep shit for running off and getting married on us."

"We mustn't tell her or Maria until they're both back and we can all get together."

"Deal," Cassidy sealed it with a very un-Cassie-like smack on Perrin's lips. Maybe after a year of being happily married she was finally loosening up a bit and cared less about what others thought.

IT TOOK SOME DOING, but Perrin found their way backstage after the opera. There was a maze of beautifully carpeted corridors and unmarked doors that led to strange linoleum hallways that seemed to lead nowhere. The soft indirect lighting giving way to harsh fluorescents, which meant they were on the right track. Or that they were hopelessly lost and someone would have to send in a search-and-rescue team after them.

Racks of clothes lined one side of the white linoleum hallway, and a line of doors along the opposite wall led to small dressing rooms. As they moved along the hall, the costumes became fancier and so did the dressing rooms. She and Cassidy peeked in one that wasn't occupied at the moment. It had a piano in the corner, an upright, in beautiful condition.

"Must be what they use to warm up their voices before they go onstage."

Then the costumes ended, and a line of cramped offices appeared along the right-hand wall.

"Hey," Cassidy pointed at a sign on an open door. "You said Bill was the Stage Manager."

Perrin grabbed her hand and dragged her in. "Let's go peek."

It was big enough for a desk, three small chairs, and a long whiteboard which was covered in incomprehensible hieroglyphics. "LR#1 blwn gel fresh #4. Cortisol III.2 4st. Strk-7a call," and dozens of other notations that must mean something to Bill, but they certainly meant nothing to her.

"His desk is awfully neat. Do we trust a man who has such a neat desk?" Cassidy leaned forward to look at a small framed photograph.

"I wish I'd brought some really red lipstick. I need to leave a really blatant lip print here somewhere."

"Perrin," Cassidy's tone brought her up short.

"What?"

Cassidy pointed to the picture of two giggling children.

"That's Jaspar and Tamara. What does that have to do with lipstic—Oh crap! This is so hard, Cass. I don't know if I can do this." Of course his kids would be as likely to be here as at the Opera offices. Finding a red-lipstick print from their dad's girl-friend would be way worse than inappropriate. It would be— "I'm such an idiot. I'm just gonna screw this up so bad. Cass, you have to tell me what to do. You're the smart one."

"Actually, it was Jo who was valedictorian at college. And personally I think that you got that 'C' in PE just so that Jo would get the honor instead of you. Remember, I saw your GRE scores in case you went to grad school and I know neither of us came close to matching yours. How did you arrange to get a 'C' in a field hockey PE class anyway?"

"Remember Ms. Kennelly?"

"Stick-in-the-Mud Kennelly? Sure."

"I made a pass at her, hot and heavy. She was totally freaked. But after that she didn't dare flunk me, despite my never attending another class. Probably too afraid I'd wind up back in one of her classes. It worked great, but don't tell Jo."

Cassidy crossed her heart like the true friend she was.

Perrin heard a voice rumbling out in the corridor, placating one person while handing out instructions to another. And his voice sounded as if he'd just finished ripping someone a new one.

"That's him," she tried not to go all weak in the knees. Knees hell! Weak in her heart, which was infinitely more dangerous—like here the stars and back kind of dangerous.

"PERRIN! YOU MADE IT!" Bill wanted to devour her, she looked glorious and delectable. That same blazer as the other night, but without the t-shirt made him want to drag her down to the floor and pick up where good manners had stopped him last night. Had he even slept last night? Yet he felt energized rather than exhausted.

He spotted the second woman just in time. Bill slammed a brake on his libido and held out a hand to shake Perrin's as if they were just two professionals.

She looked down at his hand, then rolled her eyes at the other woman, "What did I tell you about him?"

"You were right. He's too damned decent."

Perrin stepped into his arms and kissed him long and deeply enough to completely scorch any of his body's responses that hadn't already gone ballistic over the outfit.

Then she stepped back, "I, uh, may have already told her about us. Bill Cullen, this is Cassidy Knowles, my best friend in the whole world."

"I know her, you just distracted me. We sort of met at the last board meeting, Ms. Knowles. You're the one who saved Perrin's life."

Cassidy startled and turned to face Perrin even before Bill could shake her hand.

Perrin shrugged, "That's all I told him." But she appeared suddenly interested in the tiling of the floor.

Then Cassidy turned back and took his hand, shaking it carefully.

"What did I just miss?"

Cassidy inspected him closely. "You had best be worth it, Mister Cullen. To the best of my knowledge, you are only the fourth person on the planet to know that."

"Fifth," Perrin offered without looking up. "I told Melanie a while ago. She kind of already knew. Forgot to tell you she was here this week, dating an opera singer, but she's gone again. Back in five weeks for opening night."

Again some inexplicable exchange occurred silently.

At length Cassidy turned to face him once more. She was perhaps five-eight, a good four inches shorter than he was. And very trim, though with fuller curves than Perrin. But he was left with no doubt that the woman before him, having somehow saved Perrin's life once, would do absolutely anything to do so again if she felt it was necessary.

CHAPTER 8

*P*errin had the drawings spread down the entire length of her workbench. She'd had to get them back from Jerimy, because the last of the designs were being stubborn. She just couldn't see them.

The heavy colors and threads of hope and failure in the lineage of the Overlord and the Empress.

The vile reds and blacks of the court Magister and his cohorts in the clergy. The opera had set the latter as almost pure evil, bent on the destruction of the royal lineage and replacing them with their own line.

The Magister would bring about the ultimate downfall of the Tragic Prince.

The slim thread of hope would happen when his snare failed to catch Tamara as the young Empress-to-be.

But the arranged-marriage Princess, and the Prince's one True Love were eluding her. These were the two women who tore the Tragic Prince in two directions, ultimately allowing the Magister's untimely blade to make his end.

Once she had the Princess, then the Maid Confessor and

Queen Mother should follow easily enough. But at the moment, nothing about any of the four of them was being easy. Nothing!

She'd tried most of her tricks. Sketching, painting, pulling pieces randomly out of the scrap bag and stitching them together on the embroidery machine until something came of it.

And not a decent idea.

"Perrin," Raquel stuck her head in. "You have a visitor."

She almost cried out in relief. A customer needing a special dress, or a friend, she didn't care. She knew it couldn't be Bill, he had one opera coming down and meetings about getting the set construction for *Ascension* back on schedule. He said he'd be frantic all week.

"Hi, Perrin," Tamara peeked around from behind Raquel.

"Hey, you! Come here!" Without thinking Perrin had thrown her arms wide.

Tamara eyed them for a moment, then came forward and accepted the hug. Perrin kept it brief, as she would if just meeting some friend on the street. Bill hadn't been kidding, the girl was so self-conscious of every nuance of being thirteen. Of course, Perrin was also the woman who'd kissed her dad.

"So, did your dad drop you off?" She wanted to ask where he was, why hadn't he at least come in to say hello, how was he. He'd been so busy that she actually hadn't seen him since the night she and Cassidy had attended *Turandot*. They'd barely traded late night texts after the kids were in bed. But she thought it better not to ask. It was best to appear completely neutral on the topic of her dad.

"No, he didn't," a little hesitant. Then in a rush to block Perrin's next question, "I was hoping you could show me more about design and sewing. I really want to—"

Perrin held up a hand to cut her off. She too had once been a teenage girl. Her life had been nothing like Tamara's, but she knew the tones of voice that had and hadn't gotten her out of trouble. The first part was a clear lie, even if the rest of it sounded true enough.

Keep it light, she told herself.

"Wow, girl! You just told a whopper, didn't you?"

Tamara blanched but struggled on valiantly. "No. I really wanted to learn how you made those costumes. I don't get how you..." Her voice petered out as it became clear that Perrin wasn't buying the distraction for a second.

Before she could make further excuses, Perrin held up her hand.

Tamara wisely closed her mouth.

"Okay, first you sit and listen to the world according to Perrin. Then you get two choices."

She didn't look happy about it, but she climbed up on the stool across the cutting table, dropping her school pack on the floor.

"Your dad doesn't know you're here." She didn't make it a question.

"Gretchen's."

"And when he shows up and you aren't at Gretchen's, how much trouble will you have found?"

Tamara shrunk down in her seat. "Lots. Seriously grounded at least."

"Girl, he's going to put one of those house-arrest GPS ankle bracelets on you and never let you out of his sight again. He loves you so much that he'll probably end up in jail for punching anyone who gets in his way while he's trying to find you."

"No way... " Suddenly she didn't look so self-assured.

"Way!" Perrin informed her. "That's assuming he doesn't have a heart attack from worrying himself sick about you first. Lost, maybe missing in the Big Bad City."

"I'm old enough to get around Seattle on my own if I want to. Besides, he's always at work. What does he care about—"

"You have no idea how much he cares. His entire world revolves around raising you two. He's so afraid he's going to screw up, that's probably what makes him screw up half the time."

Tamara appeared to be mulling that one over seriously.

"So, time for your two choices," Perrin informed her.

"Am I going to like either one of them?"

"Not a chance."

It took some negotiation, before they ended up with a compromise. Perrin would call to break the ice, then hand it off to Tamara.

She dialed Bill's cell and put it on speaker phone. Only after she did so, did she think that maybe dialing his number from memory hadn't been the best choice. Thankfully, Tamara appeared too miserable to notice. With each ring, Tamara cringed down further on the stool.

"Hi Perrin. I have to be quick. I'm sorry, but I'm really busy right now. Gods but I miss you."

Tamara heard that one loud and clear. Her head shot up and she faced Perrin rather than continuing to study the chips in her nail polish.

"Uh, Bill. I think I may have just screwed up. I have you on speakerphone."

There was a pause, "Who else is there?"

Perrin nodded to Tamara to go ahead. She had to repeat the gesture to get some action.

"Uh, hi Dad."

"What?!" His voice roared out of the phone and echoed about Perrin's design space. If his daughter had needed any proof of what Perrin had told her, his tone said it all. She positively cowered, in shame rather than fear, Perrin was glad to see.

"Bill," Perrin cut him off. "Before you lay in, I've already done a decent job of making her feel like a total shit. She understands what she did wrong. How about giving her a one-time 'Get Out of Jail Free' card?"

There was a long silence. So long that Tamara started cringing again.

"Is she okay there with you? I could probably find someone to come and—" His voice was tight, but he was holding onto control. Barely.

"She's fine with me, Bill. I won't let her out of my sight. You have Jaspar?"

"Yeah. The little thug just shook me down for a buck for the soda machine but I'll bet he's getting a candy bar instead."

Tamara nodded her agreement.

"His sister agrees, candy it is. Take as long as you need, Bill."

"Thanks, Perrin, you're absolutely wonderf— Aw, crap! Explaining this is another problem I've left in your lap. Tamara, give her a chance. Sorry about that, gotta run." And he was gone before she could even reach out to cut the connection.

Tamara was eyeing her carefully.

"Look, girl, I got you off the hook this one time. You gonna throw me to the wolves?"

Tamara considered that for a while and then shrugged that maybe, just maybe they had a fair trade.

Perrin could see the next question building, but was not at all ready for it when it finally arrived.

"You going to marry my dad?"

Perrin managed a laugh. "Whoa there! I've only kissed him twice, wait, three times. We're barely dating. We haven't even gone out to dinner together, if you don't count the time you guys were here for pizza."

"Is he good?"

Perrin rested her elbow on the table and her chin on her palm and inspected her interrogator. How did you deal with a kid? A kid who has probably spent the last four years doing her best to be mother to a young boy and a comfort to her own father? Truth, she decided. She hadn't any basis of other kids to go on, so she would simply always tell the truth. It was the only option she could think of that had any chance of success.

"I mean, is he like you said, 'the right boy'?" Tamara added another question over Perrin's silence.

"Tamara, honey. You've gotta make a promise to Perrin."

"What?"

"Stop asking such hard questions, please?"

It earned her a tentative smile but no promises. Guess that would have to do.

"Is he good? He's almost as good a kisser as he is a dad, which is pretty incredible. Is he the right boy? I have no idea in the world. The other question I have to ask, 'Am I the right girl?' I can't believe that I am."

Tamara did another of her deep thought things before responding. "I don't know the answer either, but I can kinda see how you might be."

Man oh man. And she'd thought the questions were tough.

"LOOK AT THESE. Maybe you can tell me what's missing." Perrin had enjoyed teaching Tamara through the quiet afternoon, she was an apt student. She quickly understood right and wrong sides of fabric, seam allowances, and pinning. Cutting on the bias had tripped her up, but she was getting a handle on it. She also successfully threaded the Featherweight several times as well as jamming it up once royally.

But the unfinished costume designs had lain there on the cutting table the whole time and beckoned silently. And she was no closer to solving them.

"There's a lineage missing." Perrin had set out blank pages of paper with the role titles on them: Princess (arranged marriage), Maid-servant Companion, Queen Mother (of

Princess), and True Love (same lineage?). She'd set small snips of different fabric possibilities on each, but they all looked like crap.

Tamara stopped in her efforts to undo the latest snarl she'd made by catching a fold in the machine—yet another seam to rip out. Only way to learn stuff like that was do it wrong enough times.

She came over to lean on the table beside Perrin. Close, if not quite rubbing elbows. A good sign that she wasn't too uncomfortable about Perrin and her dad.

For a long time, they looked at the blank pages in silence. Then Tamara turned to face the room. She started doing all of the things that Perrin had done. She'd walked slowly about the room, running her fingers over a red velvet, a blue chiffon, and some black corduroy. Occasionally Tamara's hand hesitated and Perrin noted which fabrics they were, just in case she couldn't come up with any other ideas.

The girl dug through the patches bag under the table for a bit, asked a couple questions about the crazy-patch embroidery Perrin had rammed back into the bag in frustration. Next Tamara would be walking through the whole store and find nothing to help her. And then Perrin would call Bill and admit that he'd been right all along, that she was a clothing designer and not a costume designer. Crap, but she really didn't want to let him down.

Tamara was passing the rack where Perrin hung works in progress, and also some of her own clothes in case the weather changed, or she suddenly felt cold.

She stopped there, and Perrin twisted around to see what she took down.

The electric-blue knit sweater Perrin had worn to lunch last week.

"You getting cold, honey?"

Tamara took it off the hanger and brought it back to the

table. She folded it up and set it on the Princess' blank sheet. Stepping back, she tipped her head sideways to inspect it.

Perrin waited for it. Let her eyes drift over the texture and color. The knits were soft, following lines and curves, a sharp contrast to the rest of the highly structured costumes. They'd be able to accentuate or diminish based on how they were knit: ribbed, stockinette, cabled... And the blue. It was close. So close. Not electric-blue, but...

"Jewel tones," she let it out as little more than a sigh. Then she squealed. That was it! That was so it! Knit jewel tones.

She swept Tamara into a hug and then leapt up to waltz about the room with her. Both giggling madly as they went. When they passed her computer, she tapped the play button. Fleetwood Mac *Second Hand News* came roaring out of the speakers. And she did a shimmy that Tamara did a good job of imitating. They'd circled the cutting table twice, even doing an impromptu two-woman conga to totally the wrong rhythm when Tamara shouted something to her.

Perrin leaned down to hear.

"You and Dad will be perfect for each other."

"Why?" she shouted back.

"You both have the same crappy taste in music." Then Tamara did a shimmy-dip-twirl that Perrin did her best to copy as they danced another circle about the cutting table. Arriving back at the computer, she stopped Stevie Nicks in mid-throaty growl.

"Come on, kid," Perrin grabbed Tamara's hand. "We're getting out of here."

"But Dad thinks I'll be here."

"You own a cell phone?"

She held it up. "But only for emergencies."

"Fine, as soon as we're in the car, you text him. Say, 'Perrin had clothing emergency. I'm with her.' Make sure you put 'Hugs' or a smiley face or something at the end. He did a real hard thing letting you off the hook before. He deserves something nice."

They dashed out the door, Raquel and Kirstin barely having time to wave. They piled into Perrin's mini-van and pulled out onto the streets of Belltown.

Tamara dutifully punched out a text. "Is 'love you' too mushy?"

"For your dad, you can never be too mushy."

She finished the text, with a somewhat evil grin.

"What?"

Tamara looked out the window, watching downtown Seattle unfold and carefully avoiding Perrin's question, but obviously remained terribly pleased with herself. "Do you always drive so slow?"

Perrin looked down to check as they drove up the Mercer Street ramp and merged onto I-5 northbound, "I'm going the speed limit."

"But like everyone is passing us. Even Dad doesn't go the speed limit."

"Well, first, I have someone else's kid in the car, which is kind of freaking me out. Second, yeah, I usually go the speed limit in self defense. I know how easily I get distracted, so moving slower helps. Now give, or am I going to have to pull over and wrestle you to the ground for your cell phone."

Tamara studied the slowly moving landscape and gave out a long sigh of exasperation at their lack of progress. But her smile hadn't gone away.

"I just included a P.S."

"Sewing machine privileges," Perrin threatened.

"I only said, 'Perrin wants her fourth kiss soon.'" At Perrin's strangled sound the kid just laughed. "Think it got a reaction?"

Perrin just imagined Bill's reaction and hoped he didn't drop her then and there for telling such a thing to his teenage daughter. Then she imagined the look on his face and wished she could be there to see it.

"Where's Tam?" Jaspar had to tug on his dad's sleeve to get his attention. He was sitting in his office and glaring at his phone as if it had just bitten him, like that gerbil did to Tommy Hancock in Mr. Melk's class.

"She's with Ms. Williams today."

The costume lady. Wait. Hadn't she told him she'd be at Gretchen's? She never lied to him. Sometimes she got his help when she needed to tell one, but she'd always told him the truth. Or had she? What was going on all of a sudden?

"When's she getting back? I'm stuck on homew—"

"Not for a while, buddy. Look, I'm jammed up in this meeting for maybe another hour. Then I'll help you. Okay? Can you work on something else until I'm free?"

Jaspar looked at the other men in his dad's office. They had a lot of papers and drawings and notes and stuff spread all over the table. They were all looking at him, waiting for his dad.

He also had his phone out and was looking sorta pissed, like when he was trying not to scream at him or Tam for doing something dumb. He didn't scream except when they'd really earned it, but he had that look.

"Sure, Dad. Whatever."

Jaspar went back to the cubicle across the hall from his dad's office where he usually did his homework. The problem was that he didn't have any other homework except this lame book report on stupid *Captains Courageous*.

Tam usually helped him, even on books she hadn't read. She'd make a game of it, just asking so many dumb questions that eventually he'd figure out what he wanted to say.

Now she was off with the costume lady doing girl clothes

stuff. She'd gone all gaga over those dresses at the store. Bor-ring. Though getting to be in the opera was kinda cool. He'd liked that at first, even if the backstage stuff was way cooler, but they never let him work on any of that. Like he was still eight or something.

For some stupid reason he'd thought that being in the opera meant they'd all be spending more time together.

He turned to scowl at the book sitting on his desk. A story about a kid brain dead enough to fall off a ship in the middle of an ocean. Maybe he should have just drowned. Not that any dumb sister would ever notice.

———

BILL STARED BACK at the phone message. The meeting continued around him, but what had been a fascinating snarl of problems to unravel just moments before had turned into a meaningless buzz.

Clothing emergency was cute and funny. He could hear Perrin's voice declaring it like a national crisis or an incoming missile attack. It had made him smile until he scrolled the message enough to see the last line.

P.S. Perrin wants her fourth kiss soon.

His daughter had just told him that a woman, who he'd met less than two weeks before, had told his *teenage* daughter that she'd kissed him three times. And wanted to do it again.

What kind of a game was Perrin Williams playing at?

There was no possible way this could be happening. Perrin was right. Not about being toxic, but about how he should be much more cautious about letting his kids come in contact with her. What if things didn't work out? What if she was a crappy parental figure? Which the present message sure pointed to.

And this sure as hell wasn't his definition of slow. She was bonding faster with his daughter than she was with him. How was he supposed to trust someone who did that?

What if she hurt the kids somehow? Not intentionally. She'd never do that, there wasn't a mean bone in her body.

And it wasn't helping matters in the slightest how much he couldn't stop thinking about her body. The way she had responded to him for that one stolen hour. It had been incredible, as if every touch not only seared him, but her as well. He'd never responded so strongly in his life, maybe not even to... Damn it! He really had to cut that out. Adira was only diminished by the fading of memories over time. That's all that was happening. Whereas Perrin Williams was so vibrant, so alive, she shone like one of her costumes.

"Everything okay, Bill?"

He looked up at Timothy Winters, the Opera's Production Manager.

"Uh, don't know yet. Give me a sec."

He read the message again.

I'm with her.

He wondered if that was Tammy's voice or Perrin's? Perrin's. She'd been making sure that he knew she was keeping Tammy close and safe, no matter what else was going on. Maybe she was being an okay authority figure after all? She had been the one who made sure Tammy called him within minutes of entering her shop. She'd also made it clear that she'd already straightened his daughter out on lying about where she was. That was actually far above and beyond the call of duty for a girlfriend.

It was only the last line that was pure Tammy. Somehow, Perrin had decided that telling his daughter that they had kissed each other was the best option. Then, instead of any emotional storm Tammy had signed with a *Love you.* That was something he hadn't seen in far too long.

That's when he understood, Tammy was teasing him about

Perrin. Not something she'd do if she was mad or overly shocked.

For a moment, he wondered if Perrin knew about the last line. Bill had to smile. If she didn't, he'd bet that Tammy would find a way to tell her. Kids never missed an opportunity to get back at adults.

Welcome to my world, Perrin Williams.

"What do you think, Bill? Do we have time to get these plates hydro-punched or do we need to spend the extra to get them drilled?"

Bill keyed an answer into the phone, hit send, and began juggling the production schedule versus the painting and staging schedules so they could save the money with punching.

PERRIN AND TAMARA had ridden in silence for several minutes. Tamara fiddled with the radio but no one had music, all ads at the moment. They were both just killing time to see what Bill Cullen's response would be.

At long last the phone buzzed back and gave a cheerful ping as Perrin was pulling into the steep, narrow parking lot.

"What does he say?"

Tamara looked at it. Then appeared a little puzzled. "He just sent a one-letter response, 'K.' Which is short for 'Okay' when he's in a real hurry. Maybe he didn't read the P.S. part of it."

Or, Perrin could hope, he'd decided that the single response covered both messages in the text. They continued in silence, each thinking their own thoughts until reaching the store.

"What is this place?" Tamara climbed out and glared at the building.

Perrin looked up at the aged two-story, concrete-block building, with peeling taupe-blah paint. To one side was a vacant lot, some old apartments towered over it from behind.

"A knitting store, Tamara."

"But it says, The Weaving Works?"

"Don't you trust anything I tell you?"

Tamara considered, "I guess I trust you."

"Good, the moon is made of green cheese and Justin Bieber has a poster of you on his wall."

"Eww!" But Tamara was smiling as they arrived at the door. "Hey, that's cool."

Knitting in a bright sock yarn wrapped about the door handle.

"There's more of it," Perrin pointed to the bike rack in front of the store. The galvanized steel had been knit over in a succession of the colors of the rainbow. "The Weaving Works" had been boldly knit right into the fabric.

"It's called yarn bombing."

"That is just so cool!"

"You've been hanging out with Jaspar too much. You're using his adjectives."

"He's my kid brother, I don't get a whole lot of choice on who I hang out with. I would have filed a request for a girl, but I was only three when they had the punk. He's mostly okay except for being a boy. Don't tell him I said that."

"Deal." Perrin pulled open the glass-and-steel door. "Welcome to knitting heaven, Tamara."

They toured the whole store together. Racks of every color and type of yarn towered about them. Like a small, labyrinthine bookstore, its shelves stocked to overflowing with heavy yarns for fisherman's sweaters, fine yarns for baby clothes, and feathery "eyelash" yarns for when you just wanted to feel utterly ridiculous.

"Check this out," Tamara called Perrin over to the Jamieson yarns. "The skeins are so small and cute. I just love the colors."

"They're my favorites," Perrin pulled out four assorted colors. "Come on."

She led Tamara to a small mirror.

"Watch your face as I hold up each color." She started with a blue and Tamara shrugged, then an orange that clashed with her hair and her complexion.

"Eww!"

Then a black.

"That one's good."

The Perrin held up the dark green heather yarn. It played off Tamara's rich-red hair. With her fair skin, it snapped all attention to the girl's dark eyes. The extra softness kept it from being too severe beside her young woman's features.

"Wow... " Tammy offered on a long-drawn sigh.

"This doesn't mean all your clothes should be Loden green, but when you want to really knock out some boy, this wouldn't be a bad place to start."

They took the skeins back to the shelves.

"Hey Perrin. Why aren't there any guys here except for that one over there looking bored?"

"Not a lot of male knitters. Funny thing is, there are a lot of cultures where it was traditionally the male who did the knitting. Now, this is just a cozy place for women to hang out. See the big table in the corner with a couple knitters around it? There's almost always someone there to sit and knit with. Or you can bring in hard problems if you get stuck and someone will always help you out. I often think that this is how the world would feel if it was run by women."

"Cozy."

"Exactly. Now, we need the color sets for the four designs we were missing."

"You want me to help you pick colors for clothes that will go onstage?" her voice was wispy and awed.

Perrin figured it was part of that distant-and-impossibly-remote "Dad's world" and Tamara felt as if she were just a kid intruding. Like Tamara, Perrin had been plenty precocious, and that had caused its own set of problems. Well, it wouldn't ever be an issue for this girl. Not if Perrin had anything to say about it.

"You're the one that found the solution to something that's been making me crazy for over a week. You solved it, I'll make sure everyone knows that. As a matter of fact..." Perrin stepped over to the display of knitting tools and pulled down a massively ridiculous crochet hook that had to be there as a joke, it was two feet long and almost as big around as Perrin's wrist. She rolled it to the label, "Size 50." It wasn't a toy, some project actually required this monster. That was just too crazy. If she could think of what to do with it, she might buy it.

"Kneel, Empress-to-be Tamara Cullen."

"You're kidding."

"Kneel, or I tell your dad that I'm not the only one kissing boys."

"Oh man!" Tamara knelt.

Perrin tapped her lightly on each shoulder with the crochet hook, then thonked her on the head hard enough to elicit an "Ow!"

"I hereby dub you my official design assistant. Rise oh Tamara of the thank-you-for-saving-my-butt design team."

As she clambered back to her feet, several of the nearby women who had stopped to observe the goings-on offered a round of applause.

Tamara blushed a brilliant red while Perrin waved the hook as if acknowledging her adoring subjects. When the applause had turned to kind laughter and everyone had returned to their shopping, she turned once again to Tamara.

"Now, assistant, let's go choose some colors."

CHAPTER 9

"God. You should have seen her, Bill. I wish I could have shared it with you. We had the best time picking out the yarn." Perrin's voice over the phone was almost as breathless as Tammy's had been.

"Wish I could have seen it." He wished it so much it ached. His daughter had come home from her afternoon lit up like she was the queen of the world. Any lingering desire to chew her out for lying to him about going to Gretchen's died when she threw herself into his arms.

"It took her a good half hour at top speed to tell me about all the things the two of you had done. And she can talk awfully fast when she's on a roll."

Bill lay back on the top of his bed covers and stared at the dim ceiling.

"You aren't upset, are you?" Perrin's voice was soft.

"Upset? At what?"

"Well, I mean I know I shouldn't be attaching myself to her, or letting her attach to me, but she's such an amazing kid. And she wants to grow up so badly. Do you remember what that was like?"

Bill remembered joining the high-school theater as a freshman and having his entire life changed when Mary Ann, an awe-inspiring junior, had wandered across the stage carrying some tools to go fix a broken Fresnel lamp. She'd been tall, slender, with dark hair down past the middle of her back.

His worldview had altered in that moment. He'd never grown up fast enough to get her attention. Hell, he'd never once been able to tell her how he worshipped her in the two years they did shows together before she graduated and was gone.

"Yeah, I remember what it was like. I just wish it wasn't my girl doing it. And no, I'm not upset. I just wish I could have been there with her... With you. How can I miss you so much? We hardly know each other."

"You could ask me out on a date."

He could, if he could just figure out how to arrange it. *Turandot* was finally down and the set struck and returned to storage. For a while, the weeknights and weekends were his once more. His and his kids.

"Where are you now?"

"Why? Are you asking me out now? I thought your kids were asleep."

"They are. I just wanted to picture where you were, what you were doing. What I really wish is that you were lying on the pillow beside mine." And he did. Against all likelihood, he could picture her here, in the bedroom where no woman had ever been. He wanted to turn and see Perrin beside him. All her chaos, all her uncertainty, all her beauty, and all that magnificence curled up beside him. He could see it so clearly, as if she were—

"I'm in my studio."

"Oh," a dose of reality. He was sprawled on the bed thinking more about sex than any teenage boy, and she was working.

"I'm lying naked on my cutting table, just waiting for a strong man to come and ravage me."

The heat that flashed through his body left him sweating and his pulse racing.

"O-kay. That's an image I going to be glad to be stuck with for a long time."

Perrin giggled, just like a happy teenage girl who was thinking as much about sex as he was.

"How about something simpler?"

"Spoilsport," she made a raspberry sound. "Such a party pooper, you don't even want to come here. Big meanie would rather leave me all alone and unravaged in my little bed."

"Thought you were… " he lowered his voice to make sure it didn't carry down the hall to the kids, "… sprawled naked on your design table waiting desperately for me?"

"Oh no, any strong and willing man would be fine. You just happen to be the one I'm talking to. And I'm not naked, I'm wearing a flannel nightgown. Yes, all alone in my own bed."

"Not how I pictured you." Not at all. He'd thought Perrin would be one to sleep naked, or in one of those oversized t-shirts that always made a woman's legs look so amazing. Adira had been a long t-shirt type.

"No, Bill Cullen, I've never worn a little black teddy, nor am I planning to anytime soon. Not even for your fantasies. If you're going to ravage me, you'll just have to deal with a woman who wears plain white flannel nightgowns."

"Not even pink?"

"Nope, white."

"JC Penny's?"

"Caught me."

"Actually, that's an image I could definitely work with. And no, Perrin Williams, I don't want to ravage you… " he let the silence drag for several seconds. "I'm desperate to ravage you."

Her voice was soft and dreamy. "You'd better make it soon, Bill Cullen. I don't know how much longer I can stand it if you don't."

"I've have to see you. What are you doing tomorrow?" It so hard to form normal, practical thoughts with her voice whispering into his ear.

"I thought you were going to be with the kids."

"I am. I was thinking we could have a picnic."

"With the kids?" she sounded suddenly cautious and practical. He knew he should be as well.

"They do appear to know you better than I do. Maybe it's time I caught up a bit."

"You're sure?"

Was he? Even though he'd been the one to invite her, Perrin was still giving him an out. Pushing him to do what was right rather than what she knew was their mutual desperation to be with each other. Yet another layer of flighty designer was peeled off to reveal the practical woman inside.

"Some day, Perrin, you're going to have to tell me why you carry your shields so high."

Her echoing silence told him he'd screwed up. Cassidy Knowles had only reinforced Perrin's statement that she wouldn't be sharing her life history. He cursed himself for being eight kinds of dumb. To have been hurt so badly and rise above it, how much strength had that taken? How many conscious choices had she made to be a better person despite her past? He didn't even need to know what her past had been to know what effect it had upon who she was. She had risen triumphant from whatever ashes...

"I don't know if I can, Bill. I truly don't know if I can." Her voice was so small.

"I'm sorry, honey. I'm so sorry. I shouldn't have said that."

Again the interminable silence. *Honey?* He was becoming awfully attached to her. Well, it was no less than the truth, he was.

"Would you still like me on your picnic?" Her voice was even smaller if possible.

"Yes. No equivocation. No doubt. I'm not the fastest guy around, but I eventually get there. I would very much like you to join us."

Another silence.

Then, after the silence had dragged on long enough that he wondered if she was still there, he heard a quiet, "Thank you."

"IT'S RAINING!"

"I noticed!" Perrin dove into the back of Bill's car and wound up sitting next to Jaspar.

Bill made a signal to Tamara to move back. He should have thought of it sooner, but it had been her turn to be up front.

Perrin stopped her before she even had her seatbelt undone. "Don't! You'll just get wet and I'll get wetter if we try to trade."

"Some day for a picnic, Dad," Jaspar accused him as if he had personal control of the weather.

"It was sunny this morning," he glanced over his shoulder at her and mouthed a, "Hi!" which Perrin returned. It was so damn good to see her he could hardly stand it.

"I guess we could go to a restaurant," Bill leaned forward to look up at the sky through the windshield and cursed the changeable spring weather.

Jaspar declared his opinion with a loud snoring sound.

"Gotta do better than that, Dad," Tammy joined in on her brother's side. "Perrin did pizza and cool costumes last time. You're gonna have to top that."

"Ouch! Don't I get a break, extra points for being your father who can make you wash dishes every night for a month if he feels like it?"

"Nope!" the kids both roared back at him.

Perrin shot him a grin in the rearview mirror.

"What?"

"How about the backup plan we discussed last night?"

She was definitely smiling, something up her sleeve. They hadn't discussed any backup plan. Oh, she was trying to help him save face in front of the kids, bless her.

"Which one?" he asked, trying to keep up with the game.

"How about the one at CenturyLink Center, on Occidental."

"Oh right. Sure."

She winked at him as he pulled back into traffic and Jaspar started telling her all about his stage role even if the backstage stuff was the part that he found to be really "wicked."

A glance at Tammy told him that, as usual, her dad hadn't deceived her for even a moment.

"A DOG SHOW!" Both kids had screamed aloud the instant they saw the sign. Bill had spotted the poster, but they hadn't and he'd kept his mouth shut. Perrin was so brilliant it was hard to fathom.

What finally clued in the kids was a sign running vertically down a street-corner light post. Only when he approached it did he see it had been knit in English Setter white and brown with six-inch tall letters that you wanted to pet they look so fuzzy and friendly.

"Yarn bombing," Tammy informed him when he asked.

"It's cool," he acknowledged.

"Wicked, Dad. According to Jasp, that's the right word today. Get with the program." Tammy smiled and took his hand so that he didn't feel too fuddy-duddy-daddy, one of *her* phrases.

Once through the door the kids raced off to see everything at once.

Bill tried to keep up, but Perrin grabbed his hand to slow him down.

"You're not going to find a place safer than this for them to get off the leash a bit. So to speak."

He guessed that was true, but it didn't make him any happier. At least they had their cell phones with them if they found any trouble. The Exhibition Center was a tall space. Not enough to feel like outdoors, especially not with all of the steel and concrete structure and numerous pipes running across the ceiling, but enough to give an airy feel to the event.

The vast floor space was clogged with people and dogs. Teacup poodles checked out German Shepherds. Dachshunds greeted anyone who'd listen, and terriers tried to watch everything at once. The animals, all muzzled, were surprisingly well behaved. But it was hard to move without getting wrapped up in a leash or seven.

Off to the right was a vendors' area for everything from vets to dog hair-care products and specialty foods. Most of the booths had a dog sleeping at the owner's feet.

To the left were big courses for agility, speed, and whatever other kinds of competitions happened at a dog show, barricaded off with thigh-high fencing. An Australian shepherd was running the course at the moment. A large ring was also fenced off for the show dogs, presently a collection of wrinkle-skinned Shar-peis in every shade of brown, black, and tan. Toward the back, a surprising distance away, there appeared to be long rows of kennels and grooming stations for the participants.

An indoor dog show in Seattle, who knew.

Perrin had.

"You're an absolute life saver."

"I saw the rain, did a quick Internet search, and this was the best I came up with. I hope it's okay?"

"Okay? It's bloody perfect. Though I'm not taking home a puppy. Not even if all three of you gang up on me. No how. No way."

"Yes sir, Mr. Bill Cullen, sir." She saluted him.

He couldn't help himself. He leaned in and kissed her.

She let him for a long moment, then pushed him gently away. She started them moving forward again, moseying forward though he was oblivious to what was around them. All he could think about was the woman beside him.

"God that felt good."

"It really did, didn't it?" Perrin agreed with him.

"I want to do it again."

"Don't. Tamara's expecting it. But Jaspar won't be. Let it be enough that we're holding hands."

Bill glanced down in surprise. They were. He traced it back in his mind. They had been ever since the entry when she'd stopped him from rushing after the kids. It had felt so natural that he'd thought nothing of it.

"This going slow plan sucks."

She bumped shoulders with him. "This is so not slow. We really need to figure out what's going on between us soon. If there's even a chance for us, or if I'm going to hurt your kids horribly, even unintentionally. I'd rather walk out the door now than hurt them, though it might kill *me* to do so."

"Well, you're the woman three steps ahead of everyone. Any brilliant ideas?"

Perrin went silent at that. They managed two whole aisles of the vendors' area without any ideas between them. Two aisles of things they would never need in their lives. Hand-tooled leather collars fit for a mastiff. A small bookstore with everything from a photobook of the Queen's corgis to how to train your dog for sheep herding.

"They still do that?"

"Apparently."

Buffalo meat dog food. Emu meat dog food. Vegetarian dog food as if the master's predilection made any sense for the pet.

They circulated out by the agility ring so that the kids could spot them more easily. Now it was Golden retrievers racing the course at a dead run, guided by whistles and hand gestures of their trainers. At impossible speeds they were ducking through knee-high pipes, leaping over barriers, and winding through upright stanchions so close together that the dogs looked like eels while passing through.

"Could you get free Tuesday evening? Not the night, but at least the evening?"

"Why? What do you have in mind?"

Perrin shook her head, "Yay or nay, Mr. Cullen. You either can or can't."

"I'll find a way. Actually Lucy, my sister, has been wanting the kids for an overnight. Would a night as well be okay?"

They were so close together that it felt as if their bodies were about to meld, though their only actual point of contact was their clasped hands.

"The night would be wonderful." Perrin almost looked teary, though he'd never seen her cry.

"What is it?"

She shook her head part way, then hesitated, somehow knowing she'd told him too little and it was on the verge of bothering him.

"I just can't get over that you want to be with me. That's all."

"That's all?"

She nodded.

"Woman, you are going to make me totally insane yet."

"Really? Cool!" Her voice had flashed mercurially to bright, chipper, funny.

He scanned the crowd, but didn't see the kids. Eyeing her carefully, he could see the edge of the tease and tried to figure it out, but couldn't.

"Okay, what am I missing?"

"You actually like me enough for me to make you totally insane. That's cool."

"Wicked!" he corrected her. And yep! She had him pegged for sure.

JASPAR SPOTTED THEM. Dad and Ms. Williams sat at a small table with four chairs at one end of the dog obstacle course.

Ms. Williams who Tam kept calling Perrin like they were best friends. Fine, if they didn't want him around, that was just fine.

Though Tam had been cool as they'd gone to visit the dogs. And she'd said she was sorry that the boy in *Captains Courageous* hadn't at least been captured by pirates rather than fishermen, so maybe she was still okay.

But now Dad sat holding hands with the costume lady. That didn't feel right.

"Hey Tam?"

"What?" She was all involved in the dogs racing around the track.

He tipped his head toward the distant table and the grownups. Then he pretended he was more interested in the collie dogs that were coming into the ring so that it wouldn't be like they were both spying if they got caught.

"Bet they've kissed."

His sister was quiet so long that he turned away for a second to look at her. Her shrug said enough for a clear yes.

"Is she trying to marry Dad?"

Again the shrug, different meaning this time. This time Tam didn't know. He turned his attention back to the dogs.

Stuff was changing again and he didn't like this change one bit.

"Do you think we should be worried about the kids yet?" Bill looked at her nervously. He'd been doing his best not to fuss.

Over Bill's shoulder Perrin spotted the kids down at the other end of the ring. Tamara noticed her attention almost immediately, which told her that the girl had been keeping a close eye on Perrin and her dad for some time. Tamara said something to Jaspar, then grabbed her brother, held rapt watching the dogs, and began towing him by the shoulder in their direction.

"Oh," she turned her attention back to Bill. "I can make them appear if you want."

"How?" He narrowed his gaze at her.

"Easy. They're growing kids." The kids had made it about halfway through the crowds. "Ready?"

"Sure. Do your worst, lady."

Perrin closed her eyes and waved her hands over the empty table as if consulting a crystal ball. "Gee, I wonder if anyone's hungry?"

"We are!" the kids shouted from inches behind Bill who practically levitated out of his chair he was so shocked.

He stuck his tongue out at her as he hugged his kids.

"You all go find us lunch. I'll hold the table. I eat anything."

Bill led them away and she sat there.

She felt odd, as if she both was and wasn't Perrin Williams. If she was, it wasn't a version of herself that she recognized.

She knew the driven designer, consumed by the need to create beauty and joy with each of her dresses.

She knew the "cheery loon" who kept both her friends and new-met strangers on their toes. The one who could never seem to let a straight line lie on the ground untended, unquirked. The one who kept everyone at a safe distance, even those closest to her. Maybe especially.

And the woman who drove men away before they could even begin to get close—her she understood less, but knew well.

So often Perrin had wondered if that woman was afraid that she'd be tested and found wanting, or was she just plain afraid?

And she remembered the young girl before she'd changed her name on her college application, remembered her far too well. The one who took years to learn that waking in terror was not normal. The one who didn't understand for years more that she was the only one who prayed each night to wake up in the morning and learn that she'd been orphaned while she slept. Or died.

These were all at least familiar.

The one she didn't know at all sat here ever so quietly. A hundred dogs running about her. And a man who had offered her a glimpse of another world, an impossible fantasy somehow come to life. This new Perrin scared her to death.

Because she dared to want.

She could feel her heart start racing until it was in rhythm with the rushing dogs.

Look at you playing Happy Family games.

She couldn't think.

Who do you think you're kidding, you loser!

Couldn't breathe.

Run!

She had to run!

She couldn't stand!

Clawing at the table, she managed to gain her feet. A chair crashed to the floor somewhere behind her. An English Setter glanced her direction and missed a gate.

She turned to push free of the crowd too close around her.

She ran blindly into a man who wrapped his arms around her.

She fought, struggled, would have clawed if she could but the arms tightened around her until she couldn't move.

"Whoa! Perrin. Perrin!"

The nightmare never knew her name. Not that name. It

knew a different one, a name she hadn't used in twelve years. Perrin was her safe name.

Safe name. Safe.

"Perrin!"

She knew that voice. She followed the voice back. Back until she found the face that...

"Oh god, Bill. I'm so sorry." She covered her mouth and searched for the kids.

They were only now returning, heavily laden with trays of food.

She turned away, so they couldn't see her face. "Give me a minute. Just a minute."

He held her just a moment, an infinitely reassuring moment, then kissed her on the forehead and released her.

"Okay, land it there, kids."

She heard a chair scraped upright. A dog bark. The slow return of normalcy about her.

It had been years since she'd lost it like that. Years since she'd lost her firm grip of control. She stepped farther away, hoping to find and leash a few more pieces of herself. Even Jo had never seen that part of her. Only Cassidy. Only her.

"A kiss on her forehead doesn't count as number four, Dad," Tamara teased somewhere behind her.

"Number four what?" Jaspar sounded grumpy.

"So dense," Tamara complained to her dad.

Jaspar made a raspberry sound.

She could feel them waiting for her to join them. A nice, normal family. They had no wife or mother, but were a good, solid family nonetheless.

And they'd all begun to cast her for the missing role... *her!* Perrin Williams! How could they be so wrong? She closed her eyes. Perhaps if she couldn't see them. She focused on the sound of excited panting from the dogs in the nearby ring and the hum of the crowd's conversation. Perhaps if she couldn't hear them. Perhaps then she could walk away.

But she *could* hear them. And when she managed to turn, she could see them; involved in some game for which the prize was someone else's French fry. Thankfully, Bill had seated the kids with their backs to her.

Ten steps. Ten lousy steps and she could rejoin them.

Or she could turn and run.

She looked over her shoulder toward the entrance, the chaotic Seattle weather had now allowed sunshine to light the wet street beyond the glass entry doors, making it glisten. The distant view of daylight painfully bright and real compared to the industrial lighting inside the hall.

Perrin turned back and took the ten steps to the table. They were hard. Maybe the hardest thing she'd ever done. She had to count each one under her breath to make them real, to prove to herself that she was making progress.

But she made it.

She'd soon lost half her French fries to Jaspar, clearly the table's master of the game she didn't bother trying to understand. He may have been targeting her specifically, but that didn't seem likely. Bill ended the game at that point anyway. It didn't matter. She wasn't sure if she could eat much.

Bill's knee pressed hard against Perrin's own as he teased Tamara about her third career choice of the week: opera singer, fashion designer, dog trainer.

Bill's knee. It was all that anchored her in place. It was barely enough but it held.

BILL FELT her pressing her knee so hard against his. What had just happened? The woman beside him made the lost waif he'd first met appear rational.

"You gotta see them!" His son started towing Bill out of his chair and pointing toward the grooming stations at the back of the dog show.

Once he was on his feet and the table was cleared, Tamara had started leading them. But she drifted back to coax Perrin out of her chair when she didn't follow right away.

Perrin had scared the hell out of him. The stark terror on her face exceeded anything in the awful movies his kids sometimes made him watch, even the ones he wouldn't let them watch. He'd certainly never seen anything like it in real life. For a moment Perrin had been gone and the woman in her place had been terrified for her very life.

Somehow, she'd reached deep and pulled it together. He'd watched her fight some titanic battle while he'd distracted the kids. It had almost killed him to not go to her as she stood so alone in the aisle, facing whatever demons had sent her crashing into him. But he couldn't.

She was also right, they were going to have a talk, and real soon. If there was something he needed to know to protect his kids, she'd have to explain it, shields be damned. Or else they were through.

A glance back showed that Tammy had slipped a hand around Perrin's forearm, for Perrin's hands were plunged deep in her pockets. She'd looked like a ghost of herself. She was slowly recovering, but he could see the brittle layer, the near transparent façade holding her together.

He almost called Tammy away, maybe Perrin had been right about not bonding with the kids.

But he couldn't do it to her. She looked so frail, and that wasn't the woman he knew. That wasn't the woman who had brought his daughter back to him so effortlessly, and had designed those magnificent costumes.

He'd wait and see. He just hoped to God he wouldn't be left with some huge disaster to clean up.

"Here they are," Jaspar practically squealed.

In moments both kids were down on their knees. A beleaguered Cairn terrier looked up that them as eight little puppies walked all over her.

"Aren't they just so cute?" Tammy scooped one up carefully to show him the little brindle-coated pup.

Bill glanced at the owner, a big man relaxing comfortably in a small folding chair, he offered a friendly nod. "Your young 'uns know the way of it." His accent Kentucky or Tennessee, but with an overlay of watching too many episodes of *Game of Thrones.*

"Be ready to adopt in another month and a bit. The sire is over to yonder giving his all for Best in Show. Won't get it, but we won't be tellin' him." The man winked to show he was simply happy to be here.

Perrin drifted up to Bill. She tentatively reached out and touched him lightly on the hand, asking permission. He wrapped his fingers around hers and she clamped down hard, proving that all of the sewing had made her a strong woman indeed.

Not releasing his hand, she again glanced for permission, far more tentative than she'd been even half an hour before, then knelt behind the children. For a moment he feared that the life had gone out of her, as if that wild spark of life and fire were gone.

"Your dad swore that we'd never convince him to get a dog," her voice was close to normal. "Not even if we all ganged up on him. What do you think, should we try?"

Okay. So, the spark wasn't gone. She'd simply been asking if she'd screwed it up permanently. Not yet. His antenna were now out, but she was still okay.

He squeezed her hand briefly to let her know they were still okay.

"But no dog," he told the three of them.

He hoped she'd ease up on her grip soon, before his fingers went completely numb.

It took a while to extract the kids, but Bill had made it out with his fingers intact, and no dog. But it had been a close thing on both counts.

In the sunny afternoon, they'd walked along the waterfront, doing all of the touristy things together. They rode the Seattle Great Wheel, the hundred-and-seventy-five-foot Ferris wheel standing at the end of one of the piers, their gondola practically scraping against the low scudding clouds at the top of the trip. They poked into Ye Olde Curiosity Shop, making faces at the shrunken heads and exploring one of the most amazing kitsch collections he'd ever seen.

Jaspar had departed Pirate's Plunder with an eye patch that he could see through, but looked opaque from outside. Tammy found a head scarf that made her look mature and, in pulling back her hair, exposed a younger version of Adira's beautiful neck.

"That green color looks great on you, kid."

Tammy had offered one of her enigmatic smiles.

"Makes you beautiful like your mom."

That earned him the melty-happy expression he'd been hoping for.

It was only as they wandered into the Seattle Aquarium that he noticed Perrin wore an identical scarf.

"You like it? Tamara insisted we had to match."

"What color is your hair? Really?" The scarf did look good on her, mixing the blonde and the black into a soft cascade onto her back. He fooled with it a bit, relishing the softness.

"The white-blonde is about as close as I've ever let it get. It was originally a gold-blonde, but I left that behind long before I was eighteen. First goth black, then just any color that goes with my latest clothing design."

He'd like to see that original color some day. See it grown

out, all golden-blonde. Maybe in that gold dress he'd seen the first day. But it wasn't his place to tell her how she should look. And he also liked the nutty style, it made her uniquely Perrin. But he'd wager that the true blonde would be stunning. There must be something behind that eighteen line, all her stories stayed on this side of that.

And that led him back to his earlier dark thoughts. Who was she, under the woman that she wore like a fine set of clothes? Who was the terrified creature he had glimpsed so briefly? The one who'd thought that he'd... He shoved the thought aside in disgust.

He knew he was falling in love with the first woman. He'd been in love with Adira, knew what that felt like even if they were so different. Adira his quiet anchor and Perrin who made him feel more alive than he ever had other than the first time he'd held his children. It was a shock, but he could recognize it in himself.

The second woman worried him. Worried him badly.

CHAPTER 10

"Jerimy!" Perrin raced into the Costume Shop and spotted him by a rack of *Turandot* costumes. He was boxing them for storage, they must be freshly cleaned.

"Perrin!" He shouted back and met her halfway. He gave her a strong and totally unjudgmental hug. She needed that right now. All Sunday and Monday she'd been so worried, fretting at the problem like a sore tooth.

Bill hadn't changed how he treated her despite her panic attack at the dog show, but she'd felt different around him. Having revealed that awful fear inside her, she didn't know how to go back to showing him only the carefree and happy woman she'd worked so hard to stitch together over the years.

Jerimy didn't know any of that and she could just be her old, familiar self with him. He squeezed her hard enough that she had to gasp and giggle. She kissed him on each cheek before they let each other go.

"Do you knit? I need a bunch of knitters. Wait until you see. Where's my portfolio?"

"The one in your hand, beautiful?" he teased.

"Well, no, but it will have to do," she teased back and tossed it down on the table. Then she opened it and pulled out the final four drawings. She set them in a row and stepped back. These had come from somewhere deep. They were actually some of the best drawings she'd ever made, the women on the page practically breathed.

Jerimy didn't gasp, he didn't marvel, he didn't exclaim. He did something far more respectful, he went very still and silent.

When she couldn't stand it anymore, she moved in to point at the yarn samples she'd taped along the side.

"They're all hard jewel tones, but all in soft knit. Even the cables in their cloaks have a softness."

"They're pure light," Bill said from close beside her.

Perrin actually cried out a little to find he'd come up so silently that she hadn't noticed.

They were pure light. "That's the point. They are not tragic themselves, but are nonetheless caught in the Prince's tragedy. It makes them so much more sympathetic."

"I know these three women in real life. Who's the fourth one?" he pointed at the Queen Mother.

"What are you talking about?" She turned back to inspect the drawings more closely.

Bill leaned forward, extending an arm between her and Jerimy to tap each drawing in turn. So close she could feel him, smell him. Her head whirled at the wonder of him.

"You, Perrin, in two roles, Empress," he pointed to the drawing Jerimy had tacked on a corkboard on the wall, "and the True Love. Jo Thompson is the Princess and Cassidy Knowles her Maid-servant Confidant. I'd have expected that to be the other way around, but what do I know."

Perrin looked at the drawings in surprise, he was absolutely right. Without realizing, she'd used the three of them as models rather than the opera singers she'd met at the rehearsals. Of course, Jo would be the Princess, for she was honor and truth incarnate as well as being typically ever-so reserved. Cassidy's passion was a little closer to the surface though still reserved. She was the deep, quiet bond that strung them together. Bill Cullen wouldn't know that yet about either of her friends.

"Who's the fourth one?"

Perrin looked at the Queen Mother, the quiet bedrock of the world.

"Mama Maria. You'll meet her tonight."

All he offered to that was a soft grunt. He knew her mother was a part of a past she *wouldn't* talk about. He thought it was a choice, but it wasn't. She *couldn't* talk about it; not and retain her control, perhaps not even her sanity. But nor could Perrin explain Mama Maria in just a sentence or two.

"She looks nice enough."

"She's amazing." Perrin had missed her so much. But she and Hogan came back last night from their honeymoon so tonight they'd be together again. She needed a subject change for her own sake, and fast. Oh right!

"Knitting!" she practically cried it out, loudly enough for the two men to jolt. "We need knitters, Jerimy. I'm okay, but I'm not good enough to do these, and not quickly. Please, please, please tell me you know some fabulous, gonzo, out-there knitters."

"Pretty lady, do I ever! Patsy. You have a minute?"

A short, voluptuous redhead strolled over from where she'd been overseeing the packing of costumes. Unlike Jerimy, her freckles proved that her red hair was natural, though the lemon-yellow streak over the crown certainly wasn't.

"Patsy is the gonzoest knitter in Seattle. And she's a gang leader, if you can imagine a knitting gang."

Perrin looked down at her. She stood maybe five-three. She wore an opera t-shirt that fit her in a way very differently from Perrin's. She'd redone the collar to have a deep vee that exposed a well-freckled cleavage and a tattoo of a pair of knitting needles, as if her generous breasts were still being knit into reality.

"What have you got?" Her voice was biker drawl as if she led a motorcycle gang rather than a knitting one, whatever that meant. She leaned her elbows on the table and went silent for several minutes.

Perrin almost felt a need to shuffle her feet or something, but Jerimy's smile reassured her, and she waited.

"The Princess' cloak is gonna be the beast."

That's when Perrin understood what was happening, because it was something she did herself. Patsy was structuring the garments in her head, thinking how to execute them, potential problems, what worked and what didn't.

"What if we felted it, to get that structure over the shoulders?"

Perrin nodded, that would work. "As long as you can keep it light enough to get the movement we need on the lower part when she rushes across the stage."

"Maybe felt from the lower point of the shoulder blades and up, then knit onto the back of that structure for the rest of it. Shift these cables here and here as structural elements. Are the colors intarsia? Or do we alternate them like a Fair Isle? It will affect the flow of the cloak."

They reviewed it piece by piece. Perrin was peripherally aware of when Bill drifted off. Jerimy hung close by, but added little. Clearly his assistant would be the master of these costumes.

When they were done, Patsy looked up at her. "Yeah, we got this. I'll get the girls and we can get it done this week. Have to think about the gusseting so that they can be used on different singers."

"That's why I designed in this layer of buttons down the side as a common theme. I thought multiple sets of buttons might work."

Patsy nodded. "I like it. Be better if we could lose them though, wouldn't it?"

Perrin had to smile. It was fun to work with another designer who didn't see any predefined box when they were doing their art. She didn't even have to acknowledge that it would be better and that she'd trust Patsy to go ahead if she found it.

Jerimy hung the last four drawings with the others on the corkboard, completing the primary costumes for the opera. There was still an immense amount of work to be done to execute it, but the designs were all there.

Jerimy made fresh coffee, Perrin took tea, and the three of them pulled up stools in a circle to admire the display.

Perrin had always worked solo, until Cassidy had practically forced Raquel on her. She'd hated giving up the control at first, but over the last two years her tiny one-woman shop had grown past what she could handle. Russell's amazing ads and Jo's sharp marketing advice had expanded Perrin's Glorious Garb past anything she'd ever envisioned. Other than the weekly meeting where they reviewed the books together and Perrin signed all the checks herself, she rarely had to think about the business itself anymore.

Raquel wasn't a designer, but she was a very astute business-woman. One who recognized how to take care of all the things Perrin didn't give a single damn about. It had let Perrin handle all of the designs and construction, though she still outsourced some of the work to Georgie in Duvall.

Early on, she'd featured other designers work along with her own. At Raquel's insistence, all of the designs in the shop had long since been uniquely her own and it was working. They still occasionally sold items off the rack, but more and more they were moving into custom work. Raquel had shown the numbers to Jo, and Jo had concurred that the direction change was sensible, which was good enough for Perrin.

But she didn't get to often sit with other designers and just talk shop. She could get to like this, just she, Jerimy, and Patsy sitting around together. It felt normal, real, as if she belonged and was accepted. Just the way Bill and the kids made her feel. As if it was normal.

"So, Patsy, what's a knitting gang?"

For once it didn't matter that sitting here quietly was the least normal thing on the planet for any of the incarnations she'd ever invented for Perrin Williams.

CHAPTER 11

*P*errin had stepped out onto the sidewalk and was locking up the shop for the day when Bill pulled up in his car. He climbed out, even though she was clearly ready to go.

He didn't ask. He didn't hesitate.

He swept her up into his arms, drove her back against the door hard enough to knock some of the wind out of her, and kissed her as if they'd been apart for years rather than hours. She locked her arms around his neck and returned the kiss just as ardently.

She let herself become wholly lost in the taste, feel, and smell of him. His body responded and, when he went to pull back, she partly wrapped a leg around him to pull him even closer, wishing she'd thought to wear slacks rather than a dress so that she could really get some leverage. Then he leaned into her shamelessly.

Bill was starting to slide a hand under her sweater, and she was on the verge of letting him, when some teenagers in a passing car honked their horn and shouted out encouragement. He pulled back abruptly.

"Uh," he tried to help her straighten her clothes. "Hi."

She leaned in and gave him the gentlest kiss. He really was decent, even when lust was raging through him, he was decent. He was so damn cute.

"Hi, yourself. If you're going to greet me that way every time we meet, you have a winner plan on your hands, Mr. Cullen. Though I don't know what your kids will think."

He leaned his forehead against hers. "Can we, for a single night, pretend that I'm just a normal lust-filled guy who doesn't have two kids?"

"I can. Can you?"

"Probably not. But it's worth a try. For starters, you did say something about a request to be ravaged on a clothing design table. I happen to know that there's one not far from here." He eyed the darkened shop behind her suggestively.

Perrin almost wilted as he cupped his hands behind her and pulled her hips against his once more.

"If you keep doing that, you just might convince me to actually do something that crazy. Though we'd be late for dinner. And we can't do that."

"Dinner. Forget dinner. Order out. Much sex." He sounded like a caveman. A deliciously handsome, well-built, wonderful caveman. Maybe she should clothe him in furs, she did have a partial bolt of faux leopard in the shop.

Perrin kissed him again, locking her arms behind his head and pulling in so hard that her lips hurt before she let him go. He shifted down to nuzzle her neck.

"No. Later. I promise. After dinner." She managed between desperate breaths totally failing at sounding like a lusty cavewoman.

He groaned without raising his head, "You drive a hard bargain, lady."

"Bill."

He slowly lifted his head until he looked at her from a breath away. She kissed him lightly.

"At dinner, you'll meet the most important people in my world. Once you know them, then you'll know me a lot better too. I'm hoping it will let you better judge whether we can still risk being together, you know, what with the kids I'm not supposed to mention and all. Because I'm way past being rational about you."

"Says the woman being all practical." His kiss, so soft, so thorough, actually made her moan. It wasn't something she ever did unintentionally, but Bill drove it from her body. She'd have slid to the ground, if the door weren't against her back and his hands on her waist, because her knees were totally gone.

"After dinner, do we still get to have sex?" His voice was rough with need.

"Oh God, yes!" The need vibrated through her just as it did through him. Even a night of meaningless sex with Bill Cullen would be worth almost any price.

But what if it were meaningful sex?

Perrin set that question aside carefully for the moment, and nudged him gently toward his car.

"PERRIN!"

Bill watched from the doorway of a condo near Pike Place Market as a lovely woman in her late forties threw herself at Perrin. Maybe this was the Maria he was supposed to meet. Perrin leaned down and the hug they shared was so tender and so happy, he actually had to look away to give them at least a little privacy.

"Dinner," Perrin had said. She'd failed to mention that the place would be packed solid with people and the air rippling with such amazing scents he seriously considered drooling. He couldn't even begin to make sense of the crowd.

"Hey," a deep voice behind him. "Keep moving forward."

Bill glanced back over his shoulder. The guy behind him was big. A couple of inches taller than Bill and enough shoulders that you wondered how he fit through doorways.

"Wait a sec, who are you?"

Before he could answer, Cassidy Knowles came up the hall behind him. "This is the man that I told you about, Perrin's friend. Bill Cullen, Russell Morgan, my husband."

The guy suddenly loomed taller, his light eyes darkening. "Bill. Cullen." His voice deepened like a storm gathering over the infinite deep of the ocean.

Before Bill had time to duck for cover, someone was tugging on his sleeve from behind.

"Bill," Perrin's voice.

He turned carefully, keeping an eye on the big guy for as long as he could. He ended up facing the woman Perrin had first greeted.

The woman glanced over Bill's shoulder at the man Bill could only assume still loomed behind him.

"Oh, stop being so like you are, Russell," her accent was lushly Italian. "There is beer in the kitchen, now be a good boy and behave."

The big guy slipped by a little sheepishly carrying a couple bottles of wine.

Cassidy patted Bill on the shoulder as she passed. "He's harmless, but he means well."

Bill remembered the far more nuanced, but perhaps more dangerous threat Cassidy had made on Perrin's behalf and restricted himself to a careful nod in reply.

"Hello, I am Maria," the Italian woman held out a graceful hand.

"Mama Maria Amelia Avico Parrano Stanford," Perrin

corrected her and slid a hand around the smaller woman's waist. Mama Maria could never have spawned the tall, blonde beauty that was Perrin, being darkly Italian and full-figured, but they stood as close as Adira and Tammy ever had.

Bill didn't know if he should shake the offered hand, or bow and kiss it. He decided on the latter. It earned him a bright laugh and a quick hug.

"So, Perrin brings home a man for the first time. And she does not tell me before she does this. That means that she is so very worried." Maria briefly flashed a radiant smile at Perrin. "And my Perrin never worries about men. I look forward to getting to know you, Mr. Cullen."

"Bill." He tried to think of something more intelligent to add, but didn't come up with anything.

"She's scary smart," Perrin told him, leaning down to kiss Maria on the temple.

"Just like you."

That earned him Maria's full attention. "You see her?"

"I, uh," Bill scrabbled about to find an answer to the odd phrasing of the question. "I see a brilliant, beautiful, chaotic, loving, wild, confusing-as-hell woman who I can't seem to look away from. If that's what you mean, then yes."

Maria pulled him down to her level using their still-clasped hands and then she kissed him lightly on each cheek.

"Yes," she whispered in his ear. "That is exactly what I mean." Then she stood back up. "Now, go meet everyone," and she gave him a gentle push into the room.

Perrin took his hand and went to lead him forward as the latest arrival greeted "Mama Maria" and began asking about her honeymoon. A quick glance revealed a darkly handsome Mexican man and a beautiful, slim Italian woman, both in their twenties, both sporting wedding rings. They had that newly married look, both smiling so hard their cheeks must be hurting. Even fifteen years later, he still remembered that feeling with Adira. So sharp, so visceral, it took his breath away.

"Uh, hang on," he tugged Perrin to a stop, pulling her sideways slightly out of the fray. "I need a second."

She held his hand and kissed him on the shoulder, then settled. Though he could feel her vibrating with good cheer.

First he looked at the setting. It was stunning. To his left was a long table, already laden with flatware and candles and several cold dishes. The wall behind the table was covered in pictures. Formal portraits and candids, many more of the latter. Though when he leaned in, he saw that even those were magnificent. He recognized a number of the faces as being in this room.

"Russell's work. He's such an amazing artist with his camera, I just try to be as good with my fashions as he is with a lens."

"Russell, the big guy?" At Perrin's nod, all he could do was wonder. More proof that you could never judge someone from the outside; Bill would have guessed stevedore or professional intimidator for a loan shark. Of course, he *was* married to the very elegant and sophisticated Cassidy Knowles which told another story. One that he'd like to hear someday, though he doubted he'd believe it; they made too odd a couple.

The side wall was mostly books which led to a comfortable-looking seating area near a wall of windows. Beyond the windows spread the Seattle waterfront in all of its sunset glory. The condo was perched at the top of Pike Place Market. The piers that they had explored over the weekend were spread immediately below. Elliott Bay, alive with ferries, sailboats, and a tug-escorted container ship, stretched out into the distance where the Olympic Mountains rose silhouetted against the sunset sky.

"It's magnificent."

"Thanks." A man had also retreated to their safe corner as the crowd in the condo grew. "Hogan Stanford, Maria's husband. Have you met her?"

"Oh yes," Bill spotted her headed into the kitchen. "I've definitely met the Queen Mother."

"Queen Mother. That's good, I like it. Isn't she amazing?" His smile, more serene but no less radiant than the other couples, told Bill exactly who had been on the honeymoon with Maria.

"Nice tan. How was the trip?"

"You a sailor?"

"Not much," Bill looked out at the water and the several sailboats skimming along in the last of the evening breeze. "But I'd like to take the kids out someday."

"Oh, we can definitely arrange that. Make an outing of it. Russell's boat or mine. Then—"

"Did you say, 'kids'?"

Bill found himself shaking hands with Jo Thompson. She stood quite close and was not releasing his hand.

"I did. I have two of them." Jo Thompson made an interesting contrast with the other two friends. He'd only met her briefly during the Friends of the Opera board meeting. She had run it with a smooth professional demeanor.

Out of that element, she actually look twice as daunting: judge, jury, and maybe Russell as her executioner.

Perrin had told him enough to know that the three of them had gone through college together. Perrin might not speak of anything prior to turning eighteen, but she couldn't say enough about the two women she'd met twelve years ago on her very first day of school.

Perrin was the tall, slender blonde. Cassidy, the trim, and nicely figured brunette. And Jo Thompson the seriously built, raven-haired, Alaskan beauty. Bill also knew that if he didn't take some control shortly, Jo and Cassidy would steamroller him right back out the door on Perrin's behalf.

"You three," Bill offered a nod to include the approaching Cassidy. He noted with some chagrin that Hogan had wisely abandoned ship. "You must have cut quite a swath through the men."

"You've got no idea!" Perrin offered one of her ridiculous giggles. Suddenly she was in full whack-a-doodle mode. "Jo found this one guy and latched onto him for four years. I think it was just so she didn't have to deal with dating. Sneaky, but dull. Cassidy, sheesh, she was so shy that if she hadn't had Jo as a roommate and me across the hall, no guy would have even known she was there. It was all up to poor Perrin to make sure these two got laid at all."

Bill watched with interest as the two women reacted to Perrin laying out their sex lives at his feet. No shock, no surprise, and, curiously enough, no anger. The slightly manic Perrin was a wholly accepted fact and still they loved her. Cassidy had even slipped a hand around Perrin's waist from the other side as she continued.

"And no matter how much sex these two are getting from their new husbands, about which they tell poor Perrin depressingly little, they still haven't turned me into an auntie. Now I ask you, Mr. Cullen, is that fair?"

Bill looked at the two women, inspecting them as carefully as he would an opera singer about to tip off the deep end. They were expecting... Well tough! It wasn't what he was thinking, so all sails ahead or whatever sailors said and damn the consequences.

"I'm on your side, Perrin. I think that's really unfair. They should be having much more productive sex. And not telling us the all the juicy details, where's the fun in that?"

He could feel Perrin do a little dance step hop of glee against his side. Cassidy almost doubled over to hide a sharp snort of laughter.

Jo, who had retained his hand, studied him with those dark, dark eyes of hers before delivering her verdict.

"You just might do, Mr. Cullen. You just might do." Her slow smile lit her face like magic as she shook his hand solidly. He'd thought her pretty enough, but that rare smile transformed her into a great beauty.

When the two women finally moved off, probably to compare notes, Perrin threw herself into his arms.

For a long moment, he didn't care who was watching or what they thought, he just pulled her in and buried his face in Perrin's hair and reveled in the scent of the woman in his arms. He loved feeling her warmth. Holding her joy tight against him.

The dinner itself was a long, wonderful, maddening, incredible experience. At the table, Bill had ended up between Maria and Perrin, apparently a place of quite some privilege. Which raised eyebrows in some parts of the room, but not many.

Thankfully, there were a lot of stories in addition to his own. Maria and Hogan's sail up the Italian coast. Angelo, the handsome Italian chef who had married Jo Thompson, was still working on opening his second restaurant by the Seattle Center. When Bill told him when opening night of *Ascension* was, Angelo immediately decided that was a perfect night for a Grand Opening of his restaurant as well. Maybe he'd even get some before and after opera patrons for dinner.

Russell, rather than continuing to threaten Bill, started talking about some kind of a mutual marketing campaign. While a restaurant was small potatoes compared to a new opera costing upwards of five million dollars to produce, he suggested some interesting possibilities. They made an appointment for the next morning to talk about it further. He'd make sure to vet the guy personally before bothering Wilson or Chloe over in Marketing.

The Mexican man, Manuel, apparently a fine Italian *sous chef*, had taken the glowing Graziella to his family home in Oaxaca for a combined wedding and honeymoon which explained the newlywed smiles.

Angelo declared a reception dinner at his restaurant next

Tuesday, rather than dinner at Maria and Hogan's. "And, Manuel, you will not be allowed in the kitchen." Based on Manuel's reserved look, Bill would wager on his finding a way in no matter what his boss said.

Maria and Hogan had married at Christmas, but not wanted to travel until the pastry chef for the new restaurant had been trained and approved by Maria. Apparently the second week of Maria's honeymoon had been even harder on Maria from worry than on poor Ignazio trying to meet her standards all on his own. A round of toasts and many cheers were raised on his behalf, while he did his best to glow at the far end of the table, it mainly looked like a blush from where Bill was sitting.

All that news traveled back and forth over some of the most amazing food Bill had ever eaten. Lasagna, so not microwaved. A mac and cheese made with fresh-made pasta, very aged cheese, and prosciutto. A side of salmon broiled with baby asparagus, venison flank braised with a mushroom-Barolo sauce, so rich it almost killed him. Steamed vegetables tossed in a white wine, lemon, garlic sauce... The plates seemed infinite yet were all consumed. It was capped off with a pear poached in stout beer for dessert. The evening was finished by tiny cups of decaf espresso laced with Frangelico hazelnut liqueur and many heavy sighs of contentment.

"You folks do this every week?"

Maria nodded at him, "Is there anything better than family around a table?"

Bill tried to come up with something, but... "Not a one I can think of, ma'am."

"Tell me more about your children."

"Better than that, if I'm invited next week, I'll bring the kids if they'd be welcome."

"Always!" Maria replied emphatically. "Children are always welcome." She waved a hand at all the new couples seated about the table, "I expect many children to sit at this table for many years to come."

Bill lifted his right hand, where it still held Perrin's left. He liked that they were opposite handed, so that they'd been able to hold hands for much of the meal, even while they ate. He kissed the back of her knuckles. It delighted him that it was so normal it didn't distract her from her conversation further down the table, other than to squeeze his own hand back without turning.

When had he tipped over the edge? What moment had he decided that not only did he want to come back next week, with Perrin, but to offer to bring his children? That was... He could feel the blood draining from his face. Too fast. It was all happening much too fast.

Tammy, who had already been too grown up, was blossoming straight into womanhood from Perrin's influence.

And Jaspar was...what?

He'd practically thrown a five-year-old's tantrum about staying at Lucy's, though he'd been looking forward to it just days before. Bill had looked to Tammy for guidance, but she'd shrugged her shoulders helplessly. He'd tried talking it through, and finally just told him to get over it. He apologized to Lucy when he dropped them off for the horrid mood Jaspar was in. He had no idea—

Maria tapped her tiny espresso cup against his, drawing his attention back to her. "It's hard to know what to do, isn't it, Mr. Cullen? Especially when children are involved."

All he could do was nod.

"I was oh so careful with men around my son and Russell. But perhaps I was too careful. They turned into such fine boys, that I must have done something right, but Angelo grew with no father. John Morgan, Russell's father and my employer, was a good man but he was no father to Angelo. He had a wife and a son of his own. A thousand times I wonder if I made the right choice."

"He'll make a good father. They're a beautiful couple."

Jo and Angelo had begun to clear the table. When he rose to help, Maria rested her hand lightly on his arm. "Not on your first visit." Others were already rising, apparently based simply on who wasn't deep in conversation at that moment.

He settled back in his chair, not sure if he was comfortable with the continued conversation. How was he supposed to change his mind and say that he couldn't bring his children when she was being so gracious?

"Yes, it's hard to know, Mr. Cullen."

Bill turned to face Maria once more.

"So, it will be our secret. You will bring your children when you are sure and not before."

The relief was stronger than might be seemly, but he couldn't help that.

"Perrin was right, you're scary smart, Maria Stanford. She didn't mention that you are also amazingly kind."

Maria sipped her coffee, leaving him some space to gather his thoughts. Scary smart indeed.

"I don't suppose you'd care to tell me anything about the woman beside me?"

"You mean other than I wish with all my heart that she, of all women I've ever met, had been my daughter?"

That knocked Bill back in his seat. Everyone, except her new husband, called her 'Mama Maria' as if she were mother to them all. Yet from this amazing crowd of people, she had singled out Perrin.

"Really? Why?"

"Yes, really. And because Mama Maria is scary smart, you said so yourself, therefore it must be true. And there is one other thing I would tell you, Bill."

It was the first time she'd used his Christian name, as if he'd finally asked the right question, it had just taken him all evening to find it. She reached out and placed her hand over his heart.

"All the love you have in your heart for your children and your poor departed wife?"

"Yes?"

"Perrin will need that much. She will need so much before she will trust herself. So you will have to trust for her."

"Why can't she trust herself?"

"That's up to her to tell you, if she decides to."

"And if I can't trust her that much?"

"Phfft!" Maria flicked her fingers dismissively. "Your heart already knows or you would never have mentioned bringing your children here. Your mind just don't know it yet, but it is already true. Do not worry, dear boy. You will be getting there."

THEY SAT QUIETLY in his car. Bill had pulled up in front of the store, parked the car, and turned out the lights. He made no move to get out, and Perrin waited with him in the dark silence. A lone streetlight was shadowed by the trees leafing out along the sidewalk. A few other cars were parked along the block, but there was little traffic.

"I don't know if I can do this," Bill kept his hands on the wheel.

Perrin didn't move, suddenly still as a frightened child.

"No, that didn't come out right," he reached out and picked up the hand he'd held most of the night. "There's just so much inside me. It's all so jumbled up that I don't know what to do with it. It's good, Perrin. I swear to God it is, but it's big. So big."

She slowly slipped her other hand over his, trapping his fingers between her hands. Her tension eased, but her silence didn't.

"I... " He looked up at the trees, down the street, over at the out-of-business tattoo parlor. Right back where he'd started. "I don't know what to do with all that's going on inside me."

"Welcome to my world," her voice was soft. "I'm smart enough to know what's going on inside me. But I can never seem to straighten it all out. Like trying to build a costume that keeps falling apart because a key seam was never sewn, but by the time I fix it, another three have unraveled."

He turned to face her. Her face but a pale oval in the dim light.

"Can you be smart for me tonight, Perrin? I honestly don't know what to do with it all."

"Me?" He'd shocked her. Himself a little too.

"Don't see anyone else in the car volunteering."

That roused her laugh—briefly.

"I love your laugh so much." The words just came out of him. He did. It was like a thousand stage lights come alive. Her laugh shone into the darkest places and shone pure, brilliant light.

"You want me, of all the loony people on the planet, to be smart for both of us?"

He could only nod.

"Okay," she huffed out a breath. "Okay, I can try, but understand that you only have yourself to blame if this comes out all stupid."

"Understood. It's a risk I'm willing to take."

She looked away and studied her darkened shop for a long time.

He waited, one hand clamped to the wheel, the other still wrapped so warm between her two hands.

"Okay. Looks as if it's going to come out as a series of questions."

"Like I haven't had enough of those tonight. Talk about the Italian inquisition, it was a tough room."

"Hey, you asked me to take over here."

Bill nodded, "I did. Go for it. I trust you." That snapped her attention back to him. He hadn't expected those words either. Maria's words. But who else would he trust in this situation?

"Me?" her voice was a whisper.

"Yes, I do. You. The scary smart lady sitting here beside me like a blessing. So ask. Please?" He actually begged a little. Everything was so mixed up inside him.

"Okay..." her voice was shaky. She took a deep breath. "Okay. Let's start with a key one. After meeting with everyone, do you still want to be with me?"

"So much it's killing me."

"That's a good answer, Bill. That's a really good answer. I like that answer too. So if that's not the problem, then let me think what's next."

Bill sat in the dark and waited. He had kissed this woman a half dozen times, total. They hadn't had a proper, just-the-two-of-them date yet. His kids were half mad for her. And his own feelings?

"Are you afraid that if we make love, your life will never be the same?"

"Yes." The answer dragged out of him.

"Okay, we're tracking so far."

"Tracking?"

"We're both being scared silly by exactly the same shit."

That reached him. That finally punched through whatever knot had been slowly winding tighter and tighter in his gut all night. It wasn't the answer yet, but it was the first strand, broken rather than merely loosened.

"Keep going. You're doing great, Perrin."

She let go of his hand, "I can't think while we're touching." Then she grabbed it back between hers, "No, not touching you is even worse."

"That's not a question, but yes, I feel the same way."

Perrin smiled over at him.

"Okay, I think this is the final question of the first round."

"Fire away."

"Could we go inside to finish this before I freeze to death?"

"Shit!" Bill scrambled out of the car and hurried around to open her door.

She didn't lead him to her shop as he'd expected, but rather around the corner. She stopped at a door on the side street. A half dozen mailboxes hung along the wall for the various apartments above her shop and the one beyond. Perrin unlocked a door that led to a flight of stairs.

The stairway was hung with a beautiful series of quilts...or maybe it was one quilt sewn into separate works of art. It was as if he was following a stream through the seasons. Working his way upstream, the first quilt led him from ice winter to red-and-gold fall. The second stream, appearing to flow out of one quilt and into the next, followed the summer colors and included a pool with a bear pawprint and a golden flower. The third quilt started the stream flowing between banks the color of spring, eventually rising to where it flowed out from under blue-white ice, just as it had ended down below.

"Are these yours? The four seasons. They're beautiful."

"I quilt sometimes, not often." They left them behind at the head of the stairs and Perrin led him down a hall that made his eyes water. It had a green ceiling, a zebra stripe wall to one side, a yellow wall to the other with a purple-lettered poem painted on it in tall letters.

He read a few lines, it was a really bad poem.

"These, however, are so not me."

Bill considered remarking that was a good thing, but wasn't sure of how good the sound insulation might be. Besides, he remembered the last time Perrin had used those words while standing in a pile of confetti the first time she'd met his children. At least the floors were a rich, if hard worn, hardwood. None of the residents had applied "their art" to improve them.

She led him to the door at the end of the hallway.

Perrin's apartment was neither neat nor messy, it was lived in, but perhaps not very much. Clearly, her life was downstairs in her shop. There were nice coverings on the couch, a television, but no computer. Several fashion magazines. A wall of reference books on types of art: architecture, fiber, painting, sculpture of a dozen varieties, early Japanese, Italian Renaissance. The collection was all about art forms and they looked well used. This is where she obviously found many of her out-of-the-box ideas. He couldn't decide if it was an incredibly focused collection or astonishingly unfocused. Assuming the former, it was immensely eclectic within its range. She moved into the kitchen while he inspected the books.

"I don't see any on opera."

"They have books on opera art?"

"About a thousand: lighting, costume, sets, you name it. I'll get you a couple."

"Thanks."

A totally mad quilt, clearly done in one of her gonzo frames of mind, filled the wall above the couch with a dozen blocks, each in a unique style with different fabrics. Yet the colors tied it together into a curiously cohesive quilt. A wild one, but cohesive.

He found her making tea in a small kitchenette with a table that could seat only two. She still looked cold and he moved to hug her.

"No," she fended him off. "You touch me and we're going to go straight to sex, do not pass go, do not collect two-hundred dollars. And as good as that sounds, it's not what you asked for."

"I was being an idiot. Come here."

She didn't. So he tossed his jacket aside, dropped into one of the chairs, and just enjoyed watching her move about the kitchen fetching mugs and digging out a box of blueberry tea.

"Sorry, I think this is all I have at the moment."

"Kids' favorite. I've learned to like it."

She poured the hot water and sat across from him. "Ready for round two?"

"No. But let's see where we go anyway."

PERRIN LOOKED at Bill over their teacups and tried to decide just how brave she was feeling. Maria had liked him. She'd liked him a lot. Jo and Cassidy too, which helped, but Maria was the wise one. And she and Bill had talked quietly together through so much of the meal.

She'd done her best to listen to everything, while pretending not to. She'd missed a lot, but had heard Maria admonish Bill that "he already knew about his heart," he just didn't know that he did. There was no way to be sure what they were talking about, but there were things Perrin already knew about herself. Really knew. Even if they were scaring the crap out of her.

Bill waited so patiently. He'd said he trusted her.

Trusted her more than himself.

No man had ever said such a thing. Well, if he was going to trust her, how could she return less?

All it took was being brave, right? She wasn't particularly good at brave. She could do it if she hid behind crazy Perrin, because then it was someone else. And it came out as a joke that no one believed. But she couldn't go there with this man. Not when they sat quietly together in the night. Not when she felt the way she did. She'd have to be her more rational self tonight.

"Okay, do you want the scary question first or the hard one?"

"That's a choice?" He brushed a hand through his hair and she wished she had the nerve to do the same, but she didn't dare touch him at the moment. Not for his sake but for her own.

"It is."

"No third choice? Wild sex maybe?"

She shook her head. "As wonderful as that sounds, not yet."

"Shit! Why doesn't this look good? What the hell. Hard one first."

Perrin really didn't know which one was worse, but she wished he hadn't chosen the hard one.

"First, I want you to know that if you want to walk out the door afterward, I won't ever blame you."

She could see that he almost made a joke, then a denial, but finally thought better of it and set aside his tea mug to listen.

Perrin didn't know how to do this one. Maybe like she'd told Tamara about tearing up the drawings, "You gotta just do it." Well, she was about to risk tearing up her life, but she saw no other path.

So she just did it.

Perrin told Bill about a father with a taste for young girls. About a mother with a coke habit she supported by selling her daughter to anyone who came to the trailer. Perrin left nothing out, not skipping one sordid detail of eighteen years of hell that had been her childhood.

She told of her arrival at college, an escape she still wasn't sure how she'd managed, her test scores earning her a full scholarship. And how, after one particularly horrid drug-laden and abusive night, it was Cassidy who had taken her own meager savings to take Perrin home with her. The three of them had gone to her father's small vineyard just across Puget Sound on Bainbridge Island.

How Cassidy's father had been kind. Simply kind, expecting nothing in return. She'd never known such a thing was possible.

After that, for four years, she'd listened as well as she could to what Jo and Cassidy had told her to do. For four years, she'd slowly left behind a wounded child and invented Perrin Williams. Legally changing her name senior year so that the diploma would bear her "real" name.

She didn't cry as she told Bill of her true past. Tears were still locked away too deep. She'd often laughed until she cried with Jo and Cassidy. Only once since her early childhood, the first time Mama Maria had said she wished Perrin had been her daughter, had she cried for herself.

But Bill cried for her.

Tears ran untended down his face. He tried to reach for her, but she pulled back. Not trusting that she could survive the searing power of his touch and not shatter.

"I haven't had a panic attack like the one at the dog show in over five years, but I can't guarantee there won't be another. So here's the hard question, Bill. Can you still trust me around your children? Do you want to risk a woman with that past stepping into the mother-role for your children? Because that's where this might be headed, or we wouldn't be having this conversation."

With a shocking abruptness, Bill stood and whirled away, striding out into the living room.

Perrin closed her eyes, wrapped her arms around her belly to hold herself together, and waited for the final judgment and eternal damnation of the front door slamming shut.

But it didn't happen.

Not even after she waited.

When she dared open her eyes, she could see his back. He stood in the center of her living room facing her couch and the sampler quilt she'd made ages ago to teach herself basic sewing and design skills, her first-ever effort. His arms were crossed so tightly that they were straining the fabric of his shirt.

He didn't move. She waited five minutes, ten. But still he didn't move.

She stood and moved into the kitchen doorway. Almost close enough to touch him. But she couldn't bridge the gap.

"What's the scary one?" His voice was so harsh, so angry. She'd never heard anything like it, but she now knew better than to fear him. He'd never strike her. Whatever his anger, it wasn't directed at her.

She'd made it through the hard one, now she had to face the

scary one. The one even more likely to send him running down the hall away from her. She swallowed hard before trying to speak through the fear of losing him.

"I love you."

The words fell into the silence of the room and lay there untended for long enough that her stomach knotted into a hard, snarled ball.

"That's not a question." Then he turned to face her. His face was calm, though his cheeks were still wet. He stepped forward, and reaching out very slowly, brought his hands to her shoulders.

If she could have stepped back, she would have. But she was too numb, too afraid. Not even for Cassidy had she let her heart out into the world with her words.

He pulled her in, leaving the decision to stop wholly up to her, but she let him do it until she could lay her cheek on his shoulder and he wrapped his arms around her. She couldn't seem to unlock her own arms from around her midriff, so she simply leaned against him.

Bill rocked her gently, ever so gently. Then he whispered to her.

"Yeah. That's the same question-that's-not-a-question that's scaring the shit out of me too. I love you, too. It makes no sense that it could happen so fast or so completely, but I do."

Some time later, Bill's slow rocking turned into a slow dance in the middle of her small living room.

Perrin was fairly sure that she was the one who kissed him first, rather than the other way round.

He was definitely the one who swept her up in his arms and proceeded to carry her into the coat closet. She redirected him to the bedroom with giggles for his curses.

Bill set her on the bed, then sat beside her. He brushed his fingertips ever so gently over her cheek.

"Don't!" Her shout was sharp.

"What?" He jerked his hand back as if she'd burned him.

"Don't you dare treat me like I'm fragile. I'm not fragile. Earlier this evening you wanted to ravage me. So ravage me. I won't break!" Perrin was so pissed she wanted to swipe at him.

"Not fragile? Not fragile?!" His voice rose as abruptly as hers had. "Any idiot who thinks you're fragile needs his goddamn head examined. You lived through... through..." he pointed helplessly back toward the kitchen. "... that. You're the goddamn strongest and most amazing woman I've ever met. I'm being gentle because I can't believe what you just told me. *That* you just told me. That you let me in so far. How can you dare to trust me so much? That's what I'm trying to understand. I'm in awe of you, Perrin Williams, not afraid I'm going to break you!"

"Oh." If she'd been gone on him before, she was right off the deep end now. The way he saw her was incredible.

"*Oh?*" He huffed out a breath. "Is that all you have to say after my whole tirade is, 'Oh'?"

"Best, I have, Mr. Cullen."

"Shit!" he cursed. "Where was I?"

She took his hand and placed it against her cheek. "Right here." Then she closed her eyes and turned her head to rub against his fingertips.

Ever so slowly, he relaxed and began again. He traced the lines of her face. She followed the line of fire as he tested every shape and curve: cheek, chin, eyebrows, lips, and tip of her nose.

She was floating by the time he had moved down her throat. He didn't hasten his investigation of her body in the slightest as he unbuttoned her blouse, released her bra, and teased her breasts until she ached for him.

When his mouth latched onto her, she hissed at the pleasure so intense it was pain. He knew exactly what to do to drive her upward. No man had ever been so gentle. No man had ever been so intent on giving her pleasure rather than taking his own. She allowed herself to go where he led, to become a conduit of Bill's touch. Each line he drew, each place he tasted built until she was clothed in nothing but the light and heat he spread over her skin as he went.

He rolled her over until she lay on her stomach, and he continued to clothe her in his gentle brushes and kisses. He turned it into a massage. One that started at her feet and built as it flowed up her legs, over her buttocks, driving her deliciously into the bed, and up over her back and shoulders.

Just as he had made her feel clothed in traceries of light, now he stripped her bare with a deep cleansing touch. She didn't remember turning onto her back once again, didn't know when it happened and didn't care. He continued until the waves finally burned through her insides, scorching away the last remnants of darkness trapped inside her.

When he laid his lips between her legs, she exploded. She cried out as a tidal wave of pure pleasure rushed over her. No man had ever touched her like this. None had ever sent her to such places, ones she didn't even believe existed.

But now she knew.

They did exist, with the right man.

When she managed to flutter her eyes open, Perrin saw that he was still fully clothed.

"That was one hell of a ravage, Mr. Cullen."

"You're magnificent, Ms. Williams."

She managed to sit up, despite her muscles all gone to liquid.

Her fingers weren't working that well with how her nervous system was buzzing, but she managed to unbutton his shirt. His muscles twitched and quivered under her touch.

"That's a very nice chest, Mr. Cullen."

"My wife liked—Aw shit! I'm sorry." He went to turn away.

She stopped him with a kiss. "Bill. I'm not asking you to push your wife out of your heart to let me in. I know she's dead or you wouldn't be here with me. I think it's nice that you loved her so much. It really shows in Jaspar and Tamara, they'd know if it wasn't true."

"But you deserve—"

"Exactly what I'm about to take." With that she pushed him back on the bed. She dug in a drawer for some protection, then she greedily took all he could give. How many times they made love, how many times the waves rolled through each of them, releasing their bodies and clothing their hearts in such glory, Perrin didn't know.

But even as they collapsed onto each other and slid into sleep, Perrin knew that however much she'd had, she wanted more.

CHAPTER 12

*B*ill groggily surfaced. Seven a.m.

Crap! An hour late! He tried to leap into action, but his body totally failed him. Then he remembered where he was. No kids. No lunches to make, no need to double-check they had their homework in their packs.

He rolled over, but there was no one beside him. It was just breaking daylight beyond the lacy curtains. The room he hadn't seen last night was now lit with a soft light.

Everything that was utilitarian in the rest of Perrin's apartment, had no place here in her bedroom. Here there were warm colors, soft textures. Rather than a closet, rather than *just* a closet, one whole wall had been turned into shelves and hanging racks. Here were the clothes, both casual and incredible, worn by both the real Perrin and the wild-girl she presented as a smokescreen to distract others.

But where was she?

Even as he struggled to wake up enough to go find her, the bedroom door swung open. An elegant, burl-wood door harp played a cheerful chord as the door bumped lightly against the dresser.

He'd never seen anything like what came walking into the room. Perrin had said she slept in a flannel nightgown. What she hadn't said was how amazing she looked in one. It was easy to forget how tall she was because she was so slight, but the columnar gown emphasized her length. And her black-and-blonde hair stood out even more strongly against the white. The gown was of such fine material, that even the tiny breeze of her forward motion made it wrap and cling against her amazing figure.

The smile that greeted him wasn't the least bit tentative. There couldn't be any question about how they felt, not after last night. Her smile was as luminous as the morning light. Her fine features, so delicate yet so strong.

"Are you ready for some coffee?"

His brain said, "Yes." But the rest of him had other thoughts. A reaction she clearly noted through the thin layer of the sheet over his bare hips.

"I was hoping that's how you felt." She set the tray on her dresser then moved to sit beside him.

When she reached out a hand to brush his cheek, he used it as leverage to drag her against him, crushing his mouth to hers.

She lay down full length upon him and melted against him until they would be one body if not for the thin flow of soft fabric separating them.

"You," he ran a hand up her magnificent body, "requested a ravage, Ms. Williams. I think it is time you received precisely that."

"Why Mr. Cullen, that sounds like an absolutely brilliant idea."

And he did. For a moment, he considered if he should be gentle, not wanting to scare her. Then he imagined her as the Empress—the great, the powerful, the embodiment of woman. What kind of a lover could make the Empress lose herself? A gentle one would please her, but that wasn't the point of a ravage.

He rolled her onto the bed beside him. When Perrin moved to pull off the nightgown, he brushed her hands away. In some ways this too was her shield, where she wrapped herself into safety.

Well, this morning, he'd not violate that, instead he'd honor it as a part of who she was. He rubbed the fabric over her, tasted her through its thickness, drove her with his hands, though never directly touching her, until her body thrashed and she groaned begging for more.

When he could stand it no longer, he rolled her on top of him, slid the nightgown up her legs, and took her beneath the cloak of flannel now spread over both of them.

With her palms against his chest, she rose above him, the most magnificent being he could imagine, and then she drove her hips downward as he arched up into her.

Her head thrown back, her exquisite neck curving ever so perfectly, her body thrumming against his as they both greeted the morning with their shared pleasure and joy.

BILL WAS SHOWERED, dressed, and totally pleased with his morning when Perrin's phone buzzed as they were leaving her apartment. She checked the message and then made a cheer and did a little shimmy dance. Today she wore tailored wool slacks and a cashmere sweater, one of which hugged and the other of which clung.

Bill's first thought was how badly he wanted to drag her straight back into the apartment, but she was skipping ahead of him down the poem and zebra-stripe hallway.

"It's finished!" she called back to him.

"What is?" He had to hustle to keep up with her.

"C'mon slowpoke!" And she was gone.

She stood at the street corner when he caught up with her and there was certainly no need to ask what she was looking at.

A solid maple tree, with its long straight trunk rising up from a square hole in the concrete sidewalk, had been wrapped in yarn. The colors were both electrifying and familiar.

The upper half was in the conflicted color of the lineage of the Tragic Prince, the lower half, the jewel tones of the Princess and True Love. Over them both, in large, blocky letters that were actually knit into the design was simply the opera's title, *Ascension*, in the dark, forceful colors of the Overlord.

"An *Ascension* yarn bomb? That's cute."

"I had Patsy's yarn gang do it for me."

"It's a lovely piece of work." Bill brushed a hand down the soft surface.

Perrin the wild girl was looking at him...and grinning like a jackal.

Bill surreptitiously checked the soles of his shoes to see what he had just stepped in, but he had no idea.

CHAPTER 13

When Bill arrived at the Opera offices, he scraped in only minutes before his planned meeting with Russell.

He only had a moment to look up Russell Morgan online.

Bill tried to get organized, and thought of the shape of Perrin's shoulder.

He adjusted his chair and thought of the feel of her hips in his hands.

It was a struggle, but he managed to focus enough to run the search.

Russell Morgan had been a world-famous fashion photographer until he'd practically disappeared two years ago, closing his New York studio. Bill clicked over to see any images. There were several paparazzi shots of Russell with that supermodel Melanie draped on his arm.

Bill shook his head in wonder, and remembered how it felt as Perrin's strong fingers dug into his hair.

There were photos of Russell's wedding to Cassidy Knowles at a lighthouse. And some genuinely nice ads for Perrin's

Glorious Garb, Pike Place Market, and the Washington Wine Cooperative.

Bill was about to scrub at his face to force himself to focus when Nia called him to the front desk.

In the lobby, not only Russell, but also Angelo were chatting happily with Nia. It wasn't quite flirting, both men were decent enough to make sure their wedding rings were on clear display, but everything else about it was flirting.

"There's the man!" Russell's crushing handshake warned Bill that last night's threat before dinner might not have been so idle. Angelo's friendly hug and very solid thump on his back reinforced the message strongly. Angelo was not as tall as Russell, but his shoulders showed he pumped a lot of iron.

The main thing Bill pumped was a lot of paper, and as much patience with work and kids as possible. He was in good shape, Perrin had remarked on it any number of times and places on his body... Gads!

If these two guys wanted to squish him into a little ball and drop him into a garbage can, there would be nothing that he could do about it.

He skipped the standard office tour, though he did take them through the halls the long way around so they could see the more recent production photos on the walls.

Russell nodded his head as he looked at them. "Claude's work, nice. Oh, and there you used Enrique. A little dark, but he always is."

At first Bill was trying to remember the directors and designers for those productions. Then he remembered a brief meeting a few shows back as one of his assistant stage managers had reported that she'd be escorting Enrique Rinaldi during a rehearsal to photograph the production. You couldn't have a photographer running around the house during an actual performance.

Bill looked more closely, but the photographer was not

noted on the prints, only the production, date, and visible cast members. Russell Morgan was able to recognize the photographer's work as easily as Bill recognized a well-tempered singer versus a lunatic diva, in other words, at a glance.

They went down to the Costume Shop. Jerimy wasn't there, but Patsy pulled out the main clothing racks for *Ascension.*

"Damn!" Russell brushed one costume aside, then another to expose the fronts. "Look, Angelo. Look what she did. Perrin is really incredible. I swear I could take her international tomorrow. I wouldn't do that shit to her, but her designs could walk Paris."

Bill agreed, then realized that this was a leading fashion photographer, he would really know. Without saying a word, Bill pulled out the Empress and hung it in the clear so that it was fully visible.

Angelo let out a long, low whistle of appreciation. "Can you imagine how Perrin would look in that one?"

Bill remembered her arrival. The manic, sleep-deprived, stunning beauty with the blonde swirl in her newly black hair, and that dress wrapped around her.

"She was magnificent in it." He lost himself in the memory for a moment, the sheer power she had radiated, like a beacon in the night.

Only belatedly did he become aware that he had the absolute attention of the two men.

"*You* saw *Perrin* in *that?*" Russell's voice was low, dangerous.

"She was amazing. Then she crashed onto my office couch and slept for nineteen hours and twenty-three minutes."

"She does that," Angelo acknowledged cheerily.

"Your *couch?*" Russell's voice went even lower.

"By Bill's dreamy look," Angelo offered up as if he hadn't noticed Russell's tone. "I'd say they used more than the couch after they left dinner last night."

Russell took a step forward, Bill stumbled back into one of the cutting tables.

"He has this ticklish spot," Angelo said perfectly matter-of-factly then poked a single finger into Russell's lower rib cage and began wiggling it.

"Hey!" Russell leapt aside. "Cut that shit out! I'm onto something here."

Angelo went after him again, ducking what looked to be a potentially vicious headlock. "What you're onto is messing with Perrin's love life. And frankly, if there's anyone scarier to mess with than Mama, it has to be Perrin."

Russell found the headlock, just as Angelo nailed the spot making Russell squirm sideways and step back, dragging Angelo with him by his neck.

Sensing trouble, Patsy, Jerimy's assistant, had come up behind them, though Bill had no idea what the little woman could do. She barely came up to Russell's armpit. What she did was deftly slide a clothes hamper behind their knees as they stumbled back another step, and the two men collapsed backward onto the floor in a flurry of scarves, hats, and gloves.

Bill looked up at the ceiling and remembered Cassidy's comment from last night: "Harmless." *Yeah, right.*

After cleaning up, the three of them sat around one of the cutting tables on tall stools. It had taken longer to drag Russell and Angelo clear of the clothing than it had been to get it all back in the hamper.

Patsy went about her business, whistling the old Grateful Dead tune, *Man Smart (Woman Smarter)* which thankfully neither of the other guys appeared to recognize. She had members of her knitting gang coming in to start building the last costumes and she was setting up a big table encircled by comfortable chairs. Someone rolled a large knitting machine off the elevator and Patsy rushed over to help. He hadn't thought the costumes were that numerous to need a knitting machine, but maybe they were. The outfits for the court's entourage characters had to match their leaders after all.

He left her to it and returned his attention to Perrin's self-declared protectors.

"Sorry," Russell shook his head. "Actually no. I'm not a bit sorry, even if Cassidy will kick my ass for interfering. Perrin's fragile. She needs protection more than she will admit or even knows."

Bill considered pointing out that his assessment was quite the opposite, but decided that discretion was the better part of survival.

"While Russell is still blowing steam," Angelo slapped his friend on the back, as if he was choking, hard enough to echo about the room though Russell barely wavered. "Someone care to tell me what the hell am I doing here?"

Bill could only shrug. He'd only expected Russell. And he'd mainly agreed to take the meeting because Perrin thought Russell was such an artist. That he'd dragged one of Seattle's finest restaurateurs along with him, didn't make any sense that he could see.

"It's in that boy's brain," he pointed at Russell, "maybe you can beat it out of him. If not, I'm sure we could call Mama Maria and she'd be glad to come help."

That seemed to work. Russell scraped his hand back through his hair.

"Man, you try to be a little protective of your friends and suddenly everyone's threatening me with Maria."

"Is it working?"

Russell glared at him balefully, "Yeah, I guess it is. Okay, here we go. Your new opera, are you planning any opening night events?"

"We actually have a couple of them. The high rollers, bigger donors, get a gourmet catered dinner with entertainment and free passes into the final dress rehearsal. Then there's also the after-opening-night party; that's for the primary cast members and the really major donors."

Russell was nodding. "Have you contracted venues or catering services yet?"

Angelo didn't see it, still looking confused, but Bill heard it loud and clear. He'd play along as a politeness, but didn't expect it to go anywhere.

"Consuela, our head of fundraising, has the bids, but we haven't reviewed or signed anything yet. The first event is a large tent venue for three hundred people on the Seattle Center grounds: heaters, string quartets, arias by various artists, the whole nine yards. The second event is typically an indoor venue, a hundred people, maybe a little more, mostly standing, high-end finger food and a fair amount of champagne."

"He can do that," Russell assured him blithely.

Angelo caught up with the conversation. "Wait! Three hundred? Are you nuts, Russell? Is that buffet or plated?"

"Plated."

Angelo groaned.

"That's individual service for three hundred people of an appetizer, three courses, plus dessert," Bill informed Angelo as if driving in the spike. He was starting to get the rhythm of these two. It was kind of fun to watch.

Angelo's eyes had crossed. "Uh, you have any paper?"

Bill found a sketchpad and pencil in a drawer under the table and slid it across to Angelo who began scratching down some ideas and numbers.

"So, Russell."

The man looked at him suspiciously.

"Hogan tells me you have a great sailboat. Any chance of you taking my kids out for a sail?"

It was like he'd hit the magic button. Russell brightened as he talked about the fifty-footer he'd refinished and taken up the Inside Passage to Alaska with Cassidy shortly after their marriage. He even had a picture in his wallet, right next to one of a black cat and Cassidy that was absolutely breathtaking.

"Okay," Angelo resurfaced, "I can do this. I'll have to close the restaurant for the night and hire some extra staff as well. Russell, you're going to be a goddamn busboy for me to pull this off, but I can do it."

"Do what?"

Russell dug into his pocket and pulled out a crumpled printout and shoved it across to Bill.

An advertisement. It was beautiful. It had power and beauty. A picture of the Empress hijacked from one of the posters gave it a real gut punch.

Master chef Parrano's new restaurant, Angelo's Piedmont Hearth, hosting as its Grand Opening, the party to celebrate the World Premier of *Ascension*. It was a breathtaking promotion of both the opera and the restaurant. It splashed a couple pull-quotes of Angelo's Tuscan Hearth, that sounded stunning, including one from Cassidy Knowles.

Bill pointed at the last. "That's kind of an insider review, isn't it? I mean you two obviously went through the same reformatory school, but why are you getting a nice lady like Ms. Knowles wrapped up in your skullduggery?"

Russell grinned at him, "Well, when she wrote that review about a meal, I was busy messing up—our first-ever, blind date."

"Messing? *Messing?* I thought I was going to have to close my restaurant and move to Senegal to get away from the shame. You know what they speak in Senegal? French!" Angelo shivered as if nothing could be worse. "I still don't know how you ever convinced her to talk to you again."

"'Cause I'm just that good, doofus. And way more handsome than you."

"Well, it sure wasn't your brains or good manners as your cat has more of those than you by a long shot."

Bill decided that balance was a good thing, and they'd both

been beating up on Russell as an easy target. So, he turned to Angelo.

"But I have to protect our donors. I mean, how do I know your food is any good?" Angelo's reputation was unquestioned. Bill had often wished he had an excuse to eat Angelo's food, as he was sure the donors would be. But being a single dad with two kids didn't really go together with fine dining.

Russell reached across the table to punch Bill on the arm in a friendly fashion while Angelo spluttered then glared at Bill.

"We booked solid. Next two nights, but then I can set up a special. You come to my restaurant. I show you just how goddamn good I cook."

"Does his English always come apart when he's upset?"

Russell nodded his head sadly. "Maria tried to bring him up right, but he's Italian. There's only so much you can do."

Angelo spit out something in Italian that sounded both melodic and guttural.

"Right back at you, brother," Russell said with some affection.

"Okay, so," Bill had a sudden idea. "If I do *deign* to come and try your restaurant, I'll want to bring a date."

The two men sobered and shared a long glance.

Angelo answered for them, "Perrin is always welcome. Always. No matter *what* she drags in with her."

Bill had the feeling that the last part was added as an afterthought insult, no real heat behind it anymore.

"And my kids."

"Do I hafta?"

Bill tugged on Jaspar's tie. Even using a clip-on, the kid somehow was wearing it crooked.

"Hey, it's a nice restaurant and the girls are probably going to look sharp." Tammy had been consistently going to Perrin's after school when she wasn't needed for a rehearsal. But Perrin had promised him that Tammy wasn't allowed to sew until after her homework was done. He'd been checking up on her homework, as he always did, but Perrin had been as good as her word. Jaspar appeared to be enjoying the exclusive Dad time, even if that often just meant reading a book while Bill worked.

"Girls!" Jaspar scoffed.

"Look here, Jaspar. If I have to wear a tie, so do you."

Jaspar stuck his tongue out at Bill, but moved to the bathroom mirror and adjusted it himself until it was close enough. He'd inherited Bill's curling hair rather than his mother's flowing locks that had gone to Tammy. A quick brush did little to help, especially as he was a past due for a haircut. Item ninety-seven on his Dad-to-do list.

Bill was really trying not to be nervous. He'd seen Perrin only briefly as he'd picked up Tammy a few times. A couple late night phone calls did little to slake his desperate desire to see the woman.

To distract himself as they drove to the restaurant, he asked Jaspar to teach him the new Italian words he'd learned. Carlo di Stefano had, once he calmed down from his girlfriend Melanie's departure, sort of adopted Jaspar. Already the kid had more Italian than Bill had picked up over years of dealing with singers. Carlo had wisely started with cat, dog, elephant, and the like. Then he'd moved on to *giovane principe,* "Young Prince," and the other titles in the cast. Now they were ranging off into everyday life vocabulary.

While Bill appreciated it, he also cursed that now he'd have something new he had to keep up with to encourage and support his kid as if that weren't item a hundred and eighty-two.

Next year Jaspar could start a language in sixth grade and Italian was presently the favored option. Spanish Bill could keep up with from living in California and working with Mexican stagehands. French he'd at least have a head start because that had been Tammy's selection. But Italian? And ten years old, headed for sixth grade...

Life was moving too fast. It had to slow down at some point, didn't it?

He parked and they walked down to the restaurant where Perrin had said she'd meet them.

"Hey look, there's another one!"

The walk sign on the corner had one of the *Ascension* yarn-bomb banners climbing its pole.

Angelo or Russell?

Russell, Bill decided. He was the marketing brains, Angelo was the cook. He must have asked...who? Patsy? Well, that would explain the need for a knitting machine. But it didn't just feel like Patsy and her knitting gang.

It wasn't just some slap up of Perrin's designs, the yarn-bomb itself was a designed piece. Perrin, it had to be. So, Perrin had designed a couple yarn-bombs to promote the opera. That was really decent of her. Definitely above and beyond the scope of the contract. And, like the costumes, the yarn-bomb was quite attractive. A tourist stopped to photograph it with his wife standing beside it smiling.

When they entered Angelo's, Bill was taken back to his life with Adira. In the beginning they could afford one date a month out together. They'd started at the local pub with a brew and a burger. Actually in the very beginning there'd been months where Kentucky Fried Chicken had been a splurge. But over the years they'd slowly climbed up.

A good Mexican restaurant, a steak house, a nice little bistro. By the time the kids came along, "date night" had become a monthly tradition. Their last dinner out had been a massive splurge at the Allegro Romano on San Francisco's Russian Hill, just a week before she was killed.

The rich scents of fine Italian food were a slap to the face that momentarily overwhelmed him with all he'd lost. It was too much. Too fresh. Four years of dealing with it, of telling himself the next day would be better, of putting on the good face for the kids, and here it all was as immediate as yesterday and as harsh as forever.

Air.

He needed air.

Bill turned back for the door as it swung open. Out of the evening light, a vision came toward him. Perrin had somehow walked the line between dressing for him and for his children. She wore a simple evening gown of bright red. Thin straps curving behind her neck and exposing bare shoulders told him that the dress was probably backless beneath the light shawl that had slipped down to hang by her elbows. All of her sleek form was traced, enhanced by the simple lines of the dress. Elbow-long gloves of the same material only enhanced the image. It covered, but it promised.

During their one night together, he'd done his best to memorize every one of Perrin's gentle curves. Her gown invited him to appreciate them anew.

Then he focused on the woman who had arrived holding Perrin's hand.

Woman?

"Tammy?"

She managed a curtsey then a brilliant smile that she shared with Perrin. Her dress, rather than the knockout statement of bright red, was as dark and dusky as her hair. It followed the lines of Perrin's, obviously the dresses had been designed to complement each other, but it was far more demure. Where Perrin's elegantly revealed, Tammy's dress modestly suggested.

He knew Tammy had a figure, he'd helped her buy her first training bra for crying out loud, an incredibly embarrassing moment for both of them, though he'd done his best not to let on. But without him noticing, she'd started growing into her mother's beautiful figure. The dress followed her lines, which made her pretty rather than enticing. Instead of the bare shoulder-backless look that Perrin wore, it was actually as high-necked as a turtleneck. A simple silver chain an accent to the deep red material that covered her so chastely. And it wasn't merely dressing up a child in a fancy dress, she wore it as a woman would, fully aware of her own impact upon those around her.

"It's the Princess-to-be," he still had trouble equating this growing girl with his own daughter. "Tammy, you're gorgeous."

Her glowing smile and bright giggle did nothing to destroy the image.

He wrapped her into a hug, which she returned more strongly than she had in a couple of years.

He mouthed a "Thank you" to Perrin over his daughter's head.

Perrin reached out a gloved finger and brushed it along his cheek.

"So," Perrin broke the tableau and looked at Jaspar. "Are you too busy being incredibly handsome or would you be willing to escort me into dinner?"

Jaspar took Ms. Williams' hand and led her forward without any hesitation about coming in contact with a "girl." He knew that's what was expected of him tonight.

His job was to be the "little grownup gentleman" and do whatever the adults said. He could see how important this was to everyone, except him. He was like a chorus member in an opera; kill him off in Act I and no one really notices whether or not he rejoins the crowd villagers in Act III.

A glance back showed Tammy all dressed up in her girl dress

as if she was already an adult, her hand on Dad's arm like they were on a date together. Well, she wasn't fooling him. Jaspar knew that spiders still creeped her out and she hated most kinds of fish. "Dog food," she called it when Dad wasn't listening.

A pretty lady, dressed in a neat black dress that didn't make her look like she was all on display or all pretending to be grown up, greeted him with a pleasant, "*Ciao.*" It was an Italian restaurant. He'd missed that. Carlo should be here. He'd like it.

"*Ciao,*" Jaspar's reply made her smile like she really meant it. He dug for Carlo's Italian lessons and tried to make complete sentences without stumbling over them too much. "*Quattro per la cena. Il nom...nome? Cullen.*" Then he remembered to add a polite, "*Per favore.*"

Ms. Williams said something that sounded like a compliment, but he didn't care. The waitress's smile grew, "*Bueno sera, Signor Cullen. Benvenuto a Angelo's. Mi chiamo Graziella.*" Her accent was different than Carlo's. It was lighter and fit a girl. Even a grown up one. And she'd spoken slowly enough that he had time to translate "good evening," "welcome," and that her name was Graziella.

Jaspar eyed Ms. Williams without really looking. She was so tall and her hair was still that weird color that had made Tam stop wanting to be around him. The waitress, with her long dark hair and quiet face would be better for Dad than Ms. Williams. And she already spoke Italian and had treated him like an adult.

"You, boy!" Ms. Williams had said when they tore up the drawings. Sure, she'd made it fun, but everyone kept calling him "boy," like a baby. No one was calling Tam "girl" anymore. It was all of a sudden "young woman this" and "young lady that."

The waitress greeted Ms. Williams and Dad like she already knew them, and then led them to their table. She wore a ring, but it had no big diamond. And lots of girls wore rings, it didn't mean they were married.

"You have to be kidding me, Angelo." Bill sipped his espresso and enjoyed the perfect brewing of it. "No one can learn to cook that well in just thirty years. You sure you aren't at least, oh, three hundred and something."

Angelo grinned at Bill's words and sipped his own espresso. He must get a hundred such compliments a day, but still he appeared genuinely pleased.

Angelo had joined them for a few moments after the meal. The kids were polishing off their apple sorbet with caramel glaze sprinkled with pistachios as voraciously as their manners allowed.

Perrin rested one of her gloved hands on Angelo's arm, but turned to Bill. "He is always this magnificent, except if Jo comes to dinner. Then he is too distracted. We almost had to ban her from the restaurant for ruining our food during their courtship."

"Uh, but how did you straighten that out?"

"Easy," Perrin answered for him. "He married her." Her saucy wink told him that while her words had been for the kids, it had actually straightened out before that, probably when Angelo and Jo had become lovers.

Angelo captured Perrin's hand and kissed it. "It's all Perrin's doing. If not for her, my Jo might well have slipped away and my life would have been ruined."

As if Bill needed yet another reason to respect this woman.

Bill thought back over the dinner at Angelo's Hearth. It was the first time they'd all been together since the pizza night. They'd all been present at rehearsals together several times, but that wasn't the same thing. Tonight they'd had a meal as a family.

Perrin had sat across from Jaspar and beside Tammy. It was a perfect, thoughtful choice. Had she sat across from him, he'd have been too distracted and paid no attention to the kids. Instead, the children had been included throughout the dinner.

She'd made them laugh with stories of the crazy clothing that people had asked her to make. Some of them so fanciful as to be wholly impossible, yet she told each story as if it was absolutely true. By the end he believed every tale, well, except for the one about the representative from the Vulcan Science Academy's Wardrobe Mistress coming to Earth to order fancy party robes for their high council. But the rest of it she made sound at least possible if not plausible.

Tammy had talked about sewing her dress, she'd done a lot of it herself, albeit from Perrin's design. Still, it was so beautifully made that it totally floored Bill. "She made me take out the seams an awful lot of times before I made it right." Not only was his daughter a teenager, but she looked like one.

Jaspar had worked on his Italian with them, especially when he discovered that Graziella, the beautiful young maître d' who Bill had met only briefly at Maria's dinner, spoke fluent Italian. She kept coming by the table, leaving behind another few words with each passing. And, unless Bill was vastly mistaken, she'd also started Jaspar on his first major crush. Being informed that she was newly married didn't abate his ardor in the slightest. Apparently he saw that as no obstacle in whatever his plans were.

"Hey kids," Angelo looked toward them, "want to see what our kitchen looks like?"

"I bet it has a stove and everything," Tammy offered him with a laugh.

Angelo did his best to look hurt, but didn't succeed very well.

Perrin elbowed her and the two of them, thick as thieves, rose to follow before Angelo could even pretend a decent whimper.

"Where the women lead, we must follow," he told his son, and they followed along behind Angelo.

It was quite the scene.

A woman, who might have been Graziella's evil, though equally attractive twin, was hopping up and down on one foot in her impatience. "C'mon, Manuel, if you cooked any slower you'd be as bad as Angelo."

"Ah, Luisa," the Mexican chef at the center of the cook line teased back as he slid across a beautiful plate that must be the braised venison with wild morel sauce that Bill had almost ordered. "Beware, *señora*. You encourage me to follow in the footsteps of the *maestro*."

Luisa growled, dressed the plate with tiny dots of some dark sauce, and turned around with perfect timing to place it in Graziella's hand just as she breezed through the kitchen.

Perrin was leading the kids down the line to meet everyone. Without breaking their amazing flow, they greeted his kids as if this was a normal thing to do, and even described a bit of what they were doing.

Angelo remained beside Bill, off to the side watching the line's progress. He nodded once to himself, clearly satisfied with what he was seeing.

"Maria will be sorry that she missed a chance to meet your children. She starts early and usually leaves before dinner service."

"She works here?"

Angelo eyed him carefully. "With how long you spent talking to my Mama at dinner on Tuesday, I thought you would know everything. She is the best pastry chef you can imagine."

"Uh, I kind of remember that," Bill searched his memory. It was there, but way down the list. "We talked about a lot of things that night."

Angelo nodded down the cook line to where Perrin and the

kids were sampling a red sauce, though where they'd fit another bite after that meal, he had no idea.

"I've known Perrin for two years. She's an incredibly positive person, always glad to see you, always great fun to be around."

"But?" Bill could hear it clear as day. However good they were together, their relationship was still fragile. If Perrin's friends decided Bill and his family weren't good for her in some way, it could shatter what little they'd built so far.

He knew Perrin sometimes relied on them more than herself in such matters.

Trust, he could hear Maria whisper to him. *She will need so much before she will trust herself. So you will have to trust for her.*

But that didn't seem right somehow. Maybe she only let them think she didn't... No. With her past...

She still confused him much of the time.

"But," Angelo continued, acknowledging Bill's prompt. "I always assumed she was happy. But now that I see her overflowing with it around you and your children, I have to wonder about how she truly felt all this time I've known her."

Bill didn't know what to say to that one. From the moment that she'd shattered his pigeon-holing of her, by staggering into the Opera drunk with exhaustion and glowing like the Empress, he'd only ever seen her as joyous.

But happy? And that he and his family made her feel that way was something else again. A part of him worried that some addictive part of her past had become dependent on him for her happiness.

Then he had to remind himself that the Perrin Williams he knew was strong and incredibly smart. Maybe Angelo had known a different Perrin. But the one Bill knew didn't strike him as the sort of person to entrust her emotional well-being to another.

Share with them, absolutely. Care about their opinion? She

couldn't help it, she wanted everyone around her to be happy too.

Depend on them for how she felt? Not a chance.

"Well, if it makes you feel any better, Angelo, she's making me damned happy as well."

Perrin and the kids began heading back from the far end of the cook line, each bearing another serving of the dessert. Even the fierce Luisa stopped her service to meet the kids.

"Back when Russell and I were first bringing girls home to the kitchen where Mama cooked for Russell's parents, she said something to us that I've always tried to do. 'Follow the quiet voice of joy. Follow her like nothing else matters.' Best damn advice Mama ever gave me. It's why I cook. It's why I'm married to Jo. Might have made the road a little easier if we'd listened to her a bit more often."

"You ended up in an amazing spot, Angelo."

"I did, my friend." His friendly thump on Bill's back was almost as solid as one he'd deliver to Russell. It was an acceptance. A welcoming.

As he returned to the cook line, Angelo kissed Perrin on each cheek, scruffed Jaspar's hair, and bowed so deeply to Tammy that she blushed fiercely.

"Hey, where's my second dessert?" Bill complained as they reached him.

Perrin held out a spoonful of caramel-covered sorbet. "If I have to finish this on my own, I'll die of a pleasure overdose. You have to help me."

He took the bite, and did his best to relish the quiet voice of joy, as the four of them stood to the side watching the busy kitchen and eating their three desserts.

CHAPTER 14

*S*ince the dinner, Bill's week had practically hummed. The sets for *Ascension* were almost back on schedule, not quite, but that was normal with only a couple weeks to go until opening night.

The knit costumes, once completed, had totally wowed the cast members and the director. They quickly scheduled an extra photo shoot as soon as all of the primary cast were costumed. Even Geoffrey Palliser had decided to amend his contract so that the Overlord could stand beside the shining Empress.

It hadn't been hard to convince Wilson Jarvis to foot the additional advertising costs of a last-minute poster-and-banner campaign.

In a moment of inspiration, Bill had tried to contract Russell for the photo shoot. Except it turned out that one didn't just contract Russell Morgan. Even trying to do so really pissed the man off. That's when Bill had learned that not only was Russell rich, but he was also the heir to the Morganson shipping fortune. He only did projects he was interested in. Perrin, bless her, said that she hadn't had to work awfully hard to talk him down, despite Bill's bungled initial approach.

Perrin and Jerimy's makeup artist, a big Polish man named Mika Kalinski with a heavy accent, massive hands, and remarkably delicate control, had conferred at length on the final looks.

It was too late to hit the national and international press, but the new *Ascension* poster now graced the back of several Seattle buses as well as a couple of I-5 and Aurora Avenue billboards. It was hard to tell if the spike in ticket sales was due to that, or the ever-growing yarn-bombs.

Bill had finally asked Perrin once about the yarn-bomb campaign, over a lunch they'd managed to share in his office. She had evaded the question of her involvement by turning the conversation sideways into how creative they were. After that, Bill adopted a "don't ask, don't tell" policy regarding them.

The campaign grew rapidly over the next few days. At first the knit advertising had appeared only on the occasional crosswalk sign and light pole. Now it seemed he couldn't turn a corner without spotting one. The news services picked up the story, then they showed one that impossibly ran across the large bar holding stoplights out over the middle of a busy intersection. That looked dangerous to install and was probably illegal.

That was too much. He pulled Patsy and Jerimy into his office for a meeting.

"Not one of ours," Patsy didn't even take a moment of thought.

"What do you mean?"

"We've only been doing verticals on the big stuff. Also, you said this happened last night. We were busy then doing thirty tree trunks around Green Lake. Every jogger on the three miles of shoreline track this morning saw them. For horizontals it's been mostly bicycle racks. We don't mess with any traffic signs. One of my friends actually went to jail for ten days because she yarn-bombed a Stop sign a couple years back."

"To jail?" That was not the kind of publicity he wanted for the Opera under any circumstances.

"Yeah. She exactly recreated the whole sign in red and white knitting, and then built yellow sunflower petals all around the edges. The problem was it wasn't reflective. Turns out those signs are specially designed to reflect headlights back at the driver. It was really pretty, the arresting cop let her take a picture before cutting it down, but we know better than to mess with any of that."

Bill slumped back in his chair, "So how did it get up there at the corner of Broad and Western?"

Patsy whistled. "Did you get a picture?"

"I didn't have to." He did a quick search on his computer and turned the screen for them to see. It was already on the *Seattle Times* news site.

"Wow. That would be a tough installation, and to not get caught there would be even tougher. They have to have traffic cameras in an intersection that big, but we're clean. It's definitely not one of ours. No tag."

Bill looked at the picture but he didn't even know what he was looking for.

Patsy had him scroll down to another picture in the article until she found a yarn bomb on the courthouse flagpole. She pointed to the bottom, below the last "N" in *Ascension*.

He could just make out a tiny "S#1KG."

"We put that on every single thing we do. That's our gang's marker or tag, Seattle's Number One Knitting Gang. Some people go anonymous, but we felt that was like making book reviews under false names on website stores, kinda low brow not to take ownership of your own words, or your knitting."

"Then how did this happen, Patsy?" Bill scrolled back up to the picture of the street maintenance crew going up in a bucket truck to cut down the yarn-bomb.

Then she smiled. "We're going viral, boss."

And she'd been absolutely right. Over the next week after the release of the posters, magnificently designed by Russell, yarn-bombs began appearing in the oddest places. Bus bumpers, store signs that had nothing to do with the opera. They often wouldn't even say *Ascension* but Perrin's color palette was unmistakable.

The Fremont statue *Waiting for the Interurban* represented a half dozen people and a dog waiting for a bus. People were always dressing up the statues: warm scarves in winter, ridiculous sunglasses when spring finally came to the rainy city.

It was seriously bombed.

Someone had taken the poster to heart. They'd made costumes for each of the figures, following as many of the details as possible from Russell's poster. Even the child cradled in the woman's arms now wore a fair imitation of Jaspar's costume.

Russell had called and told him to get his and his cast's asses down to the statue for a group photo. By the time Bill had them there, Russell had somehow corralled a half-dozen news services into showing up, including a pair of nationals. The resulting media blitz had been amazing, and cost nothing.

Jaspar and Tammy loved the photo shoot. But they didn't stand together like he would have expected. Even Russell's attempt to coax them together had no effect. They stood on either side of the Empress and Overlord. It worried Bill, but he let it go as too far down his list of things to worry about. The kids always worked everything out.

Reports were coming in from Tacoma, even Portland was getting bombed, but most of it was concentrated in Seattle.

The day he saw one across the steel bumper of a fire truck stationed near his house, he decided that keeping his mouth shut was *definitely* the better part of discretion. That it was still there days later, smoke-stained, worn in a few places, but left in place by the crew, only spoke to the popularity of the event.

"It isn't just sales for this opera that are increasing," Wilson

Jarvis happily told King 5 News. "The Seattle community's support for this Emerald City Opera production of *Ascension* has also begun translating into a sharp increase in subscription sales for the next season. We're just thankful for this opportunity to be attracting more interest and tourism to our great city. By the time *Ascension* opens two weeks from tonight, we expect to be fully sold out, despite adding two performances. So be sure to get your tickets to *Ascension* soon."

Leave it to Wilson to work the title of the opera into every other sentence.

Bill had to miss the Tuesday dinner because of a rehearsal. It was too bad, he thought the kids would really enjoy it. At least having the kids in the opera saved him from palming them off on Lucy or a babysitter. Though Tammy was getting so grown up, maybe he could trust her to be the responsible adult when they had to be home alone. He knew there were girls younger than Tammy who made money babysitting, but still it felt too soon for him, if not for her.

He'd asked Perrin to send his apologies to Maria personally. She reminded him that this week was Manuel and Graziella's wedding reception at the restaurant. *Damn!* He'd forgotten and felt awful, but he couldn't get out of it.

After a quick round of begging Marci, he'd managed to bag two of the last tickets to the only Monday night performance when the restaurant would be closed. He'd swiped one of fundraising's best ECO-stationery note cards, thankfully Consuela stocked some without "Thank You" embossed on them in gold foil. Bill wrote a cute note, slipped in the tickets along with an invitation to come backstage after the show, and made Perrin promise to not forget it in her purse.

WHEN JASPAR TRIED to beg off from going sailing on their next day off, Bill should have seen something bad was coming.

He should have, but he didn't.

CHAPTER 15

*P*errin felt as if she were floating when she arrived at Cutters Crabhouse. It was Friday evening, a week since her dinner with Bill and the kids. The place was hopping with Seattle's finest. The crowd were all well-dressed for after-work mingling, ready to see and be seen.

Perrin even saw two of her own designs, but didn't know the women. That felt odd. Even though Raquel and Kristin were doing an amazing job of running the store, it still felt odd to be disconnected from the day-to-day contact with customers. Not that she'd have had time even if she had the desire to work the front of store again.

Her life had become a complete blur. She was in a hundred places at once, and needed to be in a thousand. Her emotions were all over the map as well.

Jerimy had insisted on her approval of his and Patsy's teams' renditions of her designs. Those had turned into wonderful discussions of what they'd each seen and liked.

Jerimy had a master's degree from NYU in Visual Culture: Costume Studies. Who even knew there was such a thing. His deep focus on Western Europe had contrasted nicely with

Perrin's self-guided education across dozens of global clothing design traditions. They discussed the rise of the pleat, the exposed midriff of the historic belly dancer, the urban Japanese woman, and the modern American teen.

Patsy, the queen of modern clothing, often jumped in with surprising variations that she'd seen. Perrin departed each meeting with so many ideas for new designs clogging her brain that she could hardly see the sidewalk beneath her feet through all the colors.

Patsy tried to keep her up to date on the wild success of the yarn bombing. One evening she'd borrowed Tamara and the three of them had gone out with the S#1K Gang. They'd bombed three seats in every Capitol Hill hospital waiting room, covering them with premade slipcovers in the palettes of the Empress, the Prince, and the True Love. It only took a minute for them to crochet the side seams to hold the premade knitting in place.

They'd all worn masks that Patsy had made, modeled on the opera's characters. Security guards had been alerted, nurses had applauded, and people stuck in drab waiting rooms for hours on end had been cheered up.

Afterward, they'd all sat around together and eaten tiny scoops of gelato in a brightly lit little shop. Tammy's eyes had been so wide as she did her best to behave as if she did this every day. Clearly, sitting with six grown women from Patsy's twenty-three to Cornelia's sixty-seven, ranked as one of the coolest things she'd ever done.

"I didn't get that grown-ups could be so much fun!" she'd bubbled as Perrin had driven her home afterward. "I want to grow up to be just like them."

Perrin had laughed, "Which one?"

"All of them at once, but especially you."

That had sobered Perrin instantly. Tamara had made it a simple statement of fact. Perrin could see how the others could be role models, but didn't quite understand how it could apply to her.

She'd talked about it in the kitchen with Bill over more blueberry tea while Tamara took a shower to get ready for bed. Jaspar had apparently sacked out early. They were careful to sit on opposite sides of the dining table in case one of the kids came in.

"Guess he was tired," Bill apologized on his son's behalf, but she missed saying hi to him. She actually hadn't seen much of Jaspar at all since the dinner she'd so enjoyed.

Bill continued, "Don't see how you could miss the role you're already playing in Tammy's life, makes perfect sense to me that she'd respect you."

At her blank look, he'd laughed.

"The girl never stops talking about you. She's actually doing better in school, which she was always good at anyway, because she's staying up late to get ahead the night before. She wants as much time working with you as she can get. She's begging me for a sewing machine for her birthday in a couple months. She's even convinced us all to watch one of those clothing design shows on television. It's a good thing that it's only one night a week, or Jaspar would be having a meltdown. As it is, he does his best to moan and complain whenever they get to a part she really wants to hear. Took him a while to figure out that she'd just rewind to listen again until he shut up."

"He's such a boy, isn't he? So much like you."

"Huh," had been Bill's grunted reply.

He'd looked surprised even after she'd explained it to him.

"Well, we're moving into the Opera House this week, the kid always seems to enjoy that. Wilson even signed up for a special rider on our insurance now to let Jaspar hang out with the crews, as long as there is always a responsible person about. The team leaders have been more than willing to have him as a junior apprentice and gofer."

Perrin wished she could see more of Jaspar, but along with the Opera's growing popularity, Perrin's Glorious Garb was receiving more attention. She and Raquel were already interviewing seamstresses to build the copies of Perrin's designs because she could no longer keep up with the orders. She'd never much liked making the same thing over and over anyway. Yet another small piece of the business to let go of.

One day she'd been going so crazy that she'd actually shown Tamara how to scale a pattern to different measurements for one of her simpler designs. Perrin hadn't been able to find a single fault with her work.

"I'd like to offer Tamara a part-time job," she'd told Bill during one of their nightly phone chats.

When he was done spluttering in surprise she'd explained.

"Minimum wage, maximum ten hours per week. Any time she spends on her own clothes are on her own, but when she'd helping me, I have to pay her. It's only fair."

"What about your time? Twenty seconds ago you were telling me how frantically busy you were."

And she was. "I wouldn't mind. I'll just… "

"You'll just charge my twerp daughter three dollars an hour for any time you spend helping her on her own projects. Any time you spend training her for your projects is your own cost, and no fudging on her behalf, Williams. She keeps a timecard, you make sure it's correct every week. If she learns something about business while she's doing this, it will make it more digestible for me. And she pays for her own materials—"

"No."

"Yes. At cost. Retail."

"Wholesale," she'd countered, caving that far because she knew Bill was the better businessperson of the two of them. All she really cared about was the design, which is why Cassidy and Jo had made her hire Raquel to run the store.

And they'd worked it out. Raquel had drawn up a contract.

Tamara and Bill had reviewed it together until Perrin was sure Tamara understood every clause and then she'd executed it, with her dad signing beneath.

AND NOW, at the end of the wildest and best week of her life in Seattle, she couldn't wait to sit with her friends. Just as she entered the front door to Cutters she spotted Carlo and Melanie leaving the restaurant. She rushed up to them.

"You're back!" she hugged Melanie in greeting. "Hi Carlo, you're looking very mellow." She offered him a broad wink and the three of them shared a laugh.

"Yes, she last night *arrivata*. Little…" he turned to Melanie and said something quickly in Italian.

Melanie translated in her soft French accent, "We did not much last night sleep. Oh sorry, translating is tricky. We haven't slept much since I arrived." They shared a smile that explained exactly why. "But now he must or Monsieur Director will be very angry with him tomorrow morning when he can't sing a note."

"Perfect!" Perrin kissed Carlo on each cheek then grabbed Melanie's hand. "C'mon, you're my date tonight. Go away, Carlo. Go sleep."

Melanie wished him a good night, kissed him sweetly enough, but Melanie appeared a little too happy for an excuse to join her.

Carlo, bemused, headed off.

"What was that about, Melanie?"

"What was what…" she trailed off and made an eloquent and graceful shrug. "We—"

"No, wait. Don't tell me. You'll just have to repeat it for the others."

"What others?"

Perrin didn't bother to explain but dragged her into the bar. Cassidy, Jo, and Maria were already at a four-top table. They all welcomed Melanie, and Perrin could detect no hesitation between Cassidy and Melanie, even though the one had married the man that the other woman had loved. They soon scared up an extra stool and all crammed around the small table.

"Well, tell us." Perrin jumped in and watched Melanie considering. She liked the supermodel. In addition to loving Russell despite all his rough edges, she'd always been so kind to Perrin about her designs.

And there was a shared pain the others would never, thankfully, understand, but had been obvious to both of them soon after meeting each other. While Melanie had faced far less physical abuse, she too had risen from a trailer-trash background and a beyond domineering mother. A past she covered with an unbreakable calm and a soft French accent.

Perrin watched Melanie's shields of caution continue to rise. True, she'd only sat with Jo and Cassidy a couple times and had barely met Mama Maria.

"Okay," Perrin jumped in first to set her at ease. Funny how a little embarrassment could actually do that sometimes. "Unlike me who is so falling in love but not getting nearly enough sex, Melanie is getting too much sex and not enough romance. How much longer does Carlo have with our Melanie? Will he make it to opening night? Your fans want to know and we want to know now. We promise we won't tell. Right everyone?" Perrin made a crisscross between her breasts and glared at each of the others until they did as well.

"You're safe now," she told Melanie. "You can trust them." She knew from her own experience with Bill that "safe" and "trust" were immensely powerful words that perhaps Melanie needed to hear.

Mama Maria looked at her with the tiniest widening of her

eyes that told Perrin she'd done it exactly right, enough so to surprise even Maria.

Melanie grimaced, then threw up her hands and laughed, a bright musical sound that turned a dozen heads at the nearer tables who were trying not to stare at the supermodel suddenly in their midst.

"Yes. Maybe. Carlo is nice, but he has…limitations."

"Perhaps he is good for fun, but not worth keeping long term." Cassidy made it a statement of perfect understanding.

Perrin leaned over and kissed her on the shoulder in thanks for making Melanie welcome.

"Yes. I should like to attend opening night, Carlo tells me such wonderful things about the music and the staging and the costumes," she rested one of her elegant hands over Perrin's.

Perrin envied her those hands. Melanie's first jobs had been as a hand model, and they were still one of the best features on the beautiful woman.

"And I am not mercenary, he is charming and fun. But maybe when the curtain comes down on the opera, perhaps so it does on Carlo and Melanie."

They stopped to order drinks and appetizers. Perrin ordered one of her usual Cosmos. Melanie tasted the white wine Cassidy had ordered for the table and, after a soft "oh my" of appreciation, she asked for an empty glass and cheerfully accepted Perrin's judgment of "wimp." Crab cakes, shrimp cock-tail, and a big bowl of steamers would get them started. The waitress left behind a plate of Cutter's focaccia bread gloriously drowned in rosemary, garlic, and olive oil.

"So…" Melanie turned to Perrin, clearly not wholly comfort-able with being the center of attention, "In love and not enough sex… Was I right about Bill Cullen? He does like you?"

"He told me…" Perrin looked around the table. Well, if Melanie didn't want to be at the center of attention having just joined them for the first time, Perrin knew exactly how to shift the conversation for a good long while. "Bill told me that he loves me."

There were understanding nods around the table. Some softening of looks, but it was something most men said too easily and they all knew that.

"And I believe him."

They all eyed her with curiosity.

"And I love him." Perrin had meant to just toss it off but barely managed a whisper.

That knocked back everyone around the table.

Mama Maria reached a hand right across Melanie's lap to grab Perrin's hand.

Perrin took a deep breath to steady herself then met Maria's gaze. They didn't need words. For five long heartbeats they held hands and looked at each other. For five poundings of blood in Perrin's ears, emotions flowed across Maria's face as they must have across her own. Fear and hope, relief and amazement, truth and acceptance, and finally approval.

That was all it took.

Then Maria's face lit with a smile that could brighten the whole world. With a quick squeeze, she sat back and apologized to Melanie for reaching across her.

Maria placed her hand briefly to her throat, where the gold chain that Perrin had given her for her wedding rested every day, often Maria's only jewelry aside from Hogan's wedding band. It had been a gift from the heart and a bond between them.

Perrin had to fight hard to keep the tears inside where they belonged at Maria's ultimate sign of hope for a marriage and a future.

The others were still gearing up to question her all about being in love—why she believed him and wasn't she just doing her normal fall-into-a-relationship thing.

Perrin wasn't sure if she was up for that, so she went for a much safer topic. She leaned in close and all the others leaned in as well, including Melanie. She glanced around to meet each of their gazes before whispering her subject change.

"Do you have any idea how hard it is to get some decent sex with a single dad? You wouldn't believe how creative we've had to be."

Mama Maria laughed. Of course she'd know what Perrin was doing, but the others all fell for the trap and wanted to know just how creative.

THE PROBLEM, Perrin had to admit that night as she crawled into bed alone and watched the ceiling spin slowly, was that even being creative had achieved so little.

She and Bill had found that their best opportunity to see each other at all was having lunch together. On days when he was too busy to even leave the office, she'd at least arrive with sandwiches to share at his desk among the prop layout plans. She'd never thought about the problems of a scepter being carried off one side of the stage, then needed at the head of a staircase on the opposite side two scenes later.

When she could coax him out of the office, they lunched in her apartment. Okay, they had fantastic sex on her bed, her couch, the floor, the kitchen—more than once they hadn't made it past leaning against the closed front door—followed by him bolting down a sandwich on the ten-block drive back to the office.

They had tried finding a moment at the Opera offices, but with the pending production the staff was increasing and there wasn't even a quiet corner. The Opera normally employed a hundred people full-time. But for a new build of a major new opera, there were over four hundred people underfoot everywhere they went.

Then the ballet that had been in residence at the Seattle Opera House after the production of *Turandot* had closed and cleared out. Once they had finished their dance, Emerald City Opera descended on the Opera House like a hammer blow.

In twenty-four hours the main electrical, pressurized air, and propane systems had been in place. There were parts of the set that would appear to burn during the dramatic second act, giving the Tragic Prince physical scars to match the psychological ones.

Forty-eight more hours and the set was in place. Impossibly, hundreds of pieces of scenery were delivered and assembled. Two trucks constantly worked the loading dock, disgorging great loads from the scene construction shop, that were then rapidly assembled. Another truck was actually parked on an elevator a story below that then delivered it directly to the stage right wing.

The crews who had been setting up in the Emerald City Opera's offices were also preparing for the move across town. The lowest floor of the offices was normally props storage. One end had been taken over by an eight-person props team. They'd even backed up a semi-truck trailer to a loading door which contained a full machine shop where they made anything they didn't already have: swords, lanterns, armor, fake foodstuffs for the grand banquet, including the tables and tablecloths. It was amazing to watch.

The other end of the ground floor was taken by fifteen electricians servicing and calibrating the lighting instruments. Massive coils of cable were stacked on pallets or dumped into bright yellow rolling hampers. Light poles and triangular steel trusses made up of those funny zig-zag metal pipes were loaded onto semi-trailers for the fast-approaching electrical move-in day.

This world was a mystery to Perrin. It was also the only place she ran into Jaspar during the whole week. But he looked to be busy learning how to wire a connector properly, so she didn't disturb him.

On the second floor, the costume department was humming—actually more of a highly organized runaway railroad train. The chorus had started coming through for fittings. A dozen seamstresses were fitting pre-made pieces to measurements cards. And altering the many costumes that didn't work out quite right. A man they planned to use as a village cartman had recently joined a gym and his shoulders no longer matched his card nor fit his intended uniform. A woman was four months pregnant, still able to sing, but her form-fitting gown no longer fit her form and had to be switched with someone else's.

In the middle of the floor, a temporary makeup department had been set up. There, Mika worked with five other specialists to turn the photographs of the designs he and Perrin had developed into face cards for every single character: base powder Ben Nye BV71, Sandy Rose CR3 cheek rouge, auburn eye pencil blended with... The list went on to define the lip outline which emphasized them at a distance, degree of blending or highlights, aging lines on backs of hands and neck, wigs, prosthetics like latex scars, stage blood to be coordinated with costuming as they'd be laundering it out of the costumes after every performance.

A couple of the major roles, the Prince, Princess, and the True Love had several face cards. For Carlo as the Prince, sometimes he had a makeup call between two scenes as his look evolved: hope to scars to loss of hope to premature age to destitution and ultimate failure as he dies in the arms of the Princess who loves him. His final aria ending with a demented cry for his murdered True Love.

"So Bill," Perrin asked after they'd stolen a kiss in the office's central freight elevator, "Is it always going to be this difficult for us to have sex?"

"Make love?" He'd brushed a hand down her body that electrified every single nerve ending.

"Oh man. You have to cut that out."

"Cut out this?" he kissed her fiercely for two seconds while groping her wildly. "Or stop telling you that I love you?"

Perrin made sure that her clothes were straight by the time the elevator stopped even if her pulse was thoroughly chaotic.

"Okay," she struggled for a breath then nodded for him to open the heavy steel gates that split horizontally across the middle to raise and lower. Just as he put his hands on the heavy strap to start them moving, she rubbed her palm downward over the front of his pants then whispered in his ear.

"Don't stop doing either one." She shoved the door down so that it clanged open and walked out onto the main office floor, leaving Bill to trail somewhere far behind.

CHAPTER 16

"Today's a dark day," Tammy informed Perrin as she slipped into the back seat of Bill's car. Jasp was being a total pill. Sure it was his turn up front, but he hadn't even offered to move back for Perrin. Perrin had shrugged it off before Dad could dig in.

"What's a 'dark' day?" Perrin had on a nice blouse of pale blue, so plain it was almost a shock. But Tammy was learning. She could see just how well made it was and how perfectly it fit, not clinging, but not loose and sloppy like some generic store thing. It didn't have to be wild like their red dresses to be amazing. That's what she wanted to do, make clothes that made her look that nice. Even Perrin's jeans fit way better than Tammy's despite how long she'd spent poking around the mall's racks to find a pair that fit exactly right.

"Dark day means the stage is unlit. Everybody gets a day off. So today's pretty much the last time we're gonna see Dad even close to sane for the two weeks until opening night."

"At least you get to see me at rehearsals," he called back as he pulled into traffic.

"Yeah, that's righteous," Tammy replied. It was Jasp's latest word, though it tended to make Dad snort with laughter when they used it. She wondered if Jasp had figured it wrong. "If you think he's been busy these last couple weeks, just wait. It's cra—"

"That's what I wanna do," Jaspar cut her off. It wasn't his normal kind of cut-off.

Something was wrong and she didn't know what it was. And it wasn't just today. With Jasp she always knew, but not this time.

"I'm gonna do what Dad does. I'm gonna know all about electricity and machine tools and none of that costume crap."

Dad glanced up into the mirror in apology to Perrin, and Tammy could see the look. When had she grown tall enough to see his eyes in the rearview? Very righteous.

But Jasp missed it. He usually caught onto adult stuff faster than she did. Tammy had found she had to figure out things that Jaspar saw right away and blurted out. He was just a stupid boy in a lot of ways, but he was always "people smart."

She hated when he descended into one of his troll moods. It reminded her too much of when Mom died. That had been bad for all of them, Jasp had refused to believe her for weeks that Mom was never coming home again. And Dad had been mostly out of it. She'd learned to anticipate and defuse the troll, but she always knew why Jasp was doing it. Tammy couldn't see this one yet. She'd have to get him aside later.

"I have to worry about the 'costume crap' too," Dad tromped down on him. "Though between Perrin and Jerimy I have to worry less than usual." He looked at Perrin again in the rearview mirror.

Wow! Did Dad have any idea how much he was showing how he felt about Perrin? They were way past fourth kiss.

Tammy was losing track of everything. When had that happened?

In reply, Jasp hunched down in the front seat and glared out the window.

PERRIN NOTED that Russell actually looked pleased rather than amused when Jaspar declared his boat, the *Lady Amalthea*, as "righteous."

"I named her for a unicorn who turned briefly into a princess but decided she was better off as a unicorn."

"Smart lady." Jaspar declared.

While the guys were bonding over the boat, Perrin climbed aboard and gave Tammy a hand to steady her. It was a beautiful Saturday morning and there were a lot of boats headed out from the Shilshole Marina. There was a fresh wind, which meant good sailing, but the weather was warm enough she'd probably only need a light windbreaker once they were under way.

Perrin had always liked the boat, she was like her owner in so many ways. She was just as pretty as Russell was handsome, but she was rough around the edges too. The two of them matched. Russell had spent a year refinishing the 1940s sloop—he'd taught her that meant one mast not all the way at the very front. But for all the *Lady's* fine finish, she was narrow inside.

"It's called a Pullman-style cabin," Russell told the kids on the guided tour before they left dock. They'd all climbed together down the narrow ladder until they were standing well below the waterline. "Like those railroad cars in the old movies where you sleep down one side and walk down the other."

On one side of the off-center aisle down below was a galley, a table for seating four people that could turn into a narrow bed for two, a tiny bathroom that he gave them detailed instructions on how to use, and the boat ended in a double bed up forward.

Perrin had dug out some good stories from Cassidy about

what a motivated girl could do on that particular bed. They shared a look that made Cassidy blush, even if she was smiling brightly. Perrin kissed her on the cheek to make up for it and received a hug in return.

On the other side of the aisle was a narrow bench, long enough to sleep on if you stuck your feet into the space behind the ladder. Russell called it a pilot's berth. "Because it's closest to where the pilot needs to rush in case of an emergency," he pointed at the ladderway back to the cockpit. A tiny wood stove, an awkward bench and a tiny closet completed the way forward.

Cassidy had raided Angelo's restaurant to create a massive basket lunch. Nutcase, Bill's small black cat, was the only other passenger, almost as rough-mannered as her owner, but also sweet to the core. The kids both took to her right away.

Russell lost a lot of ground when he insisted that the two kids had to wear life vests, but made up for it by producing small racing vests that didn't inflate until they were submerged, rather than the big, poofy orange things.

Russell recruited Jaspar and Bill to help him get the boat away from the dock, though Perrin had seen him do it single-handed any number of times when Cassidy was too busy to help. Perrin preferred just being a passenger.

"It's nice to let myself be taken care of sometimes," Cassidy leaned back, seated her sunglasses firmly and smiled up at the warm mid-morning sun. "Nothing better than a spring day in early May."

Perrin made sure that she and Tamara were slathered in sunscreen and both wearing floppy hats, even Tamara's Mediterranean complexion would crisp out on the bright water. Perrin herself had learned that the hard way last year. The air felt so fresh and cool when you were gliding over the water. She'd burned red as a lobster on her first trip and had to finish the outing lying on a cool bunk below, being tossed about at the mercy of the waves.

The three of them sat in the cockpit and let the world go by.

Perrin talked about some of the new designs she was working on, including Melanie's dress. Tammy tried so hard to pretend that she could still breathe normally after Perrin told her she'd get to help on the whole dress that Perrin had to hug her so that she wouldn't hyperventilate.

Cass understood perfectly and began teasing Tamara about being careful not to become too famous or Cassidy would have to chase her off, because nobody was allowed to compete with Perrin. It forced Tammy to laugh, breathe, and think of something else. Meanwhile the boys coiled lines and unwrapped sails. In moments they were headed out.

Her favorite moment was after the sails were up, but not yet drawing wind. Russell would nudge the tiller aside with his knee, lean down to kill the engine, then wink at his wife as it spluttered to silence. He did it every time. A shared memory Cass had never explained and Perrin didn't want to intrude on. Sort of like the moment she and the kids had torn up those awful paintings. That memory was theirs, not for others.

The boat dug in, suddenly at the wind's call, there was a visceral surge that echoed deep in her body. It was a place of peace, a perfect moment.

Bill dropped down beside her and slid an arm around her waist just as Perrin realized quite how alike this moment was to when she was lying in Bill's arms. Quiet, peaceful, powerful. Centered.

She leaned against him and closed her eyes, letting the motion of the boat just take her where it wanted to go. As long as Bill's arms were around her, she knew she'd be safe.

TAMMY SAW her chance after lunch.

Jasp had been sticking close by Mr. Morgan, learning all about sailing. He'd obviously geeked out when Mr. Morgan taught him how to steer. She couldn't quite bring herself to call him Russell, even if she felt fine with Cassidy. He was nice enough, but he was so big and imposing and so...male. At least she supposed that's what it was, but whatever, she stuck with using Mr. Morgan.

Tammy wouldn't have minded learning to sail too, but talking with Cassidy and Perrin like grownups, and watching her dad with Perrin was occupying her mind.

She wondered how Perrin would answer the question now about whether she was trying to marry their dad. There was no way to get her alone to ask. She and Dad were way attached at the hip.

But now Jasp had gone forward alone to sit on the front hatch and stare out at the waves. So Tammy left the cockpit and headed up to the bow. The couple of ropes no bigger around than her thumb that ran like a railing along the edge of the deck didn't look like enough to stop anyone. There was a thin netting between the lines that didn't impress her much either. The boat was tipped way over and the water was rushing madly by just inches below the edge of the deck. From the cockpit, it hadn't looked like they were going so fast.

She backed off. The walkway down the other side of where the cabin stuck up through the deck was high out of the water. She tried that side. A glance back showed Cassidy, Dad, and Perrin all laughing together. Mr. Morgan, clearly keeping an eye on everything, nodded easily at her from where he sat at the tiller, clearly telling Tammy that she was right to go along the high side of the cabin. Lesson learned. She decided he was okay and hoped that he wouldn't laugh at her too much for how she had to edge forward on the tilted deck clutching the thigh-high thin rope with both hands.

Earlier, Jasp had been trotting up and down the deck as if it was nothing. She didn't have the feel of this yet. Every time they hit a wave, she was sure they were going over, or at least that she was. Finally she made it, awfully glad she was wearing the life vest.

She edged up and squatted beside Jasp, "Hey, Troll."

"Go away."

Usually that nickname at least earned a courtesy laugh.

"C'mon, Jasp. Give. What's up with you?"

"With me? Up with me?!" He spun to face her, his skin suffused with deep red, and blotchy as if he'd been on the verge of crying. He hated crying.

"Yeah. With you!" She learned sometimes you had to face his steam with your own steam. "You've been grouchy all day."

"Like you care."

"I do. Honest."

"Yeah. You care, just like Dad does. Only not about me. You two only care about *her*." He made the pronoun sound awful, like it was acid or evil goo.

"That's not true." Tammy glanced back down the long deck to where Perrin sat curled in Dad's arms. They'd been like that the whole trip. It wasn't true, was it?

"Are you blind?" Jasp hadn't bothered to look back, he was just staring over the bow again, out at the rushing waves, blinking hard at the wind. Wind that was dragging tears straight back from his eyes and into his hair so she hadn't noticed them at first.

"Not blind, troll. She's neat, that's all."

"She's not neat. She's trying to shove us out."

"No!" Tammy protested. "She's not like that."

"Idiot!" he shoved her away and she fell on her butt.

She shoved against his shoulder hard enough to knock him off the hatch. He tumbled down the sloped deck and landed hard against one of the vertical metal things that held up the lifelines every couple feet.

He cried out. Jasp struggled to stand, reached out with a hand to steady himself, but his arm hung funny and it didn't work. The boat dropped down over a wave, making them almost weightless at just the wrong instant. With another cry, Jasp stumbled and fell over the lifeline into the water. His life vest inflated with a loud pop, then he disappeared toward the back.

She screamed.

That's the only part of what happened next that Tammy clearly remembered, her own scream. How it tore at her throat, at her heart. How it hurt her ears and echoed from the sky. She'd already lost her mother and now she screwed up and Jasp was gone in a single instant. Just like that. Only this time it wasn't some drunk driver who did it. It was her.

Mr. Morgan's shout and dive over the side were a blur. At some point, someone, Perrin maybe, remembered Tammy was alone at the bow and came to get her.

The rest was just images. The boat rocking in the water, no longer moving. A wet Mr. Morgan and a crying and shivering Jasp. Phone call for an ambulance to be at the dock.

And tears. She'd cried herself sick and remembered throwing up somewhere, maybe off the edge of the dock. Someone carrying her. Mr. Morgan? Whoever, they'd still been wet. Her own clothes now clammy down one whole side of her body. She and Perrin in the car, her dad with Jasp already gone.

She knew she'd have nightmares forever of Jasp falling into the water and never coming back.

Just like Mom.

CHAPTER 17

*P*errin knew what she had to do—and hated it. Hated the situation. Hated herself most of all. At least she was used to that part of it.

She sat in the farthest corner of the painfully white hospital waiting room. As far as possible from Jaspar, now behind some anonymous curtain in the ER. Far from the three yarn-bombed chairs she and Tammy had done together a mere few days ago. And close by the sliding glass doors she'd have to use in a few minutes.

She wanted to run through them now and out into the fading Seattle afternoon. Run and never stop, but there was one thing she had to do first. So she waited, her hands clasped in her lap until all feeling had long since left them, staring straight ahead at a poster about identifying different reactions to various types of bug bites. Normally, it would creep her out, but she was too numb.

It had all gone wrong so fast, that's what she couldn't wrap her head around. One moment she'd been curled against Bill, laughing with Cassidy and Tammy, and the next a screaming Jaspar had gone shooting by the stern. Russell had been in the water so fast he hadn't been ten feet behind the boy. So fast, Perrin didn't even have time to be afraid for him. Cassidy had turned the big boat back to Russell and Jaspar so fast it was a miracle.

But on the drive to the hospital she'd learned that it wasn't an accident, not merely a bad wave and a clumsy ten-year old. Tamara had sobbed out her story, unheeding and unaware of where the axe had fallen.

This wasn't just a bump in the road, it was the end of the line. It was going to kill her own heart to walk away, but she had to. But first...

Bill staggered out into the waiting room looking haggard. He scanned the weekend crowds, about two-thirds of the chairs were filled, before spotting her and coming over. He dropped into the seat beside her. The dark rings under his eyes showed the awful toll the last few hours had taken on him.

"Well, that was fun."

She couldn't make herself laugh, not even as a kindness.

"Clean break. Bit of a mess because of all the jostling, but they have that sewn back up and the bone reset. They gave him a painkiller, so he's resting easier now. Tammy won't leave him, not even when he yelled at her. Can't figure that one out, he never yells at Tammy like that. First one he goes to when he's hurting, even before me. She just sits there like a ghost, holding onto his foot like she'll never let him go." He scrubbed his hands over his face then offered her a weak smile, "How's your day been?"

"Bill... " her throat closed. How was she supposed to say what she had to say to this poor, exhausted man? A deep breath didn't help, mostly because she couldn't make her diaphragm take one.

Finally catching her mood, he sobered and turned to face her.

"I only stayed to say goodbye... " she didn't even pause for a breath, the only way through was absolute truth to the end... and speed. She had to say it fast or maybe it really would kill her. "The reason they fought is that I'm the problem. I've taken you and Tamara away from Jaspar and he's angry. He's so angry and hurt. He'll be even angrier that you're out here now with me. Your children need you and all I'm doing is driving them away. Don't come after me. I won't talk to you. I won't see you. I owe that to your children."

She stood and walked out the door before he could respond. When she made it through the door, she saw Cassidy and Russell had arrived from putting the boat away. She did the only thing she could think of, she turned in the other direction and ran—it was all that was left for her to do.

RUSSELL CAUGHT Bill around the chest before he was five steps out the door. It was like running into a wall.

"Go!" Russell shouted at Cassidy, who had already taken off after Perrin.

Bill pushed against Russell, but to no effect. Ten, twenty, thirty seconds later, whenever he stopped his futile struggling, it was too late. Perrin, with Cassidy trailing far behind, was long out of sight.

Russell's clasp turned into a friendly arm around the shoulder, with a grip that not even a grizzly bear could break free from. Russell led him back inside.

"Wonder what got into her?" Russell offered it conversationally.

Bill didn't know. Her words had made no sense. His kids were crazy about her. It was because of Perrin they were in the opera production, becoming more involved every day. Tammy couldn't stop talking about her. And Tammy was really smart about people. Her response made Bill trust Perrin all the more.

Quirky as she was, the woman daily proved her ability to be a positive role model for his daughter.

So what had happened?

"She couldn't mean what she said, could she?" he asked Russell.

Russell guided him back to the very chairs he and Perrin had been sitting in moments before. The big man opened his mouth to respond but the fear was too big for Bill to give him a chance to speak. The fear just kept stumbling words out of Bill's mouth.

"About never coming back? About never seeing me again? She couldn't mean that?"

Russell's face turned grim, "She said that?"

Bill could only nod.

"Shit," Russell muttered under his breath. "You never know with Perrin. Mama Maria practically adopts her, Cassie worships her, and to me she's flighty and damned stubborn. You wouldn't believe how good that woman is at getting her way."

Bill buried his face in his hands. He understood the stubborn woman, the one who drove herself so hard. She'd done six months of work in the last four weeks, totally charming Tammy and himself in the process. Charming? Dammit! He loved the woman. He even loved her for her pig-headed protection of his children.

"Dad?"

Bill jerked his head up at Tammy's voice.

"He's asking for you. I don't think he wants to see either of us, but he'd rather it was you than me." She looked around, her face still tear-streaked, her eyes almost blood red. "Where's Perrin?"

Behind Tammy, Cassidy came in through the door still breathing hard. She shook her head once, "no."

Bill rose, nodded to Russell and Cassidy, then, wrapping an arm around his daughter's shoulders, they went to see his son.

PERRIN WAS SO LOST. She'd zig-zagged through streets, alleys, backyards. No way she could face Cassidy, but Perrin's long legs and the speed she'd learned so many years ago in college field hockey had outdistanced her quickly.

It was her own self she couldn't seem to get away from. She glanced up at a street sign. Yesler and 34th. She forced herself to turn away when she saw the *Ascension* yarn-bomb climbing the crosswalk sign's pole that she'd been leaning against.

She became aware of the traffic sounds, the afternoon cooling into darkness, the pedestrians eying her strangely as she leaned there trying to recover her breath.

She was so totally lost.

And she had nowhere to go. She had no bolt hole, no safe place where none could find her. When had she let go of that? *Stupid!* Where was it now that she finally needed it?

Perrin could *feel* Cassidy rallying the troops, Jo and Maria. She knew how relentless they could be, Perrin had done the same for Jo and Cassidy a couple of times herself.

Now when she needed to be alone, she had nowhere safe. They'd check her store and apartment, thankfully she'd left her cell phone home for the day so she didn't have to feel guilty... guiltier for not answering when they called her.

She couldn't go to a hotel. For a day out with Bill and the kids she'd stuffed her apartment key in one pocket and her driver's license and a twenty-dollar bill in the other. Twenty bucks wouldn't even buy her a bus ticket out of town.

"Shit!" Her curse startled several people she hadn't noticed waiting for the light.

Out of options, all she could do was select the least painful one.

Turning north and west, she started walking slowly back toward downtown.

MAMA MARIA OPENED her condo's door even as Perrin stood debating whether or not to knock.

"Oh, I was just headed back out to... " she trailed off as she studied Perrin. Then, with a gentle hand on her shoulder, she guided Perrin inside.

She didn't say a word until she had Perrin seated on the couch by the night-darkened windows, a cable-knit throw blanket around her shoulders, and a big mug of steaming tea she could barely hold against the chills. The warm afternoon had long since gone to a dark, cool evening. Her sleeveless blouse wholly insufficient to protect her.

The front door opened and closed behind her, making her twitch. The tea burned her fingers and spilled on the blanket. Maria didn't embarrass her even more by trying to help. She simply turned to Hogan who had stumbled to a halt at the entry to the living room.

"Yes, Hogan. She's found. Could you let the others know, and then make us dinner, just for the three of us I think. Tell the others that tomorrow is soon enough for questions."

After Hogan nodded silently and headed into the kitchen, already dialing the phone, Maria sat on the couch beside her.

Perrin managed to set down the tea, wiping her fingers on her pant leg before she wrapped the blanket more tightly about her. Then she simply leaned forward and lay her head in Maria's lap. Lying there, she told the story of the day between bouts of shivering, partly from the cold, partly from self-loathing.

She should have seen it. In retrospect, had seen it. Jaspar going to bed early to avoid her when she knew full well he felt bedtime was for "little kids" and was always pushing the limits; her one visit to their house a perfect excuse. Somehow arranging never to sit by her at the opera, not even when his sister did. Perhaps especially not when his sister did.

When they'd first met, the boy had been such a bright and shining light. Somehow she'd missed the change as he shifted toward the Overlord's darkness.

Maria just let her talk, slowly brushing at her hair until she was done. Run dry of all emotion.

"I have to leave, Maria. I can't stay. Not even in Seattle. I would think of them all nearby. Worse, I might see them. I can't do that. I can't."

"You were never dumb, Perrin my girl."

"Except about men."

"You were never dumb," Maria made it such a definitive statement that Perrin couldn't argue. "Perhaps less than sensible at times, but you always knew exactly what you were doing even when you were screwing up."

"I know this time too, Mama Maria. Honest I do."

Maria pushed her upright until they were facing each other. She was silent for the longest time, just looking up at Perrin with those dark eyes that demanded honesty.

"I didn't say that I won't hate leaving, but it's the best for everyone, Maria. You know that."

"Not best for you, my girl."

"I can't put that ahead of what's best for Bill's family. I know I should, but I can't. I care about them too much. It will be okay. I'm used to it being hard."

"And do you think that you'll hurt them less by leaving?"

That one she didn't have an answer to. She'd seen Bill's eyes as she'd said goodbye. He'd been devastated before the words even registered. She was thankful that Russell had stopped him and Cassidy had followed in his stead, because she might not have had the heart to run away from Bill. Tamara would be shattered as well.

"Oh God, Maria," Perrin clasped the blanket more tightly and folded both fists over her aching heart, "anything I do makes it worse." She hung her head.

Maria raised her chin with a gentle hand. "So, we do this one step at a time."

"We?" It was the most heartening word Perrin had ever heard. Because she certainly couldn't do this on her own. "What next step?"

"You already know, sweetheart." Maria pulled her down enough to kiss her on the top of the head, just as she had the day she'd told Perrin she'd wished to have had Perrin as her daughter. "You know, you just wish you didn't."

Perrin thought a moment, then nodded.

She knew.

It was so hard, but she knew.

BILL COLLAPSED at his dining room table, too exhausted to breathe, way too tired to make a drink or eat any dinner. At least they were all home.

Back at the hospital, on the way back into ER to see Jaspar, Tammy had spilled about what exactly had happened on the bow of the boat and why they'd been fighting to begin with.

Perrin. Of all idiotic, dumb-ass, idiot moves he'd made as a single father, that one took the cake. Perrin had opened a new world for Tammy, giving her a gift of such magnitude that his daughter was growing and changing daily as she scrambled to take it all in. And Perrin had done the same for him, showing him that a part of his heart he had thought forever dead, still existed. Hell, his heart *thrived* beneath her shining radiance, her Empress' touch upon his heart proving to be a benediction beyond price.

But he'd missed what was up with Jaspar. Missed how many times Jaspar had come in to ask for help with homework. Because Tammy wasn't around anymore. "Just another hour, buddy." Which had turned into two or three as he worked to keep the opera on track. He'd barely registered when Jaspar had drifted away to the technical crews to get away from him as well.

Crap! There had to be more ways he could screw up as a parent, but he didn't know what they were.

He'd known better than to confront it head-on with Jaspar. It would be too obvious that Tammy had told him and it would just drive them all further apart.

He wished he could ask Perrin, she was so good at these things. But she hadn't answered any of his surreptitious calls made out of earshot of the kids. He didn't know if she ever would again. Russell's statement, about how Perrin always got her way, scared the shit out of him. It wasn't that she was manipulative, but she was tenacious as hell when adhering to what she believed to be right; a trait he appreciated under any other circumstance.

He still hadn't worked up the nerve to call Maria, and now it was probably too late.

He lay his head on the table trying not to think of his son in a drugged sleep with a cast in his bedroom. Or of Tammy, refusing to leave the chair beside Jaspar until she'd fallen asleep against the foot of the bed and Bill had actually carried her to her own bed for the first time in years.

The buzz of his phone jerked him from his stupor. He fumbled it from his pocket. Just a text. From a number he didn't recognize. He almost deleted it, but decided it couldn't hurt to look.

I'm okay. So sorry.
Tell Tammy not to come tomorrow.
I will call. But not yet.
-P

Bill blinked hard, could feel the burning in his eyes. He

wiped at them and his hand came away wet. Who knew he'd be the one in the relationship who cried. He thought he was done with that after Adira's death—thought there could be no tears left after he'd shed so many.

All he could think was how hard it must have been for Perrin to send that message after the things she'd said.

And how desperate he was to cling onto even this tiniest thread of hope.

CHAPTER 18

"*Y*ou look *très misérable,* Perrin." Melanie's light greeting did nothing to cheer Perrin. She sat alone in her design studio and wondered why she bothered. A place where she always found joy and inspiration now only felt empty. She kept wanting to glance over her shoulder and see Tamara's intent frown as she concentrated on pinning a seam exactly right. To hear the girl's laughter at the simple joy of learning something new.

And each of those thoughts was accompanied with the void where Jaspar stood. She didn't know how he looked when upset, happy, sad, mischievous... Perrin had inklings, but they weren't anchored in her heart the way Tamara's were. It wasn't that she loved Tamara better, a grown-up couldn't afford to do that between children, but Perrin certainly knew her better.

"Perrin?"

"Sorry, Melanie. I didn't sleep well last night."

"*Non.* That is not so. You did not sleep at all and your heart, I can see how your heart is hurting. The little girl, she is not here."

Perrin did her best to close the topic. "Only me today. Let

me show you the sketches I made for you." She pulled them out of the portfolio and spread her drawings across the cutting table.

Melanie watched her for a long moment and then came around the table. She turned to inspect the sketches, but not before pulling up a stool so close that their hips touched. She wrapped an arm around Perrin's waist and pulled her close as only a true friend would with another. In that position they went through the design in detail.

Melanie pointed out a line of the hem that she had seen Donatella Versace put on the Paris runway just last week. To avoid being labeled derivative, between them they restructured the lines.

Perrin slowly shifted beneath Melanie's kindness and her shared passion for original fashion. The model's casual, friendly embrace, her deep insights, and her gentle understanding did almost as much as Maria's no-nonsense kindness. Cassidy would have worried and fussed. Jo would have been her typical quiet, steadfast, pillar-strong self at a loss as to how to help and never understanding how much being herself did just that. Melanie simply let Perrin be her own, upset self without comment or judgment.

When they were done, there was a peace between them. The design would be stunning. Not merely analogous to the opera costumes, but uniquely its own statement. Enough so that Perrin knew she'd need to dig Russell out of his cave to make sure he was there to photograph Melanie's arrival at the opening. Which was another thread of her life she'd have to re-tie.

And she'd have to get him to talk with Wilson Jarvis about how to turn the Emerald City Opera opening into a red-carpet event that the entertainment news would cover. Yet another future payoff for Seattle and the Emerald City Opera. She had almost a dozen designs that Raquel had sold from the store that would be walking the lobby on opening night, though none were like Melanie's showpiece.

Melanie tried to coax her to go out, to call her friends and make an afternoon of it. It was tempting, she definitely had some fences to mend there. But there was another one, far more important. And just because it was hard, she wouldn't shy away from it this time.

———

JASPAR SAT in his dad's office. Getting the day off from school almost made up for having his arm in a cast. Tomorrow he'd get some good mileage out of it from classmates, even more than having sailed the big boat. 'Course Dad had called the school and gotten all his homework assignments, so it wasn't a totally free ride. And he couldn't do squat downstairs with the crew with his arm in a cast.

Dad had been cool about it all. Clearly Tam had filled him in, but he hadn't gone all parent-fake about it either. He'd made a point of settling Jaspar in the office, rather than out in the cubical he normally used for homework. And the stuff he was doing was neat once Jaspar started paying attention to it. More than once Jaspar had forgotten all about Kipling's story of Kim's adventures in India to listen to what his dad did to make the opera run.

When she got off school, Tam had been so afraid to come up to him that he'd given in way sooner than he planned. She sat on the couch and was all girly, offering to get him a soda, seeing if he wanted help with anything.

When Dad was out of the room he asked her quietly, "Why are you here anyway? Why aren't you with her?" No need to explain who he was talking about, though he hadn't meant it to come out so nasty. Tam looked miserable, right on the verge of tears for like the hundredth time since he'd been hurt.

"Dad said it was better if I didn't," she sniffled hard. "I checked Dad's phone. She sent him a message saying she didn't want me to come."

Man the waterworks really were going. Tam was really, really sad about it. He didn't want that.

"What was the rest of the message?"

She told him.

Jaspar had to think about it a bit. He had a funny feeling that the most important part of the message wasn't the part that Tam cared about. Ms. Williams had said she was sorry.

By itself, it might mean she was sorry that Jaspar had broken his arm, but that didn't fit the rest of it.

And it didn't fit what a mess Dad was today, like he hadn't slept or anything. Twice he'd seemed to forget what he was holding in his hands. When they'd gone out to lunch together, though it was embarrassing that Dad had to cut up his hamburger so that he could eat it, his dad didn't eat much of his own.

Ms. Williams had said she was sorry and said that she would call, though *not yet.*

Almost every night for the last month he'd heard his dad talking with her. He couldn't make out the words, except once or twice when he'd snuck up outside the bedroom door, but you didn't talk that much to a girl unless you really liked her.

Dad came through the office, said something about Jerimy and the costumes. Did the kids want to go downstairs with him?

Tam, rather than leaping up as she had about costumes even before Ms. Williams first showed up, checked in with him. Jaspar tipped his head a little so she'd know he was fine with it and it was okay if she went.

She double checked, which made him even less angry at her. He did the finger flick for her to get gone, like when he was sick and she was hovering too much. She went, but Jaspar told Dad he was fine, wanted to read his book. What he really wanted to do was think.

He didn't like that everything had changed. And he didn't like that it had happened so fast. Tam was done with middle school next month. When did she get so old? And girl-shaped. Like he didn't even recognize her, though he could see that boys sure did. Even grown-ups would stop to watch her go by. They used to always say, "What a cute kid." Now it was all, "What a beautiful girl." Like she'd changed and left him behind. And those dresses.

Jaspar squirmed around on the couch trying to get more comfortable, but his arm was hurting and it wasn't easy.

Tam had looked even more like an adult in her costume and those dresses she kept making with Ms. Williams. She was good at it too, everyone said so. Maybe it was more than just wearing them. Even before Ms. Williams, she was downstairs with Jerimy and Patsy a whole bunch, like she really cared about that stuff. He'd always been able to find her there when he needed something.

It wasn't like the electricians, or even better sailing that whole big boat with no one but Mr. Morgan paying any real attention to him. But maybe she liked it that much.

Jaspar slowly became aware that there was someone standing at the office door.

Ms. Williams.

"Dad and Tam are downstairs."

She nodded, but didn't move to go to them, just stood there.

"What?" Dad would harass Jaspar about such bad manners, but he wasn't here.

"Can I come in?"

Jaspar shrugged a yes and then wished he hadn't. His arm really hurt.

She didn't just breeze in like she seemed to always... Oh no! She was gonna do one of those serious adult-conversation-with-the-kid things. He really didn't want to deal with one of those right now.

She sat down on one of the chairs and faced him.

He knew he was going to be rude, could feel it building up.

"I really screwed up, didn't I?"

It took Jaspar a moment to figure out what she was talking about. He'd expected her to start with his arm or the book open on his lap or something safe. Even Dad usually did that, pretty much everyone except Tam did that.

"It's not that I like Tamara better than you, I just know her better. I understand girls better than guys. Before your dad, I hadn't met all that many guys that I liked enough to be friends with. Russell and Angelo married my best friends, but even them, it took me a long while. I'm really sorry for how I treated you, even if I didn't mean to."

Jaspar had to blink at her, as if she was turning into a different person without even moving.

"What I brought for you today isn't some lame bribe to try and make it all better. It's for the opera. Anything else, well, I just hope you'll give me a chance to try and figure it out better than I have so far." Then she opened the long bag she'd brought in. First she pulled out a dark cloth, elaborately sewed in the same colors as his costume.

"What's that?"

"It's a sling for you to wear with your costume." She spread it out on the couch beside him where Tam had been sitting. "It will cover the whole cast and just make it look like your character was wounded in sword practice or something."

"But I don't have sword."

She reached into her bag again and pulled out a wooden sword complete with belt and scabbard just like the one Carlo wore as the Prince, only smaller. It had been painted to look so real he had to touch it to make sure it was wood.

"This way you can still go on stage and your character will still make sense."

On stage. He hadn't even thought about how that might be a problem for a kid with a cast. But she'd thought of it and figured out how to fix it.

"Thanks," he tried to think of something more intelligent to say.

She nodded and stood up to leave.

"You gonna wait to see Dad and Tam?"

She shook her head now.

"You're making my dad and my sister really sad."

That stopped her in the door as if he'd just stabbed her with his new sword. He hadn't really meant to.

Ms. Williams took a deep breath before turning to look at him, her hand braced on the doorframe. "I know."

Now Jaspar got why she'd said she was sorry. Why she'd said the rest of the text.

"You know what, Ms. Williams?"

"What?" She didn't let go of the door frame.

"It might be okay if you called Dad tonight."

She was silent for the longest time before she nodded to him and whispered, "Thank you, Jaspar. I don't know if I'm ready, but thanks." And she was gone.

He was still thinking about what it all meant when his dad came back.

"Hey, nice sword. Where did that come from?"

He shrugged and ran his hand down its smooth length.

Tam came in and spotted the sling lying where Perrin had left it beside him on the couch.

"Hey, that's cool. A sling as a part of your costume. It matches perfectly, and the sword explains your injury." She got the costume part of it right away.

But Tam didn't get the rest of it, not yet. It always took her a couple extra moments while she thought about and tested a new idea. She was right more often than he was, just slower to make sure of it. Maybe about Ms. Williams she'd been right and he'd been wrong.

Dad figured out where the sword and sling had come from fast enough though. He dropped into a chair as if Jaspar had just hacked his legs out from under him.

CHAPTER 19

*P*errin skipped the Tuesday dinner to work on Melanie's dress and the one she'd wear herself to go with it for opening night. Actually, she'd have to make three more. As the costume designer, she'd been given three tickets to opening night, and Carlo had obtained two for Melanie. So between them they'd invited Maria, Jo, and Cassidy. The men had all agreed to pitch in to help Angelo as the restaurant's opening neared and he descended into near total panic.

Five dresses total. With Melanie's to play off, the other designs had come together quickly and easily. The dresses would be similar in look, though matched to each woman's figure of course. And each would be primarily in a single color from the opera that best highlighted their complexion: Cassidy's black, Jo's sky blue, Maria's red, and Perrin's gold. Melanie would be the montage that each of them complemented. They should all arrive together in a limo. That would create a proper sensation.

Jo and Cassidy hunted her down later that night, coming to the shop and banging on the glass.

They'd tried to make sure everything was okay and ask how

could they help. They tried to force food on her from a care package Maria had put together before sending them over. They tried to get her to stop for a moment.

Perrin didn't have time for any of that.

In minutes she had them working in the studio; and they cut, pinned, and sewed to her direction. It didn't take long for them all to settle in and work together. They talked and they laughed —it was so…normal. Perrin would never know what they talked about and didn't care. All she cared about was how much she loved these women and how much they loved her. She made a point of telling them so several times as they worked.

Then she had one more idea. One she didn't even need to sketch. It was a promising idea, but she wasn't ready to work on just yet.

JERIMY'S CALL TO meet with Richard, the lighting designer, brought Perrin to the Opera offices. He also tactfully informed her that Bill would be over at the Opera House overseeing the first staging rehearsal walk-through that afternoon, which she greatly appreciated.

She, Jerimy, and Richard sat at the big cutting table, all of the primary costumes turned face-out on racks in front of them. Jaspar sat quietly off to the side watching. She was starting to understand that about him. Tamara would think something through. Jaspar followed his instincts.

Jasper was an older soul in a way, despite Tamara's mothering of him. His mother's death had made him more like Cassidy. Actually they'd both lost their moms at about the same age. Cassidy had become an adult that day, as had Jaspar. He'd been a bit more buffered by Tamara's care, but Perrin could see the similarity of the effect.

Jerimy turned off the lights in this end of the Costume Shop.

Richard had set up a pair of lights about ten feet apart and laid out a dozen different colored gels. The colored transparent sheets fit into steel frames that then slid into slots at the front of the lighting instruments.

"Now we can see what challenges you've set me."

The white light was the closest to what Perrin was used to working with. Fashion runways were brightly lit so that every detail could be seen. There was some coloring, but not much. And most of her designs were designed for wear in daylight, office light, or at some party. Again, all shades of white.

Then he put a pale blue in front of one instrument and a soft pink in the front of the other. It was as if the costumes had jumped into three dimensions.

Jaspar had moved up on Jerimy's other side, "Could you do that again?"

Richard slid the two gels out of the way and then dropped them back in.

"Okay, thanks." With that single demonstration, Perrin could feel Jaspar neatly filing away whole categories of information. Just as Cassidy had during college when she also took classes at the Culinary Institute of America just up the highway. Each new bit of knowledge neatly filed, creating an order to the chaos that surrounded them.

Richard turned on a third light in between the other two, shooting forward from a low stand directly in front of them.

"This one is called Bastard Amber, that's its real name."

"But it's pinkish, why do they call it that?" Perrin left Jaspar to ask the questions, though she would have asked the exact same thing.

"Hold your good arm in front of the instrument."

"It's warm," Jaspar commented.

"Right. These instruments throw a lot of heat. Wait until you're onstage with half a hundred instruments on, you'll really heat up. Now watch your skin." He dropped in the gel.

"I don't get it."

"You look more natural," Perrin told him. "Your skin is warmer, more alive, but the costumes looks kind of the same."

Richard slid the gel in and out a few times.

In exasperation Jaspar had her trade places with him.

"Her skin is so light, you can really see it," Richard said before dropping the gel back in.

Beyond the bright light, she could see Jaspar nodding. "I couldn't see it so much up close. It's kind of too much for her, isn't it."

"Try some of the others."

Jaspar started holding one after another in front of the lens without putting them in the slot.

"The red makes her look all blotchy, even worse than the fake amber."

When he tried a green filter, Perrin did her best to make frog noises.

"Ick! What's that for?"

Richard laughed, "You usually use it behind people for landscape scenes, underwater like for the Rhinemaidens in Wagner's *Ring,* or even a darker one for dangerous forest."

Jaspar made a couple more changes then declared, "This one makes her look nicest."

"Good eye. That one is a good match for her skin. But now look at the costumes behind her."

"Uh," Jaspar studied them. "It's okay if she's the Princess or the True Love, but it totally sucks if she's the Empress."

"Well, I'm no Empress, so we're all safe there." Perrin turned around to look at the costumes as Jerimy and Richard laughed. "You're right, Jaspar. That's nasty."

They shared a smile.

"You see, Jaspar," Richard began making notes, "there's no perfect lighting. It's a balancing act and compromises."

Mika came in with the makeup cards and they soon passed

beyond where Perrin could follow. It was a language as unique as her own about texture and line. It was the language of light, and she could see Jaspar absorbing it just sitting there at Richard's side.

———

TWO NIGHTS LATER, Perrin almost didn't answer when she saw Bill's number on the phone. She wasn't ready to talk to him yet. There was too much to un-say and too much that couldn't be said yet. Not while everything was so out of order. She wouldn't even know where to start. Well, perhaps he would know.

Finally, steeling her nerves, she answered.

"Hi, Ms. Williams."

"Tamara," she fell back and was thankful for the stool behind her when she landed on it.

"Uh, I have to be quick. I had to use Dad's phone to get your number. You aren't mad at us, are you? At...me?" The girl's voice nearly cracked from the strain.

"Oh God no, Tamara. Never mad at you. Feeling like an idiot six different ways, but never mad."

Tamara sniffled slightly. "That's what Jasp said, but I didn't believe him. Guess I should have. The little troll is always right. Jasp wore the sling and the sword today at rehearsal; it looked great."

"That's good." Perrin knew she was missing something. Jaspar had told Tammy that Perrin wouldn't be mad. Did that mean that maybe Bill wasn't...

"We don't have rehearsal tomorrow night. Can you come over for dinner?"

It was a good thing she was sitting down so that she didn't fall down.

"Uh, who's asking?"

"Jasp's idea. Something about maybe we just needed to try each other on for size. I make a pretty good lasagna."

"I'll bring a salad," some autonomic part of her responded.

"Cool, we'll be home by six. 'By—"

"Tamara?"

"What?"

"Does your dad know?"

"Nope. Don't tell." And the connection went dead.

———

PERRIN HAD FOUND a new level of "near meltdown nervous" that she'd never known existed. If she could have called back to beg off, she would have. But if she called on Bill's phone, she'd get Bill. And she didn't have the numbers for the kids' emergency-only cell phones. Her level of nerves definitely ranked as emergency, the national-level kind, call out the Red Cross and the National Guard. But she didn't have their numbers.

She couldn't even think of what to wear. She almost called Maria before deciding that she just needed to breathe deeply. She wasn't going to dinner with the King and Queen, no matter how it felt. A dress was too far over the top. A skirt probably too much as well.

What would she wear for a casual evening at home? Tattered and faded Vassar College sweatpants and a fleece hoodie sweatshirt were her usual first choices. Too far the other way.

She really needed to get a grip.

Perrin finally settled on jeans and sandals with some crazy-colored socks that Patsy had made for her from something she called magic yarn, the opera t-shirt, and the fleece hoodie just because she needed the extra level of security.

She was fifteen minutes early and drove past the house to park on a back street to just sit and wait. As the minutes stretched, her nerves became so bad, she knew she wouldn't make it the whole time without deciding to go home. With five minutes to go, she drove up to the house.

Perrin had sat in the kitchen once before, after dropping off Tammy, but she'd been too wired to notice much. Now she was so hyped up that she noticed everything.

Their house was in the Greenwood neighborhood, just a few miles north of downtown; a remodel of a remodel of a remodel Bill had informed her. The street was steep and narrow, enough room for two cars to pass if they were careful and everyone parked close to the one curb.

The blue-gray two-story house with forest-green shutters and trim had a surprising amount of privacy in the crowded neighborhood. It stood on a rise a dozen steps above street level behind a massive old hawthorn tree. The porch light was on and she could see the living room light through the original diamond-cut window.

When she klonked the big brass door knocker, it felt as if it echoed throughout the quiet neighborhood. "Here be an interloper!" it announced. The desire to turn and run surged through her again, defeated by being too nervous to do any running. She thought she heard someone call out, "Dad, can you get the door?"

Oh crap!

Then the door was open. Bill stood there, backlit by the bright living room and looking really, really good in bare feet, jeans, and an open flannel shirt over a blue t-shirt.

"Perrin?" he barely managed a whisper.

She might have to kill Tamara and the conspiring Jaspar later, but for the kids' sake, she took the bit. Clearly it was up to her to make it work.

"I was invited to dinner by your children. That is, if you're willing to invite me into your house."

"The kids?" His eyes widened and his jaw dropped like in an old, silent movie.

She tried to fight down the smile, but knew she wasn't succeeding. "I brought a salad." Perrin held out the covered bowl as if that would make everything make sense.

Bill closed his mouth, then both his eyes. He opened one as if checking that she was still standing there. Then he looked up toward the ceiling, "Thank you, God." He almost launched himself at her, but stopped when she warned him off with a slight shake of her head.

His careful nod acknowledged both the wisdom and the regret of that choice. Then he held open the door and she walked in.

"Well at least that explains the lasagna mystery."

She looked over at his whisper.

"It's Tammy's signature ultra-special-occasion dish. She cooks a couple nights a week to help me out, but we don't get her lasagna very often. It's good. That little sneak."

The front door opened right into the living room. It was comfortable rather than being austere. More bookcases than art. A couple of well-used couches and chairs sat on a rug that had definitely seen years of children. A big, octagonal coffee table that appeared to have sixteen different projects on it, as well as three relatively clear spaces where they probably set their dinners on most nights. A big television hung to one side, though not one of the monsters—available, but not the center of attention. She could easily see them all hanging out here together.

Bill took the salad bowl, brushing her hand as he did so. The electric shock shook her. Distance and time had increased her reaction to him rather than decreased it. Standing here, barefoot in the center of his domain, he was so incredibly, perfectly male. His eyes darkened just looking at her. Well, at least that hadn't changed between them.

Perrin turned away to continue the tour.

A wide, carpeted stairway led up to what must be the

bedrooms. Off the other side of the living room, was a pair of rooms connected with an open arch.

"Our offices, though they spread bigger projects out over the dining room table for weeks at a time. We actually don't get to eat at it much." Perrin peeked in. Two smaller desks were in the front part of the room. They were mostly neat, though it was easy to see which was which. The wall around Tamara's had numerous fashion magazine photo spreads torn out and taped up. The growth looked fairly recent. Jaspar's was actually neater, mostly dinosaurs and a half-dozen well-done model airplanes dangling overhead from bits of thread. A book open on the desk had a diagram just like the one Richard had used to map out his stage lighting design.

Beyond the arch, was Bill's larger desk, that looked as if it had been hit by a hurricane. A new facet to the man, so terribly organized in his public life. She liked that he had a messy side.

"It's all so...normal, Bill. You've made a magnificent home for them."

He stood beside her looking about the room as if he'd never seen it before. His glance at her registered that he was aware in this moment of just how different it was from her own childhood, and that maybe she could judge better than he did.

"Think about it. How many kids share an office with their dad?"

"I, uh... It just seemed the right way to use the space when I did it." Then he finally nodded, acknowledging that maybe he hadn't done so badly after all, as if there was any doubt.

On the far side of the living room from the front door, they stepped into the connected dining room and kitchen, separated only by a long counter with a gap in the middle. It was the only part of the house she really remembered from her prior visit. Last time Jaspar had been asleep, or had been pretending to be, Tamara headed that way, and the front room was dark. Now there were lights on everywhere and an oldies station playing.

Bill rolled his eyes when he saw her noticing it. It was as if the kids thought she and Bill had been adults in the 1960s rather than the twenty-first century.

Jaspar greeted her with a quick wave from where he was busy half-tossing a fourth setting at the table one-handed. Apparently that was all he was willing to offer, but she was glad to wave back.

"Scamp," Bill accused him and received back a glowing smile for his insult.

Tamara ran out of the kitchen area and, after only the briefest hesitation, threw herself into Perrin's arms. They held each other hard, like sisters too long apart. She kissed Tamara on top of her head. Then, continuing to forget all of her hard-won thirteen-year-old decorum, Tamara rushed back into the kitchen to make sure everything was all right.

The last room was a big space beyond the dining room. It had tools, toys, some miscellaneous furniture, and a forlorn-looking vacuum cleaner. A room they didn't use much.

"The house was really too big for us, but the kids fell in love with it, and it's right near a very good school."

Perrin smiled slightly as she moved to help Jaspar light candles and Bill headed into the kitchen to assist his daughter. Perrin only now noticed that once through the door, she'd relaxed. Somehow, all of her nerves had remained out on the porch.

BILL CONSIDERED SIMPLY SLIPPING under the table in a small puddle of contentment. In some ways this meal had been less casual than the dressed-up dinner at Angelo's. It felt a little foreign to be eating at the dining table. Also, he'd been far more aware of the dynamics as the conversation had ranged over school projects, books, and the upcoming opening at the Opera.

Tammy was so glad to have Perrin sitting at the table that she was even more incoherent than Bill was. Jaspar was now the one he was being forced to see differently. How was it that his children kept growing up around Perrin? One moment Jasper would be wondering aloud what it must be like to ride an elephant as Kim did in Kipling's tale. The next, he'd be watching Perrin's and Bill's own interactions as if they were lab animals to be observed.

Tammy had told Bill more than once that Jaspar was really smart about people. Now he could see it. But he could also see that his son would make a fearsome poker player some day—he was far too good at keeping his thoughts to himself. He felt sad, the boy's spontaneity was another thing Adira had taken with her to the grave.

"Okay, Tamara," Perrin sighed happily. "You have to feed that lasagna to Angelo some night, it will make him crazy it's so good."

Perrin's compliment had Tammy positively beaming. She was first to stand from the table and started to gather plates.

"Cut that out," Bill told her. "You cooked. Cook doesn't clean."

"But Jasp can't—"

"Grownups will clean up. We still know how. C'mere."

She came straight into his arms.

He held her tightly and whispered in her ear. "You did it perfect, honey. I'm so proud of you." Then he raised his voice, "Now scoot, I'm sure your homework is waiting for you somewhere."

She scooted, with a hop and a skip she hadn't had since Jaspar broke his arm last week. He was shocked at how much he missed it, how easily he took her naturally bright nature for granted. He had to cut that out and remember what a gift she was. That both of them were.

"And you," he aimed a finger at Jaspar who was just clambering out of his chair. He was already a little gawky, just as Bill had been at that age before he'd started to really hit the growth spurts. "I don't know what your part was in this, but whatever it was, you did it right."

"Thanks, Dad."

Oddly, rather than coming to his chair, he went to stand by Perrin. The two of them had some form of silent communication that he couldn't follow.

"You're okay," Jaspar finally informed her so quietly Bill could barely hear it.

"Thank you," Perrin mouthed just as softly.

Then Jaspar was gone.

"What was all that about?" Bill asked her.

Perrin went coy. Her black-and-blonde hair swirling across to hide her features as she stood and looked down to begin gathering plates.

"Perrin?"

"Jaspar and I appear to have negotiated a truce, perhaps even a peaceable settlement."

"Really, how did you do it?" Bill looked out into the living room as if he'd be able to discern the change inside his son wrought by the amazing Perrin Williams, but Jaspar was long gone.

"I didn't," she headed to the kitchen with the first stack of plates. "He did. Jaspar's the one who invited me tonight, convinced Tamara to cook her best meal for me."

Bill tried to get out of his chair to help. Really he did. But he couldn't seem to manage it. His children were just as mysterious and astonishing as the woman making herself at home in his kitchen.

CHAPTER 20

*P*errin arrived several hours early for the opening
night of *Ascension*. She dropped off a clothes bag
with Jerimy, though strictly forbade his opening it. Her opening
night dress still hung at her shop, where she'd meet up with her
friends for the "official" arrival at the Opera House, but she
couldn't wait.

Though the theater was pretty quiet still, the air vibrated. It
took a little time to track down Bill. Perrin had expected him to
be at the center of some whirlwind, instead he was sitting
quietly reading through his own notes in his office.

She leaned on the door for a while and simply enjoyed
watching his neat movements. Studying a page of the score,
adding a tiny note in the margin, then checking it again before
moving on. She could watch his hands for hours and never
know discontent.

"Anywhere we can go for a quiet picnic?"

When he turned to smile at her, she raised the wicker basket
with the red-and-white cloth that she'd put together herself in
some fit of excessive domesticity.

"I have the kids. They're next door doing their homework. I

know it's Friday, but with performances tonight, tomorrow, and Sunday matinee, I figured sooner was better."

"Sounds perfect," Perrin readjusted her libido a bit, but not much. She'd expected the kids to be around and had filled the basket for four. "But somewhere quiet so that you get a break. All three of you probably need it."

The kids didn't complain for a second about escaping schoolwork. Bill took her hand, and Jaspar didn't appear to mind, though it was clear that he noticed.

"There's this one place…" Bill led them to an elevator that went up several stories.

Perrin could hear in his tone that it was a place that had other possibilities if they were ever alone here. The elevator opened to another linoleum corridor, but through a heavy door they entered another world. A narrow steel catwalk led off into the darkness. Tiny lights hung on the railing about every ten feet.

It was Jaspar who pulled her up to the edge and then pointed down. They were at the very top of the stage, way farther above the floor than the audience ever saw. Down below she could see the set like a doll's house.

What on stage was a thirty-foot high wall of impenetrable forest, looked like a child's play set from up here. It was actually a series of a dozen trees that would disappear upward into the "fly loft" where they stood right now, an area just as big and tall as the stage right above it. The space was also occupied with other pieces of sets, lights and cables, and a dozen things she couldn't even identify.

The rest of the forest, she knew from looking it over at stage level, was three stories tall and full of shape, texture, and color, but it was barely five-feet thick. The back was made of thin tubes of square steel, knit together as intricately as her costumes. They were made of interlocking eight-foot sections that rolled around on wheels. From up here she could see the

Prince's castle sat off to one side, the Princess' homeland off to another, so massive up close, they were play toys from here.

Bill led them up a narrow flight of stairs and through a small door.

She couldn't make any sense of the space.

This time it was Bill who led her across the plywood flooring toward a low wall.

"Careful," he took her arm. "It's a bit of a drop."

At the rear of the platform, she understood where they were. They were in the ceiling of the auditorium. The deep red seats ranged in neat rows far below. So close, you could almost jump to it, a steel gantry had a half-dozen big lights.

But the platform itself felt safe and secure. Perhaps ten by twenty feet surrounded by a knee-high wall, it would be a perfect place to stack equipment and hold a quick meeting before installing it.

She looked around at this inside view of the Opera House world when Jaspar came to stand beside her.

She clamped a hand on his shoulder to make sure he didn't go over the low rail unexpectedly. He just grinned up at her.

"See," he pointed with this good hand. "Jim, Marissa, Camille, and Jess sit there and run followspots. That's those big lights that they can aim down at the stage and steer to follow people. They let me try it once, it's fun but getting it so smooth that no one notices you doing it is tough."

Beyond the gantry, the inner structure of the ceiling ranged off into the distance, a maze of steel supports, air conditioning pipes, and tiny walkways. He pointed out everything with a clear command of what it was called.

"This is your idea of romantic?" Perrin asked Bill once they turned the floor that was actually the auditorium's ceiling into a picnic area.

"No one will look for me here at least."

Jaspar helped Tamara spread out the lunch as much as he

could one-handed and they all sat. Sandwiches, sodas, and laughter told her she'd done well.

She hadn't worried about that though. Old Perrin would have, making sure each thing was thought out, planned, replanned. New Perrin had simply made lunch and was enjoying herself. Her usual mode was to sort of sit outside herself and observe how naturally, or unnaturally, she was interacting with those around her and make the necessary adjustments. Now she sat inside herself and simply observed that she wasn't busy second guessing herself.

When at length they returned to the main stage, Bill looked relaxed and the kids excited, exactly what she'd been hoping for. Though she'd never have pictured a picnic in the ceiling. Once on the stage, Bill pointed up to where they'd been sitting. That's when the nerves hit her, it was so far up in the air. She closed her eyes and looked away quickly. A fall from there would break far more than an arm like Jasper's fall on the sailboat.

Most of the crew leaders had shown up during their absence. It was only minutes before Bill was whisked away.

Jaspar and Tammy took her on a tour of the Opera House. Both tugging on her hands, often in different directions to show off favorite places.

From Bill's office, Tammy led them down the hall to visit Jerimy. She admired it as if new, though it was one of the only spaces she'd seen before. Smaller than her design studio, it had two sewing machines and a bin of fabrics, zippers, and the like for emergency repairs. A bank of washing machines was for removing stage blood before it set and made a stain. All of the clothes would be dry cleaned between every performance.

Next was the Green Room where Jaspar headed for the sugar until he noted Perrin watching closely and he turned for a fistful of trail mix instead.

Mika was already set up in the Makeup Room, six assistants hopping to his commands to make everything ready for the steady stream that would be coming through. With the chorus, they would be adorning well over a hundred people during the next two hours. Perrin retreated out of his way as quickly as Tamara would let her.

She liked the way that the technical crews made time for Jaspar. And not just because he was the Stage Manager's kid, they appeared to genuinely like him. He introduced Perrin to so many people that she never stood a chance of remembering their names.

The bewildering lighting setup in the back corner of the stage was clearly Jaspar's favorite. The console reminded her of when the TV news showed the controls of the space shuttle. Screens everywhere, rows and rows of sliders, a bank of controls for the intelligent lights, which sounded creepy... Jaspar seemed to know what it all meant and how to use most of it, though he was careful not to actually touch anything as he explained it.

She didn't like to be reduced to saying "Uh-huh" at appropriate places, but maybe that was all he needed from her in this moment. Perhaps that he wanted to share it with her was enough. She'd have to ask Bill later, maybe he'd know. But maybe not. He'd surprised her when he'd tried once to explain that he wasn't some amazing father acting from a secret fathering manual. He insisted that he was just making it up as he went along. Perrin decided that for the moment, "Uh-huh" was going to have to be sufficient.

Even more bewildering was the sound console. Not for the singers or the musicians, they didn't need any help he informed her, "not even Tam," he said with some pride. It was for sound effects, backstage monitors so that everyone could hear where they were in the opera, even the headphone system. It seemed that everyone had on a set of headphones all hooked into little battery packs clipped to their belts.

By now, people were scurrying around everywhere with

intense purpose. Almost everyone. A whole group of men and women dressed in black right down to their sneakers and gloves, lounged backstage. They would be nearly invisible in the shadows as they moved set pieces that looked so real up close even if they had looked like toys from above.

When the kids headed to makeup, she retreated to the tall stool at Bill's station, just off stage right, not ten feet from where the actors would be onstage. "Stage right" was different from "house right" for the audience. Perrin heard people switching effortlessly between the two. It made a subtle invisible barrier between performer and observer, the switching of whose right and left was important.

Bill's station included a half-dozen little computer screens. One showed the overly early arrivals milling in the lobby. Another, a view from above the audience, showed the three-thousand vacant seats. A third offered a clear image of the still-empty conductor's stand in the orchestra pit, though Perrin could hear a piano tuner checking the concert grand down there.

One of the pair of larger screens showed the closed red curtain as seen from the audience, but it would show the full stage when it opened. The second one had an incomprehensible display that Bill told her he mostly ignored because it was the feed from Richard's lighting control console.

The biggest screen on Bill's console was the cue list. Every few minutes, Bill would breeze through, brush a hand down her arm that sent warm shivers up her spine, then start checking items off the list.

"Two hours to show," he called over a PA that she could hear echoing about the backstage area. "House open in an hour-fifteen. Chorus to makeup and costumes." Then he was gone again.

Four assistant stage managers swirled about. One was Bill's hands and feet on the stage left offstage area, another chased cast members, a third worked with crew chiefs from lighting, sound, and the prop master who had set up long tables at strategic points in the off-stage darkness, every single piece sitting in its tape-outlined area. The fourth one appeared to be everywhere at once.

"Be dead without Jenny," Bill had remarked as the so-named assistant whisked him away to check on some last-minute detail.

"Pretty excellent, huh?" Jaspar appeared at Perrin's elbow, now dressed as the Young Prince, right down to his sling and sword.

"It makes my head hurt there's so much going on," Perrin confessed. "Is it always this crazy?"

Jaspar scanned the goings-on about him with a practiced eye. "No… " then he grinned at her,. "usually it's much worse!"

"Gee, thanks so much!"

He just smiled.

She'd learned during lunch when to recognize that Jaspar had something to say. She did her best to sit quietly and wait.

"Are you and Dad okay again?" His question sobered her.

Perrin had made a promise to herself to only speak truth with Bill's children, so she shrugged. "I think so. Remember, I've seen way less of him than you have."

Jaspar offered one of his sage, ten-year old nods. "Hadn't thought about that. He sure gets mushy when he talks about you."

"Seems fair. I get mushy when I talk about him."

He shook his head, "No, you don't. Not mushy. You get all quiet and happy at the same time."

Perrin desperately needed a subject change. "I made a surprise for you for the party after the show."

"More clothes I bet," he groaned but gave her a smile as he rested his good hand on his sword pommel to show his thanks.

"You'd win that bet."

He was right, she did feel all quiet and happy as he trotted away toward makeup and she left to get ready and meet her friends.

PERRIN CLIMBED out of the limo with Melanie, Jo, Cassidy, and Maria. She moved Melanie to the center, so that their dresses would work correctly together. The flashes were blinding. Russell brushed by close in front of them, kissed Cassidy quickly, and whispered, "Don't squint, and smile," before moving off to a new angle and raising his own camera.

Only Melanie appeared at perfect ease. The others looked a little wild, but then they shared smiles among themselves and it was somehow alright. Arm in arm, like they were following a red-brick road, her friends moved forward with her.

E! network stopped them along the way. Totally overwhelmed by the big glass eye of the television camera, Perrin kept her mouth shut. Melanie, barely missing a beat, stepped in and answered their questions emphasizing repeatedly that the woman beside her had indeed designed both these dresses and all of the costumes for *Ascension*. Her acknowledgement that she was indeed still seeing the Italian tenor star of the opera was brushed aside so quickly that Perrin barely saw it go by.

E! had apparently already done backstage interviews with several of the stars. When asked where the amazing ideas had come from Perrin couldn't answer, "While listening to Bill Cullen's lovely voice."

Melanie cut her off gently when she tried to stumble out an answer and led them inside.

"Never answer such questions," Melanie advised her quietly as Perrin slowly regained her equilibrium. "Designs always come from your heart, somewhere mysterious and unfathomable. It makes your line of designs more unique and enhances the perceived value of your work. Coco never explained her work nor should you."

They drank overpriced champagne from tall, thin flutes and waited for the time to go in. Perrin began noticing that there were distinct categories of men and women approaching them.

Cassidy was soon at the center of a small circle of vintners and wine connoisseurs, apparently oblivious to her best friend's beauty. Jo had board members of both Pike Place Market and the Opera, as well as one of her former law partners, clustered close about her. Her quiet power so enhanced by her dress that each word she softly spoke stilled the group for them all to listen.

Perrin with Maria close by her side, was swamped by women wearing her designs. They were no competition for the power of the five new dresses, but still the gathering created a spectacle that kept many heads turned in their direction. Melanie continued to run interference for her because it was all far too big for Perrin.

It was a huge relief when an usher rapped three notes on a small brass xylophone announcing it was time to take their seats. It was the same three notes as the little wooden door harp on her bedroom door. It provided memories that made it easier to smile and remain calm.

The opera itself was a bit of a blur. She knew the story and the music so well that she could simply enjoy the emotional journey without having to pay attention to all of the tiny details.

Carlo sang beautifully of hope and love; his first costume, for he alone had needed several, attempted to deny the foreshadowing of his pending failure that the music so broadly suggested.

The Magister's dark tones rose in threat until cut short with a magnificent low note produced by Geoffrey Palliser as the presence of the Overlord. He and the Empress were announced with overwhelming musical force and power. Perrin barely felt

Melanie's squeeze on her arm at the magnificence of the costumes under Richard's lighting.

Carlo ceased being the singer and became the character. The Prince struggling against his fate despite its inevitably. Perrin could see the parallels of Bill as he struggled to hold his family together despite the tragic loss they had suffered.

When the Princess and the True Love both vied for the Prince's favor, Perrin felt as if she were being torn in two. She wanted both to win; both to triumph and achieve that which they sought.

The True Love's murder by the Magister's least servant came as such a shock that Perrin barely masked a sobbing breath, many in the audience did not. The Empress' intervention too late, the Overlord a moment behind. The Prince broken forever at her loss, crying out from his madness. The haunting tunes somehow captured Perrin's running rhythm as she'd run away from the hospital. How had she ever done such a thing to Bill?

Before she could truly hate herself, a light, sweet soprano offered the faintest glimmer of hope. The Empress and Over-lord-to-be, Tamara and Jaspar, rekindled by the very darkness that surrounded them, glowed forth brighter than beacons in the night.

The opera, so dark, so rife with doom, was rescued from the very brink with a gentle duet of the elder Empress and her protégé. The Overlord's final benediction offering hope for all.

All but one. *Ascension* closed with a grim reminder of human fragility: the softly weeping lullaby the Princess sang to lull the mad Prince who lay with his head upon her lap.

A shocked silence was all the stunned audience could offer. It stretched out long enough for Perrin to glance at her friends. They all wept unaware, untended tears trickling down their faces. She checked her own cheeks with a hand, dry, though not through lack of—

Practically as one, the audience erupted to its feet.

ASCENSION HAD LIVED up to all of the hype created by the yarn-bombing and other advertising efforts.

Bill told her that Seattle audiences were notorious for not giving standing ovations and had never demanded an encore in the four years he'd been at Emerald City Opera. *Ascension* would be headed straight into the majestic heights of major opera house repertoire, an unprecedented opening. No one was even worrying about the reviews. Well, not much.

She let the others go ahead to the restaurant while she rushed backstage. With Jerimy's assistance, she'd helped Tamara and Jaspar into their matching outfits from the bag she'd delivered earlier. These were the idea she'd had when she'd made the other dresses for her friends. The children were now attired to be the shining stars of the emotional progression she'd made with the five dresses and with the opera itself.

Tamara's dress was easily recognizable as the Empress-to-be, but shifted in two ways: into high fashion and unbridled joy. It wouldn't be appropriate for any lesser party, but it would be a smash hit tonight.

Jaspar's suit combined the fulfillment of the Young Prince's eternal promise with the Overlord's majestic power. She'd designed the sling right into it, in a way that turned the "accident" of both the sailboat and the supposed sword accident, into a representation of the small cost of his ultimate triumph.

Jaspar had declared it "Most excellent!"

Perrin had to agree.

By the time they were ready, Bill had arrived, changed into an elegant charcoal suit for the party. Hand in hand, the four of them walked through the warm May evening for the couple blocks to Angelo's new restaurant.

Perrin felt as if she was floating on air, Bill with Tamara on one arm and her on the other, and Jaspar holding her down to the earth with his good hand in hers.

Forewarned, Russell had been waiting at the entrance with his camera. No matter what else happened, Perrin knew that whatever her past might be, she would have photographic proof of just how much joy was possible.

CHAPTER 21

*P*errin followed Tamara and Jaspar's instructions to the letter, and once again been unable to resist arriving at Bill's house early. She went with casual but pretty. The same outfit she'd worn the first time they met: the flirty fall skirt, clingy spring blouse, and the same filmy batik summer scarf. She'd substituted the leprechaun-green hat for the winter woolen just as a fun tease.

And not one single color of the opera, which was actually a relief.

When Bill answered the door, she handed him the large pizza she'd brought with her.

"What are you doi—" He smacked his forehead. "That's why the kids wanted to sleepover at Lucy's. Why those conniving, sneaky, pint-sized—"

"Would you rather I leave? If I do, I take the pizza with me." She offered him her most innocent smile as she reached out to take back the box.

He yanked it out of reach, wrapped his free arm around her waist and hauled her against him so fast she barely had time to laugh before his kiss crushed down on her smile.

"The pizza's still hot," she teased him.

He dropped it to the floor, landing it flat she was glad to see, and dragged her to the sofa, the bedroom being much too far away.

The pizza was long gone cold by the time she let him leave her long enough to reheat it, so that finally they could have some dinner in bed.

IT WAS in the shower the next morning that Bill learned something new about Perrin.

"You're shy." It was so unexpected that he actually said it aloud.

She didn't turn to meet his eyes as she rubbed a soapy washcloth over one of those impossibly long legs of hers, foot propped on the edge of the tub.

"How many women are you, Perrin Williams?"

"What?" that made her look up at him over her shoulder. "I'm not schizoid."

"No, you're impossibly healthy. Both of body, which we've gone to some trouble to prove once again, and of mind, because you are the most magnificent woman I've ever met. Not schizoid. But definitely multi-faceted, like a jewel."

"How Irish are you, Bill Cullen? Because that sounded like total blarney." She switched legs, offering him something else to admire.

"The name is, but I don't really know. We're pure American melting pot mutts. So fess up, how many Perrin Williamses are there?"

"You tell me." She pushed him out of the flow of water to rinse herself off, with her back still mostly toward him. Okay, there were scenes like this in movies. It was just odd that he was in the middle of one. He leaned back against the end of the shower stall to enjoy the view of the water sluicing through her hair and down her back and hips while he thought about it.

"Okay, there's the Perrin Williams born the day she met Jo and Cassidy. Still wild and crazy, but finding ways to control herself, to break from her past. Then there's the amazing designer who had to find a creative channel for all of the incredible energy and joy that had been buried for eighteen years too long and was desperate to find expression."

She turned beneath the water to face him, the shower still cascading over her, blurring and softening lines, only her face clear of the water. She looked amused, but not very.

"I think I count two more, three if you count the sexual goddess whose body I can never tire of."

That earned him a brief smile.

"There is the quiet genius who really doesn't want to be noticed. The scary smart one. The one who, whenever anyone even glimpses her existence, ducks behind the old familiar cloak of craziness as a distraction."

That widened her eyes and wiped away any remaining hint of amusement. He reached out and brushed his hand over her cheek, she leaned briefly into the caress, then returned to watching him quietly.

"I'm not sure that anyone other than Maria has ever seen her clearly."

Perrin slowly shook her head, then added softly, "And you."

"And me. Cassidy knows she's there," he continued. "That's why you're so close. But she can't quite hold focus on that Perrin."

"What's the last one?" Her voice barely sounded over the falling water. She hooked one hand over her opposite shoulder, masking her breasts. Bill was aware of the protectiveness of the gesture, even if she probably wasn't. One last shield?

"It's the Perrin Williams that I always see. Though, now that I think of it, maybe I'm the only one. No, my kids do, too. But

I'm guessing that even you don't. She has a quiet center and a heart that is so open that it's always right there. It's the heart that let Jaspar and Tammy come straight in with no games, no defenses. They've learned to love you, but you loved them from the moment they roared into the Costume Shop before the first piece of paper was torn. She's the Perrin who shines before me every time I look at her."

"I don't know her."

"Oh, but you do, my love." He moved forward and kissed her ever so lightly, though her crossed arm still separated them. "Every time you are with me, those other Perrins aren't the ones that leap to the fore. Except at that first meeting with Wilson in your shop when I was being such a jerk, you've always showed me the true you. Every time you turn shy, it's because you think you don't know her, but you do. She is the Empress, powerful *and* vulnerable. She is the Princess, gorgeous *and* unaware at the same time. And she is most definitely the True Love, brilliant *and* caring *and* sharing. She is so loving that she can't help but pour her heart out into the world. And Perrin? All those many facets of you... "

"Yes?" her voice was slow and careful. Immensely cautious.

"That's who I always want beside me when I wake. I want her to be the mother of Jaspar and Tammy. And I want to have a child with you, Perrin Williams. That child would be a true miracle with you for a mother."

She narrowed her eyes, having to blink them a few times to clear them of the water trickling out of her hair.

"Did you just propose to me?"

"Yes, I did." Bill hadn't really planned on it, at least not yet, but he'd meant it with every cell of his being.

"In the shower?"

He looked up at the spray still cascading over them and slid his hands onto her hips, pulling her partway out of the water.

"Well, at the time I thought it was a waterfall in a tropical paradise, but this would appear to be a shower that we're standing in. So yes, I seem to have proposed to you in the shower."

"Oh."

"Oh? That's all you have to say, is 'Oh'?"

"Would you prefer if I said, 'Oh yes'?"

"That was sort of the point of asking."

Without breaking eye contact, she slid her arm out from between them, and wrapped both of her arms about his neck. Pulling him beneath the water with her, she kissed him hard.

Then she eased back just a bit, the water streaming over them. Her impossibly brilliant smile lit her blue eyes and stunned him speechless as she so often did.

"We have to ask the kids, but otherwise that's a really big, yarn-bomb sized, 'Oh Yes!'" Her kiss was wet, but there was no question about it being totally heartfelt. Perrin had always kissed him with her heart wide open.

But she had never before kissed him with the taste of tears running down her cheeks.

CHAPTER 22

*P*errin had insisted that she had one last load to fetch at the apartment before the move was complete. Bill thought they'd left it clean, but he must have missed something.

The family had all sat together and decided that she should move in and unpack in the days before the wedding, so that after the ceremony she would simply be home when she arrived. She and Tammy were even staying in Cassidy's spare bedroom tonight, so as not to spoil tomorrow, neither the wedding nor the first homecoming.

Perrin's home studio was mostly put together in the spare room off the dining room. A small cutting table, an eight-foot set of shelves full of fabrics on one side, an open-style closet down the other. At one end, beneath the row of north-facing windows, stood the Featherweight sewing machine. And by the door, a pair of small desks.

She'd insisted that the kids would always be welcome there to do their homework or anything else, even if she was working. When he'd asked where his spot was, she'd pulled out one of the tall stools from beneath the cutting table. His name had been knit into a soft seat covering. Now he understood why this end of the table had no cutting mat—his desk and hers were one.

Over Tammy's, Perrin had mounted a massive crochet hook on which had been carved with burned-in letters, "Chief Assistant Empress Tamara Cullen." Over Jaspar's hung a wooden sword, exactly like the one he'd worn on stage, with the same-style letters saying, "The True Prince Jaspar Cullen."

The kids had almost died when they saw them. If either of them could have loved Perrin more after she did that, they would have.

Bill had offered to go with her for the last load, but she'd insisted it was a one-woman job. Then she'd turned right around and asked the kids if they wanted to go with her. He'd watched them drive off in her van, as perplexed as ever about what she was up to.

He knew that she would keep him on his toes for years, no, for decades to come. He also knew that it would always be a joy. Even when there were hard times, she would stand beside him and him beside her with joy.

Tomorrow, they would all stand together as a family for the first time. They had made it a combined wedding, adoption, and name change ceremony. She'd tried to hold onto her own fabricated last name out of respect for their mother, but the kids had overruled her.

At the wedding, Tammy would stand as maid of honor, with Jaspar making sure his dad didn't screw up or collapse from sheer nerves.

Despite his probing, Tammy had only said that her and Perrin's dresses were, "Totally Killer!" It was the same judgment Jaspar had declared when he and Bill had tried on their tuxes together. Bill had checked, but the girls had been smart and kept Jaspar in the dark about the dresses. Bill was trying to be patient, but it was really hard.

He finished breaking down the last of the moving boxes and

stored them in the garage. They were gone long enough that he'd just finished installing the last shelf she'd asked for when they pulled into the driveway.

Bill could hear the excited laughter of the three of them as they came into the house, the best sound he'd ever heard. He went to meet them in the living room.

The kids were grinning like lunatics, of course they'd been doing that all week as the wedding came closer and closer, but then so had he.

Perrin looked tall and beautiful and majestic. He noticed two things.

"Your hair!"

"See, I told you he'd notice," Jaspar informed Tammy. "Our dad's not a total dork."

Bill chose the safe course and ignored the aside.

Perrin had dyed her hair gold-blonde and cut it short fully revealing her astonishing neck and delicate face. For the first time since college, Perrin Williams had returned to her natural hair color and perhaps the first time ever, ceased hiding behind her hair.

As if she'd finally become herself.

"You've bypassed the Empress, my love," he moved down the hall toward them. "You've tipped right over into goddess."

Her smile was radiant. This was the Perrin he'd always seen.

It was as he leaned in to kiss her over the kids' heads, that his mind fully registered the second thing.

Tucked in the crook of Perrin's arm lay the tiny brindle-colored Cairn terrier they'd seen at the dog show. It had grown from one handful to two.

"I kept the breeder's card," she scratched the dog behind the ear. "She was just finally weaned last week. We figured if three-to-one couldn't win the vote to adopt her, maybe we just needed a fourth vote. All in favor, raise your paw."

The kids each shot up a hand. Perrin lifted the paw on the

tiny ball of fluff—who perked up both of her ears at the attention—as his fiancée grinned up at him.

"Oh man." Well, it took a wise man to know when he was beat. Just as it had taken a wise man to see the real Perrin, then be smart enough to fall in love with her, and tenacious enough to win her heart.

As their children danced around them, he raised his own hand to make it unanimous.

KEEP READING

Keep reading for an excerpt from book #5:
Where Dreams Are Written
And reviews are a HUGE help.
Thanks for joining my journey, Matt.

IF YOU ENJOYED THIS, YOU MIGHT ALSO ENJOY:

WHERE DREAMS ARE WRITTEN (EXCERPT)

A WHERE DREAMS SEATTLE ROMANCE

*M*elanie stood, poised, at the edge of the "wedoption" of her friend Perrin. The ceremony had tradition, spontaneity, and so much heart. A wild mix, just as Perrin was. She had taken vows with her husband as his two children stood by them in Angelo's Tuscan Hearth Ristorante in the heart of Seattle's Pike Place Market.

It was Perrin's new ten-year old son who had named the ceremony. The wedding of Perrin and his dad, and her adoption of Bill's children—the "wedoption." The kids were adopting Perrin as much as she was doing so for them.

It was all so sweet that Melanie felt mushy and sniffly inside, not that she'd ever let it show. She pulled out no handkerchief, had no pockets in her sleek dress to carry one. She only showed emotions carefully, and never mushy and sniffly ones. Being one of the fashion industry's leading models, she'd learned long ago that showing her own emotions was almost never appropriate. Everything she presented, both on the runway and off, was very carefully considered. She occasionally wished she could simply react, but that never seemed to work out.

She let her present boyfriend, Carlo, swirl her into a dance across the space cleared at the middle of the restaurant.

"That was *magnifico*, Carlo. Your *Ave Maria*." The operatic tenor, just finished with a highly successful production at Emerald City Opera, had indeed filled the restaurant with liquid soaring tones that evoked the sanctity of a small church set in the Italian country-side rather than Angelo's fine dining restaurant in the Market.

"This place and Angelo's food made it simple. It looks and smells so Italian, I sing from heart. The couple..." he slipped his hand from her waist for a moment to toss a kiss to the sky.

"Yes, *molto bello*." Melanie had dressed carefully, to not outshine the bride, but she needn't have worried. One of the most innovative designers working today, Perrin had judged herself and her maid-of-honor daughter perfectly despite their sharply contrasting coloring. Perrin's golden hair and fair skin and Tamara's darkly flowing curls and her birth-mother's dusky complexion had both radiated in Perrin's designs.

"I could marriage her myself. So pretty." Carlo swirled her among the other dancers with effortless control. Carlo's French was as poor as her Italian and his English was non-existent. So, she always spoke in her school-girl Italian and he spoke to her in a child's rudimentary French. That way they always understood one another and the inability to discuss more complex topics had not been a major issue. Carlo was not a deep man.

But he was a kind and considerate lover. Also, his Mediter-ranean-dark skin, classic Italian good looks, and international fame had made them a stunning couple, frequently gracing the tabloid covers. But his limitations had soon become apparent and were now wearying. Soon they would be finished.

"I have received call on phone," he whispered as they pulled together for a slow passage of the song. "Marko Lerano has taken ill and they need an Alfredo for *Traviata* at La Scala."

"That's such wonderful news for you. La Scala," at least she thought it might be, so she offered her support. "When do they need you?"

"I have already called the taxi. They say the tickets at the airport will be. You keep hotel room as long as like."

Well, that was abrupt, but she knew such contracts were rare, vital to a career, and lucrative. Still...

"There is more, isn't there, Carlo?"

He nodded sadly.

She needed no other cue, she was about to be dumped. People didn't dump Melanie, she dumped them. She considered getting angry, but she wasn't, and hated people who put on a show for others. This was the perfect opportunity for a drama queen: a large audience, grinding someone else's celebration to a total, upstaged halt. Why did some women do that? She'd never understood.

What she did know was that, being Italian and male, it would be hard for Carlo to say the next sentence. They had done well together but she too had known it was over, for her at least. She wouldn't have minded if he had been left to pine away for her *un petite moment,* but if such was not to be, *c'est la vie.* She could at least be kind.

"It was a good run, Carlo, *oui?*"

"*Si.*" His appreciation shone on his face and the sagging relief in his shoulders. He kissed her on each cheek. "You are wonderful woman, Melanie. Never let persons tell you not."

"You're wonderful as well," she patted his cheek.

He leaned in for a final kiss, but if they were done, they were done. He was wise enough to hesitate then pull back and nod. And just that easily, their six months was over. Moments later he had led her gracefully to the edge of the dance floor, offered a final bow, and, after offering congratulations to the groom once more, slipped quietly out of the restaurant.

She stood pillar-still at the edge of the room as dancers

swirled about the dining room floor. Those still at the tables shared stories and smiles among candlelight and buffet dishes.

Melanie sought inside herself for pain, or relief. And found neither. Merely irritation that she had been dumped. The Ice Queen they often called her, due to that perfect mix of self-composure and immense female allure she could project. It had earned her so many accolades: four swimsuit covers, Victoria's Secret signature model, ever increasing offers of obscene amounts of money from *Playboy* that she kept refusing.

Melanie didn't need the money and would never pose nude. She had caused two major photographers to be fired for taking candid shots while she was changing clothes during a shoot; her contract was very strict on that point. She wore sheer and skimpy, posed naturally with a well-placed arm and little else, or wore only a Godiva of her trademark waist-length blond hair. But that's where she drew the line. The stories of those high profile firings had ensured that all her photographers were very careful around her. Neither of those images had made it out of the studio; the second one she'd had to shatter a five thousand dollar camera in order to make her point. But it had been made and no one in the industry was likely to forget it.

It was *Playboy's* first offer years before that had led to the final fight, of so many, with her mother. She had taught her daughter many lessons. Melanie had discarded most of them, but two lessons she took to heart: care with her money, and only the work mattered. The professional standards and practices Melanie had worked out on her own.

Carlo had left her by two towering vases filled with lilac and rhododendron, not far from the front door; the flowers nicely accented her maroon dress. She could easily slip away, but found herself unusually reluctant to do so. Melanie never stayed until the end of a party—it might look too desperate—but she remained despite that.

People came and greeted her and were greeted in return,

having no idea that for only the second time in her life she had been dropped by a lover. She could forgive Russell because he hadn't known that's what he was doing at the time. Carlo however, was a sign. Of what? That things were changing?

Jo, one of Perrin's best friends, and her husband Angelo dropped by.

"So glad you could attend," Jo's touch was friendly as they traded cheek-to-cheek kisses. It really touched her and she let her façade melt enough to let them know it. Angelo was Russell's best friend and knew of their failed relationship all too well. And Jo, the calm, cool clear-thinking powerhouse lawyer who now managed the Pike Place Market. Of all the people she knew perhaps Jo was the only one who didn't judge her as anything more than who she was—inside.

"The food. Angelo. *Zut!*" Melanie flapped her hands as if she couldn't think of enough to say. And she couldn't; his cooking really was that good. Yet another reason she was still standing on the far side of the room from the banquet table. He was one of the best Italian chefs in the country and she'd already had too much to eat, but would eat more if she happened to pass too near the sumptuous table.

He positively beamed.

How odd that she and Jo knew each other so little, but knew each other so well. They had cemented their relationship in an airport bar over two photographs, both by the same photographer. One photo, the moment she had fallen in love with Russell as he captured an image he didn't understand; the other of the same moment for Jo and Angelo, though they hadn't yet known.

She and Jo didn't need to speak to recall the moment where they had set the photographs side by side and Jo's life had changed as she saw the images of herself with her future husband. Jo simply held her hands a moment longer and pressed their cheeks together, no air kisses, no need for whispered words, just understanding and acceptance—both rare items in Melanie's world.

The couple moved on but Melanie felt a better than before they'd arrived.

She took a glass of champagne from a passing waiter so that her hands would have something to do. She didn't really want any. The merriment that resounded around the crowded dining room brushed by her as lightly as the smell of Angelo's amazing marinated lamb—that must be wafting out the windows to tease the tourists walking the cobblestones of Pike Place Market this cool May evening.

Perrin, Jo, and Cassidy—friends since college. And Angelo's mother Maria. They were all so close. You could see it in every gesture. What would it be like to have such friends? She watched them, all happily married. Perrin and Bill dancing to a Fleetwood Mac tune that for some reason was causing their children no end of amusement. Jo and Angelo now with Maria, all tasting the latest dish to come from the kitchen. More food. *Impossible.* Cassidy and Russell also moving across the dance floor.

Melanie took a sip of champagne to hide the pang of envy. Russell was so handsome, having just the right kind of roughness to him, and disgustingly wealthy. Though she had been very careful and was quite well off herself, so that had been less of a factor. Still, they would have been a perfect couple...for about a year. Whereas he and Cassidy looked quite content enough to be together the rest of their lives. Again, she resisted the sigh of longing.

Marriage and lifetime were not for her. Still, she could envy the group of friends their stable husbands and their close friendship.

While the other three women were starting college together, Melanie had dropped out of high school to pursue her modeling career. By the time they'd graduated, Melanie had nailed her first swimsuit cover and had put out a restraining order against her ex-manager mother ever contacting her again.

That had been the day she'd legally dropped her last name forever—she wanted no ties to her past. She'd earned her GED through a correspondence course and her business skills through the college of hard knocks and intense study.

Melanie now hid her desperate, New Jersey past behind careful emotional control and a soft French accent acquired from a learn-at-home computer program and perfected on international photo shoots.

Yet Perrin had made her feel included and welcome rather than the supermodel outsider unexpectedly in their midst. And those who Perrin accepted, her friends accepted without question. It was so unlike Melanie's own world where everything was move and countermove; where the only things that mattered were image and your latest contract. The one escape she allowed herself was into novels, everything else she kept focused on her career.

She allowed herself to simply observe the wedding reception crowd packing the restaurant, taking microscopic sips of champagne to portray herself as content with standing alone.

Angelo's Tuscan Hearth was warm with mahogany tables, blues and yellows on the walls and the midnight dark tablecloths. The wall art was all photographs of the old country by Russell. She had never looked as good as when he was the one photographing her—his retirement from fashion photography had been a blow to the industry.

The dance floor had become more crowded in the few minutes since Carlo's departure. The women wore DKNY, Lauren, Armani, and a fair number of innovative Perrin's Glorious Garb designs. Perrin's work stood out, by not suffering from the classic couture problems. Wearing her designs, a woman could walk out the door and not be out of place strolling through Pike Place Market. They would stand out for their beauty or eye-appeal, but these were not runway-only showpieces.

Perrin's fashion design friends, her new husband Bill's Emerald City Opera companions, and both of their personal friends all jostled happily together, mingling one table to the next. It was a joyous event, laughter an ingredient more common than the regional wines or the amazing food. If she knew how, she would swirl down into the crowd and appear to be enjoying herself. But the artifice usually so readily at hand eluded her and she remained, standing among the flowers.

Perrin swirled by in Bill's arms, laughing and shining with joy—a joy she had created in herself, despite her past.

Melanie found that the most surprising thing of all. She had always seen herself as too damaged to find a true relationship, yet Perrin's past had been far worse than hers. Here she was, Perrin outshining them all so effortlessly.

The bride's dress was a conceptual and technical master-piece. The dress, and the complementary one that Tamara wore, emphasized a fairy lightness, a magic that made them both appear to float about the room; both too joyous to touch anything as mundane as the real world. The diaphanous gold over a form-fitting sapphire sheath—like sunset glistening on the ocean. On Tamara's emerging curves and mahogany red hair it modestly promised the woman yet to come.

"Truly, Perrin," Melanie had told her over appetizers, "even in Milan, such work would be valued." It was no less than the truth.

Russell came by, nudged her slightly closer to one of the flower vases and snapped a couple of quick photos. He may have retired from fashion photography, but his skills had grown rather than diminished. Without doing it consciously, she had watched him move through the room, arranging groups but making them look candid.

Jaspar, Perrin's new son, had taken to following Russell

around and the two were now consulting on which shots to take and how to set them up. The boy drank it up like a sponge. Russell with children. Melanie put a hand over her heart to stop the pain at the image. He would be such an amazing father even if they were not to be hers.

The shutter clicked again. She stuck her tongue out at Russell, but pulled it back in before he could raise his camera once more. He laughed, then he and his protégé moved on to other subjects.

She felt her phone buzz. Business. She always let the business line through no matter where she was, except during the wedding ceremony itself. Early in her career, jobs were offered, negotiated, and scheduled in the time span of a week. Now, if they didn't reach you immediately, the job could be gone before you called back. This was a text.

There was only one line: *Sorry. Swimsuit cast now set. Maybe next year. Sue.*

This should have been a contract, not a brush off. This should have been a shot at the cover; her chance to tie Elle for the record of five covers. Instead, she wouldn't be in the issue—for the first time in eight years. There had to be a mistake, but no matter how many times she reread the message, it didn't change. She never begged. She was Melanie. The demand for her modeling time was constant and costly. But this one time she texted back to make sure.

Sue answered immediately, *So sorry. If in my hands, you'd be in. S.*

White lie there, Sue was the editor-in-chief and could easily override any underling's decisions, but you never burned bridges in this industry. So, she wrote back a quick *Thanks and looking forward to next year. M.* White lie back.

It happened.

To others.

Not to Melanie. She'd never lost a contract before. Ever. Not since that photographer's cat had scratched her moments before her first big hand-modeling contract when she'd been eleven. The scar had healed long before the memory of her mother's head-wrenching slap for the lack of caution.

Melanie stood on the periphery of the wedding crowd and used all of her control to remain calm. Passive. *Immobile.* She had known it was time to start planning for her next step. She'd seen too many girls fall by the wayside with no backup plan and many, unlike Melanie, had not been careful with their earnings. There was always some seventeen-year old with perfect skin waiting to be discovered.

But she hadn't been ready for it yet. Tyra had her talk show and acting. Iman had her cosmetics and had married David Bowie. Naomi was still working, though not as often as she'd like, for a variety of reasons. There were whole chains of super-model restaurants, as if the skill in the studio and on the runway somehow translated across industries, which it almost never did. And there was only one Kate in the world, only one Claudia, only one Heidi.

It wasn't the death knell of her career, but people would hear that she'd lost the swimsuit issue. Soon, not this year but probably next, her contracts would start to go down instead of up in both money and frequency. She hadn't worked this hard to become second-rate. Even if Victoria's Secret renewed her as their signature model, the writing was on the wall.

She moved along the edge of the room to find a chair in which to sit, her *équilibre* was not being reliable at the moment.

Russell, of course, chose that moment to emerge from around the gently flickering fireplace and step in front of her.

She sighed and strengthened her shields.

"Wow! You look like you've just been gut-punched, Melanie. What's up?"

Russell. Of course. The one person who could see when she was upset. Kind, frequently oblivious, and married to Cassidy

Knowles instead of to herself. Russell didn't know everything about her but he knew more than anyone else ever had. Ever. Including how to read the Ice Queen's true emotions if her guard had slipped in the slightest.

There was a time that hadn't been true, but her single failure at making their relationship a lasting one had changed everything, and now he could read her when no others understood. She had been the one to make the mistake of falling in love with him; he had been the one to not notice and leave her behind.

"I appear to have just lost my boyfriend and the next swimsuit issue in the same ten minutes." The shock of saying it aloud cut her inside, despite wearing her cloak of calm for the rest of the world.

"Carlo dumped you? Where *is* that slime? I'll kick the cringing dog for being so stupid." Russell was tall, taller than she was if she hadn't been wearing heels, and began scanning the crowd looking for him.

"Already on his way to Italy, I fear."

"Does he have any idea what he just threw away? Idiot." He sounded truly angry on her behalf.

Melanie smiled to herself. Although Russell had done the same to her, worse because she'd been in love with him as she'd never been with Carlo di Stefano, he was ready to leap to her defense. She pulled Russell close for just a moment, to share an instant of his strength, then kiss him on the cheek.

"Hey, no falling for my husband." Cassidy came over to join them, she said it with a smile.

"*Excusez-moi.* Too late." Melanie could have bitten off her own tongue. Not that it was a secret, for Melanie had told Jo and whatever one of the three friends knew, they all knew. But the truth behind her words shifted her light joke over closer to envy.

Cassidy's gentle hand of sympathy on Melanie's arm made it

both better and worse. The understanding was kind though, and Cassidy was always kind to the very core.

"What's going on that's made Russell so angry?"

Melanie told her.

"You lost the swimsuit contract?" Cassidy sounded deeply shocked on Melanie's behalf. She at least understood which bit of news was actually important.

"Wait," Russell spun to face her from his continued search for the departed Carlo. "You *what?* Is Sue even dumber than Carlo?" Melanie had met Russell while working on a swimsuit issue, had become a key model for Russell Morgan Inc., and shared his bed for almost a year. "I'll give her a call and—"

"And," Cassidy interrupted his growing tirade, "ruin any chance of her ever working with Sue again. No, Russell." Though she was half a head shorter than Russell and looked even more slender than she was when compared with his broad-shouldered frame, it was clear that Cassidy was indeed the right wife for him. She smoothed out Russell's hair-trigger emotions so effortlessly that neither of them probably noticed. They were that much in sync. Like Perrin and Bill, they were each so much better together than apart. Melanie would have gotten right up in his face and they'd have gone at it.

Once again, Melanie felt the stab of envy. Would she ever find a man to love her that much?

"*Now* what am I supposed to do?"

Silence. No one answered. Because no one was there.

Josh Harper stood at the doorway and listened to the odd quality of his voice echoing about his empty Chelsea condo on New York's Lower West Side. No wife, not anymore according to last week's small sheaf of papers and a court ruling. No lawyer, done and paid off the following day. Not even a realtor,

"Just leave the key on the counter. The new owners will be changing the locks tomorrow anyway."

He didn't know anything anymore. The underpinnings of his life had been abruptly pulled when the woman he'd adored had decided she was no longer interested in men, or being married to one. No acrimony. No alimony, their incomes were near enough identical. No hurt, at least on her side, just sadness and apologies and a chaste kiss to end the five happiest years of his life.

With the wondrous and painful insight of perspective, he could now see what she meant, who she really was that neither of them had noticed. But that did nothing to ease the pain. Rather it only added to his sense of feeling foolish. He'd been naïve...or dense...or stupid enough to marry and love a woman who...wanted another woman.

He ran a hand over the Gaggenau cook top where they'd made a thousand meals together, the big double oven that had delivered turkeys and pies to large gatherings of friends. Mostly her friends, he could now see. Mostly women, though she swore that hadn't been conscious.

Josh still couldn't understand the echoing emptiness that had so recently been his cozy home. That had included his wife. Worse, she'd known for over half a year but had delayed telling him because she couldn't figure out how to approach the subject without hurting him.

At least she didn't have a girlfriend yet, she'd always been true to him just as he had to her.

One thing was clear, he needed a fresh start.

A completely fresh start.

And he could afford one. With his half of the money from the sale of the condo and furnishings, added to his half of their savings, he was set for a while. For several years if he was careful.

Josh pulled out his phone as he stood there at the door with his computer bag over his shoulder, his only constant companion. He'd left a dozen or so boxes, mostly cookbooks, with a storage company that would ship them if he ever figured out where they should go. His other belongings hadn't even filled the trunk of his BMW waiting for him downstairs. Perhaps he'd been too severe in shedding his past, but that was done now too.

He hit speed dial on his phone. When Shirene answered, he kept it simple.

"I quit."

"Don't be an idiot, Joshua. You can't. You're my senior editor. Your prose is part of what makes *Gourmet Week* hum."

"You have my four emergency articles already on file in case I was sick or something went wrong. Well, it's gone wrong. Consider them and my unused vacation as my thirty days' notice."

"No, Joshua, my friend. For ten years you've dedicated your life—"

"To reporting about food. And it was fun. But it's not what I set out to do in the beginning. It's not what I want to be doing ten years from now. Call Elric, he'll come aboard happily and do a great job for you. Give you a fresh viewpoint."

"But Joshua—"

"I'm so done, Shirene."

There was a long silence before she finally responded, "If you ever need a job in the industry, I get your first call?"

"You do."

"Promise?"

"Promise."

"And if you need a friend to talk to, you call me anytime, day or night?"

"You're the best, Shirene." A friend to talk to. That finally gave him an idea of where he was going. "If you're ever in Seattle, give a shout."

"Seattle? Whatever is in Seattle?" Spoken like a true New York publisher.

"Me. Bye." Josh hung up, tossed the keys on the counter, and closed the door behind him without looking back.

Keep reading.
Available at fine retailers everywhere:
Where Dreams Are Written

ABOUT THE AUTHOR

USA Today and Amazon #1 Bestseller M. L. "Matt" Buchman has 70+ contemporary and military romance novels, and action-adventure thrillers. Also 100 short stories and lotsa audiobooks.

Booklist says: 3x "Top 10 Romance of the Year" and among "The 20 Best Romantic Suspense Novels: Modern Masterpieces." NPR and B&N say: "Best 5 Romance of the Year." PW declares: "Tom Clancy fans open to a strong female lead will clamor for more."

A project manager with a geophysics degree, he's designed and built houses, flown and jumped out of planes, solo-sailed a 50' sailboat, and bicycled solo around the world...and he quilts. More at: www.mlbuchman.com.

Other works by M. L. Buchman: *(* - also in audio)*

Other works by M. L. Buchman:

Contemporary Romance (cont)

Love Abroad
Heart of the Cotswolds: England
Path of Love: Cinque Terre, Italy

Where Dreams
Where Dreams are Born
Where Dreams Reside
Where Dreams Are of Christmas*
Where Dreams Unfold
Where Dreams Are Written
Where Dreams Continue

Science Fiction / Fantasy

Deities Anonymous
Cookbook from Hell: Reheated
Saviors 101

Single Titles
The Nara Reaction
Monk's Maze
the Me and Elsie Chronicles

Non-Fiction

Strategies for Success
Managing Your Inner Artist/Writer
Estate Planning for Authors*
Character Voice
Narrate and Record Your Own
Audiobook*

Short Story Series by M. L. Buchman:

Romantic Suspense

Antarctic Ice Fliers

Delta Force
Th Delta Force Shooters
The Delta Force Warriors

Firehawks
The Firehawks Lookouts
The Firehawks Hotshots
The Firebirds

The Night Stalkers
The Night Stalkers 5D Stories
The Night Stalkers 5E Stories
The Night Stalkers CSAR
The Night Stalkers Wedding Stories

US Coast Guard

White House Protection Force

Contemporary Romance

Eagle Cove

Henderson's Ranch*

Where Dreams

Action-Adventure Thrillers

Dead Chef

Miranda Chase Origin Stories

Science Fiction / Fantasy

Deities Anonymous

Other
The Future Night Stalkers
Single Titles

SIGN UP FOR M. L. BUCHMAN'S NEWSLETTER TODAY

and receive:
Release News
Free Short Stories
a Free Starter Anthology

Do it today. Do it now.
www.mlbuchman.com/newsletter

www.ingramcontent.com/pod-product-compliance
Lightning Source LLC
Chambersburg PA
CBHW020718130726
47899CB00011B/388